A Traitor in the Family

A Traitor in the Family

NICHOLAS SEARLE

VIKING
an imprint of
PENGUIN BOOKS

VIKING

UK | USA | Canada | Ireland | Australia
India | New Zealand | South Africa

Viking is part of the Penguin Random House group of companies
whose addresses can be found at global.penguinrandomhouse.com

First published 2017
001

Copyright © NJS Creative Limited, 2017

The moral right of the author has been asserted

Set in 12/14.75 pt Dante MT Std
Typeset by Jouve (UK), Milton Keynes
Printed in Great Britain by Clays Ltd, St Ives plc

A CIP catalogue record for this book is available from the British Library

HARDBACK ISBN: 978–0–241–29636–3
TRADE PAPERBACK ISBN: 978–0–241–29637–0

www.greenpenguin.co.uk

For C, always

The events and characters portrayed in this novel are entirely imagined. Should similarities be noted between this story and the activities of real people, including members of certain august, once-proscribed organizations, they are neither intended nor mere coincidence, but unavoidable.

1989

I

While her husband prepared to murder a young man he had never met, Bridget O'Neill was completing her arrangements for Christmas with her in-laws.

She worried over the mince pies in the oven, her offering for the festive meal. Her mother-in-law was a forceful woman and defensive of her territory. In principle Bridget's mince pies were acceptable. Always sweet shortcrust, never flaky pastry, and packed full of the mincemeat she made herself. It had become something of a tradition, almost inadvertently, as Bridget down the years had sought to find something that wouldn't provoke sharp looks and sarcasm.

Marie O'Neill would make herself a martyr in the kitchen throughout Christmas Eve, sighing audibly and increasing the volume if those in the front room showed no signs of having heard her, emerging every so often with a red face and strands of grey hair plastered to her forehead. The O'Neills would take their meal that evening, leaving the next day free for celebration.

For all this, unlike Bridget, Marie O'Neill was not domesticated. She had grown up among the privations of the Second World War and lived through troubled times since, as an activist both when single and after she was married. The O'Neills were a staunch family and Marie was a hard woman. She'd demonstrated not the slightest interest in the fact that Bridget had not provided her with a grandchild. She'd lost her eldest son to the dark forces of the English, shot down three years earlier in an SAS ambush in County Tyrone, but had shown, in Bridget's presence at least, not a flicker of acknowledgement, let alone emotion. She was a tough woman, to be sure, and flintily vigilant.

Glancing anxiously at the oven every so often, Bridget banked up the fire for the night. She had packed earlier in the day and the next morning would walk to the village to take a bus to Dundalk. It would mean getting up at five thirty. Francis would not tolerate her being late at the meeting point. But this hardly mattered since Bridget rarely slept well and at that hour was often nursing a cup of tea in the kitchen.

Finally she opened the oven door. They looked all right. Shortcrust would never have that golden-brown sheen but there was consolation in its crumbly, buttery texture. The tops had swelled plumply but there was no messy brown ooze down their sides. She would give them a few minutes to cool, then wrap them in baking parchment and put them in a Tupperware box. Not ideal – they could have done with longer out of the oven – but needs must. It was late and there would be no time in the morning.

Schmaltzy Christmas songs blared on the radio as they neared the outskirts of Calais, interspersed with the peculiarly French rapid-fire enthusiasm of the presenters. The talk was all of Germany's first Christmas as a single country since the war. Later there might be something different to report.

He was a good driver, John Boy. He'd see them right. Cautious. He kept a safe distance between their car and the red tail lights in front, despite drivers, in a hurry even at this early hour, accelerating past them and cutting in, taking their space. Patiently, John Boy slowed each time to create the gap again. The process repeated itself but John Boy remained unperturbed, attention on the road. At home, he was a driving instructor and the New Year would see him back in the passenger seat being similarly patient with young learners crashing the gears of his Austin Maestro.

Germany had produced no surprises. They'd driven around the Rheindahlen army base unhindered in the car they stole in Essen. Another of John Boy's skills. Brian was handy to have on board as well. With a German mother, he was bilingual. They let him do the talking. He had nerve too. Even though this was his first foray in earnest, he'd been calm. Francis hadn't needed to nurse him through as much as he'd anticipated.

They'd drawn up plans of the base which they had then carefully transcribed on to graph paper with different headings. The officers' mess became the engineering building, the parade square the muster area, and so on. It all squared with the legend they'd built for themselves, backed up by a chartered surveyor's office in Dublin. It was so close to Christmas that to check their story would be impossible anyway. The office would be closed today, Christmas Eve. But it was good practice.

Brian's linguistic skills, and his boyish charm, had found them a small house in the Taunus that could be rented informally as and when they needed it. No forms to fill in; cash in hand. Quite an achievement, Brian said, because in Germany people tended to bow to bureaucracy. He found the place in the small ads of a local Frankfurt paper. The owner had inherited it on the death of his father and was concerned about tax. They agreed that Brian would give him a call in the New Year when their plans for bird-watching had advanced. The distance from the main area of British bases was good. It allowed them to lay off and relax, while the autobahn system enabled them to be on target swiftly.

They'd dumped the German Opel in Nijmegen and immediately found a large, anonymous Ford that would suit their purposes. Now they approached the port.

It was four forty and still pitch black. Perfect, thought Francis. The eager beavers wanting to get home early. They approached the holding area before embarkation and John

Boy reversed effortlessly into a space on the distant side of the car park, near the entrance. Cars had begun to gather, not too many. As the car stilled and the engine ticked away its warmth, Francis felt the tension rise inside. Which of them could fail to sense it? They looked intently in different directions, as if searching for meaning rather than for threat and safety in the gloom of their small corner of France. Francis wound down his window and looked across the wet tarmac. Floodlights illuminated the main drag near the booths that would soon open for the six-thirty ferry. In the distance trucks accelerated on to the ship.

Closer by, he heard English voices. People from three cars had congregated and a hot flask was being shared. The children were excited, tracing small circles and figures of eight around the cars and the adults. 'Careful of the traffic,' shouted one of the dads. But there was little danger. There were perhaps nine cars in this vast space, including the one in which Francis, John Boy and Brian sat.

A small Nissan drove in and parked separately from the other vehicles. Like them, it was right-hand drive and it bore the distinctive pattern of registration plate for which they were looking. Three letters, two numbers, then B. British Forces Germany.

The driver emerged and stretched his arms. His wife got out of the other side, tipped her seat forward and with some difficulty lifted a baby from the rear, swaddled against the cold in a bright blue padded polyester suit. Maybe a year old, thought Francis. The man helped a little girl out from his side. She was fractious. 'Daddy, I'm hungry,' she said plaintively. She might be four years old.

Brian exhaled loudly in the back.

Francis turned to him. 'You OK?' he said.

'Yeah,' replied Brian quietly, eyes alight, body tense.

Francis looked at John Boy and nodded. John Boy started the engine and it murmured quietly. Simultaneously Francis and Brian climbed out of the car and pushed their doors to with quiet clicks. They looked ahead. No one had noticed them, it seemed. They nodded to each other again before pulling the balaclava masks over their faces.

They walked slowly, Brian one pace behind Francis, calmly approaching the family by the Nissan. Francis focused on them; it was Brian's job to scan the horizon and alert him to any trouble. He could see that the young serviceman was of Asian descent. It made no difference to Francis.

The little girl noticed him first. She looked up with large brown eyes. Francis found himself smiling reassuringly, even though his mouth was hidden by the mask. He had the gun in his hand and sensed Brian turning behind him as they had practised, protecting his back.

There was no drama. He walked smartly up to the young soldier, palming the little girl away brusquely with his free hand, and before the man could react placed the barrel against his temple. He pulled the trigger and there was the customary somewhat disappointing pop. It was always the same outside. Indoors was different. He felt the force though, sure enough, recoiling through his tense hand, rippling instantaneously up his straightened arm and into his shoulder and neck, flaring his brain and making his eyes blaze with a kind of exhilaration. There was the normal explosion of matter and blood from the opposite side of the man's head and he crumpled. Gone.

Francis looked at the woman holding the baby. Her mouth was open and her eyes stared and he noticed her dirty-blonde hair. He shrugged, more to convey helplessness than indifference.

A commotion had begun near the other cars and men were running towards them. But the Ford was already there and

Francis and Brian climbed in calmly. John Boy pulled away quickly but smoothly. Francis saw by the car clock that it was between four fifty-five and five a.m.

They had earlier reconnoitred the route to the motorway. They were heading south-east on the A26 within four minutes.

Brian was repeating, 'Fuck fuck fuck fuck fuck.' It was beginning to get annoying.

'You all right, Bri?' said Francis.

'Fuck,' was the reply.

John Boy glanced in the mirror but said nothing. He continued to drive calmly, his attention fully on the road.

'First time is always the worst,' said Francis. 'Need to keep our heads now.'

'I didn't expect it to be like that. Fuck.'

'No one ever does. It's a shock. You'll get over it. We need to keep to the plan now. You all right with that?'

'Suppose so,' said Brian.

'Well, if you're not, say so now.' Francis and John Boy hoped not to have to deal with such complexities.

'I am, Francis,' he said.

'Good. Don't worry. It's normal. No one's going to give you a hard time.'

They drove for two hours, barely speaking, listening to the radio. It did not hit the news until they were approaching the Villepinte rapid transit station. As they got out of the car, Francis and John Boy pulled off their boiler suits and boots and placed them discreetly in the suitcase that lay on the back seat and already held their balaclavas, weapons and gloves. They put on their shoes. Brian watched for anyone showing an interest in their activities.

Francis straightened his tie and combed his hair. He checked his pockets for passport, wallet and ticket. With a nod, he said goodbye to Brian and went into the station with John Boy. Brian would take the car back to the remote clearing near Eindhoven they'd selected for the purpose, douse the interior with petrol from the jerrycan in the rear footwell and torch it. He would then walk the two miles or so to the nearest station, in time to catch the eleven o'clock train to Düsseldorf, giving himself ample time for the connection to Stuttgart. He would spend Christmas with his maternal grandparents at their farm, where he would burn the boiler suits and gloves and hide the two handguns.

Francis and John Boy strolled into the station and bought tickets to Charles de Gaulle airport from the machine. Brussels would have been quicker, marginally, from Calais but it was smaller and fewer flights went to Ireland. At the airport they waited quietly in the queue and checked in for the eight forty-five Aer Lingus flight to Dublin as Michael Brennan, chartered surveyor, and his colleague Patrick O'Leary. They noticed no special security measures at the airport.

They were met at Dublin airport by a driver. Travelling north, they turned off the motorway to go into the centre of Dundalk, where Bridget O'Neill waited patiently for her husband with their luggage. John Boy alighted, she climbed into the car with Francis and they sped on to Belfast. They were to spend Christmas with Francis's parents in the small terraced house off the Falls Road in which he had grown up. They arrived by eleven thirty and Francis had time for a cup of tea with his old ma before he strolled up to Finnegan's Bar, greeting his parents' neighbours as he went. In the bar he was on his loudest and best form, buying pints for people he'd not seen in years. He made sure his presence would be noted by the inevitable touts hanging around. No doubt he would be buying one or two of them a beer.

*

Christmas here was unlike anything she had experienced at home. Home, that elastic concept. She supposed home was where they had lived for the past eight years, that cold and never completely dry cottage outside the village, set among the green of the border counties. It was considered bandit country, but as her husband was one of the key bandits she knew she should feel fortunate. However, home for her – as, she imagined, for many women of her age who had not found relative contentment and peace upon leaving – remained her parents' house, even though there too she had at times felt imprisoned.

When she was a child, her mother would prepare the Christmas lunch while her father sat in his chair impassively watching the television: extravagantly sweatered celebrities visiting sundry children's hospitals, and reruns of cartoons. Bridget and her sister would be allowed to open their presents, fold the wrapping paper and dispose of it, then help their mother peel the vegetables. At eleven thirty her father would go to the village pub, long since closed now, and she would wait with her mother and sister for her maternal grandparents to arrive from the other side of the village, he with a twinkle in his eye and a smile that her mother considered mildly imbecilic, she always ready to criticize the arrangements. Some years her mother's sister would visit from the South, with her silent husband and two sons, one Bridget's age and the other two years younger, and with her tales of prosperity in Arklow. They never reciprocated by visiting them in their three-bed detached on the new housing estate.

Life had been different back then, beyond memory almost, though it was only the late 1960s, just before the dark days that endured and would continue for ever, or so it seemed to her. South Armagh had been becalmed, merely bypassed by life, not besieged as now. Bridget knew that this was not the fond invented memory of a childhood that had never existed. The present was a grim struggle, observed on all sides by unseen eyes.

At some point her father would slope back in, not as combative as usual, minding his Ps and Qs, and the rite of a solemn, subdued meal would follow. When the washing-up was done and the guests departed, they would watch television together.

Bridget was brought back to the present by her mother-in-law as she held raucous court in the living room, drinking a rum and Coke and smoking a cigarette with a film-star flourish.

'I'm telling youse I could drink any man here under the table,' shouted Marie O'Neill, jabbing her finger in the general direction of the room.

'Aye, sure now,' said one of the neighbours, whose name Bridget did not know. 'There'll be no one taking you on, Marie.' He laughed, not entirely kindly.

'Ah well, screw you, Desmond,' she said, almost toppling from the arm of the sofa into the lap of Norman from number six.

'Chance would be a fine thing, Marie. A fine thing,' Desmond called back.

'Not a chance in a million. Not a hope. If you were the only boy in the world and I were the only girl . . .' she began singing, 'I'd slit me fecking throat.' She roared with laughter.

The first Christmas she had spent with the O'Neills she had been alarmed. The edge of the shock had worn off slightly over the years. A raw unease remained which she was sure must be evident, however much she smiled. Yet no one seemed to notice. It was quite possible they were too preoccupied with their drinking and shouting and singing and fumbling and fighting to notice her watching nervously; or maybe she was a better actor than she thought.

Bridget knew where her father-in-law would be, down the road at the Shaughnessys. She had noticed the glance between Sean and Pauline Shaughnessy just before Pauline left the house. She was equally sure that Marie, too, had seen it, just as she was certain that Marie had observed Sean fumbling at Bridget's breast on the dark landing that morning as she tried silently to fend him off. She had considered telling Francis, but she knew he would find any excuse not to confront his father. 'Just a bit of Christmas fun, Bridget. Lighten up.' So much for her brave Fenian warrior.

Bridget noticed Liam watching her as she strove not to look anxious, perched on her stool in the corner of the crowded little room. When she had first met the family, Francis's younger brother had been no more than a boy. Now he had developed a youthful charm, though Francis had told her he mixed with the wrong bunch and had been in trouble with the boys as a result. Liam was a watcher and she felt some measure of alliance with him. She returned his look with a reserved smile and his gaze moved so casually that she wondered whether he'd been looking at her in the first place.

Everyone knew young Liam was the cross the family bore and the shame of the street, not a patch on his two older brothers, not one of the boys, just a common criminal. Few concealed their contempt or their watchfulness, as if he might nick a fiver from a wallet or a handbag, but Bridget liked him.

The O'Neills had eaten their turkey and pudding the previous evening and attended Midnight Mass at St Ethelburga's. Before leaving, they had watched the late news and seen that Private Singh, shot in Calais by the IRA that morning, had not died but was in a coma and on life support. The reports were vague. He might be moved to a military hospital in England once his condition stabilized, or he might be left in a permanent vegetative state. Sean O'Neill had smirked sidelong at Francis, whose only expression was of mild boredom. No one had spoken.

Soon after the mince pies, assessed by Marie as 'not bad', Bridget had seen Liam pull on a thin jerkin and slink out of the door with a backward glance, like a misbehaving dog that feared discovery and punishment. Now he was preparing to make his next furtive departure.

Francis sat in the easy chair in Gentleman Joe's office, sipping whisky. Joe was behind his desk, leaning back in his chair, holding his glass contemplatively, the bottle open in front of him. Kenny, Joe's bagman, stood by the door.

'I hate fecking Christmas,' said Kenny.

'Compliments of the season to you too, Kenny,' said Joe. 'Just relax. We all need our time of rest. And this is the centre of the Christian calendar. Is it not, now, Francis?'

'I suppose so,' said Francis.

'You suppose so . . .' said Joe ruminatively. 'Well, I suppose I suppose so too.'

It was two years earlier that the Prods had come calling for Joe Geraghty. He'd been visiting an old people's home out near Dunmurry where an old volunteer from the 1940s was living out his days when his car was ambushed. Kenny, when drink had been taken, would describe it all vividly but with a professional's detachment. He'd been driving and Colm Hawley was in the front passenger seat. Colm had been one of the movement's thinkers, a man with six children advocating a political solution, arguing that the military campaign was heading up a blind alley. But Joe, the big man, was the target and the Prods' intelligence had been good. They were laid up in force and a hijacked truck blocked the road. Kenny skidded the car into a J-turn and faced back towards the M1, shouting at Joe to lie down. The bullets shattered the rear window and thudded into the front seats. Kenny had been hit and was bleeding profusely but managed to drive on, just maintaining control and consciousness. Colm was slumped forward in his seat, dead.

Francis had been part of the team dispatched to exact

vengeance on the two shooters, identified by Joe's Security Team. It was a routine job once they knew where the bastards would be drinking and Francis's role was to guard the outside while Mikey Sullivan and Peter Boyle went in and offed them. A different team was sent to lift the tout who'd reported Joe's prospective visit to the RUC. He'd been left in a ditch over Newtownards way. The news had been taken to Kenny's hospital bedside as some form of solace. God knows what Colm's wife made of it. The tout had been only too willing to name his RUC handlers, who were now on the list in Joe's little black book.

Since that time, Joe and Kenny had gained a reputation as the Odd Couple, inseparable, Kenny constantly moaning.

'Well, I never could stand Christmas anyway,' said Kenny.

'Will you listen to yourself?' said Joe. 'Enough now. Have you nothing better to do than to stand around complaining? Go off and do something useful. Francis and I have things to discuss.'

'Yes, boss,' said Kenny, looking into his glass as if calculating how many slugs would be required to empty it.

'Carry on like this, Francis, and you'll be going down in history as a hero,' said Joe. 'You're royalty as it is.'

'It's just a job, Joe,' began Francis. 'Just a job.'

'Well, you're good at it. One moment, Francis. Would you be so kind as to shut the door behind you, Kenny?'

'Boss,' replied Kenny in the affirmative.

'Now then, Francis. The soldier still lives.'

'Sorry, Joe. I thought it was clean enough.'

'No, no, don't be fretting now. How could you know? It's almost better. He'll stay in the news for a few days at least. Will he, won't he? Do they switch the machines off or not? No. Couldn't be more pleased, the boys and me. I'm to congratulate you formally on the action. The message comes from the top. The very top. You'll have more work in the future, that's for sure.'

'Thanks, Joe. It means a lot. Joe?'

'Aye, Francis. What is it?'

'I was wondering . . .'

'Yes?'

'I need some time out of it. Just a couple of weeks.'

'Ah, yes. Got to you, has it? I understand.'

'No, nothing like that. It's just . . . I've been invited to a wedding.'

'Oh yes. And?'

'Tony Simons and Cheryl Maguire. When I was younger I used to hang around with them.'

'Aye, I recall the names. Don't they live abroad somewhere?'

'Yes.'

'Ah. I see. America, is it?'

'No. Singapore.'

'Right. And they're not coming home to tie the knot?'

'No, Joe.'

'I'm with you.'

'So I was wondering . . .'

Joe Geraghty shook his head. 'That's a tricky one, Francis. That's a fast ball, I'll tell you. You know what I always say to volunteers, especially ones as important as you. You want to keep yourself beyond suspicion. You don't want any of the boys to have reason to doubt you now. The struggle –'

'I know, Joe. It comes first. But I was wondering . . .'

'Whether I could make an exception. It's a difficult one. At least it's not America. America would be a total no-no. But even so . . .'

'I'll not plead with you, Joe.'

'And little good would that do you. Now let me think about this.' He looked from his glass to the bottle and decided against taking another measure. 'Tell you what, Francis. Let's deal with it like this. I'd rather you decided not to go. But you're not going to do that, are you?'

'No.'

'All right. Let's just keep this to ourselves, then, shall we? It's up to me, but I'd be expected to tell others. And if I did we both know what would happen next. It's the example. If I'm seen to be letting you go off like this, what about the next boyo who comes and asks me?'

'I understand, Joe.'

'So we'll keep this between us. Not even Kenny.'

'Fair enough.'

'I'll watch your back. We say nothing to anybody, but if I get reports back I'll say I sent you off on some errand.' He looked thoughtful. 'I'll have to magic up a cock-and-bull story. But that's my problem. Leave it to me. How does that sound?'

'Grand, Joe. Thanks.'

'Never say I'm not a generous man, Francis O'Neill.'

'I'd never say that.'

'I'm sure you wouldn't. You all right for money?'

'You can always do with a bit more. But I'm fine. I'll find the fare somehow.'

'I'll see if I can rustle up a bonus for this job. I always look after my boys, don't I?'

It had been more than fifteen years before. As a teenager he had been proudly presented by his father to the great Gentleman Joe Geraghty down at the club. He remembered the day, and the induction that followed it, with a shuddering vividness.

'Yes, Joe.'

'Well, you just be discreet about your going and coming. Tell no one. And I mean no one. You're a marked man, remember, in more ways than one. And I don't want any unnecessary explaining to do with the boys here if you're seen on your travels. Understand?'

1990

2

What was it, then, this place that she came from? In the scheme of things. What did it amount to, the anonymous scattering of dwellings in the misty lushness of the very south of the North? Very little, Bridget told herself.

She was not prone to such thinking, to this way of looking at the world. She had been brought up to be sensible and, largely, she was. This disconnection, though, this sense of living outside herself, had set her going. Set her racing, more like. She sat imprisoned in her seat, pinioned on the one side by Francis, spreading all over the place in sleep, and on the other by the cold vinyl lining of the aircraft's fuselage. Oddly, noise seemed to be magnified and muffled at the same time: the constant droning roar of the engines and the air rushing through the cabin disrupted normal thought and set her mind on an unfamiliar course. Hence this. And the vain search for sleep in all this discomfort and noise, and all these people, snoring and coughing and moaning, added to the effect and unsettled her further.

Very little, she repeated to herself. Just like herself: unprepossessing and insignificant in the scheme of things. Less significant than ever these days.

She had grown up in the village. Her paternal grandparents had lived in what was now the North, while her mother's parents had a cottage along the back road to Dundalk. Her father laboured in the local foundry and wanted nothing more than a quiet life.

When she was young in Carrickcloghan there'd been a pub,

a butcher's shop, a baker's, as well as a small grocery store and the post office run by old Mr Kennedy, where she'd worked after leaving school. Mr Kennedy's father had started up the little shop, where he sold newspapers and stationery. The post office had come later, after the war. Mr Kennedy said that his father had been so proud that he'd bought a safe in anticipation. There'd been a stir in the village when it was delivered from London in 1951, so her parents told her when she got the job.

She'd always been keen on her studies at school, always been good at her languages and her literature. She'd applied to Queen's University to study English. The reading, she loved it, from Agatha Christie to what she thought of as *literature*. She tore through Shakespeare (though later found she preferred Marlowe), she devoured Austen, the Brontës and Dickens and then discovered early twentieth-century poetry: the War poets, Pound, Eliot and, the dearest of them all, Yeats.

Her university application was successful and she'd felt intimidated but excited. She spent the summer reading and putting together the clothes and other belongings she'd need in Belfast. Then her sister, two years older, left to work in a bank in Cork and her mother persuaded her to put university off for a year or so. It all seemed so long ago now, that craving for culture. To be sure, she still read – though was reliant on the mobile library and found herself consuming cheap romances as often as what she would call proper books – and found her solace there. But it was a resigned escape and no longer offered the thrill of excitement to come.

In those days her job and her books had almost been enough. Until the arrival of Francis O'Neill, that is.

As the post office clerk, Bridget had been entrusted with one of the two keys to the all too large safe, that testament to Mr Kennedy senior's unfulfilled ambitions – of what, Bridget had no idea – and dealt with the cash and the stamps and the certificates piled forlornly in the corner. The key was like a ceremonial item that Bridget kept diligently tied round her neck until she placed it in the drawer of her bedside table at night. The post office had never been robbed, unlike most others in the area, a fact that Bridget ascribed to Francis's influence. Mr Kennedy had not asked for the key back even after she and Francis had married, despite his evident disapproval of all that Francis represented.

The post office had closed so suddenly that she was told by letter in the Saturday post not to turn up for work on the Monday. There was a cheque covering the pay that was due to her and a little more. She had gone there to leave her keys but Mr Kennedy had already left. She let herself in and everything was gone except for the massive safe, which was presumably too cumbersome for the removers. The second key had been left in the heavy door, which instinctively Bridget closed and locked. For the remembering of it, she still kept the two keys at home. Later she'd realized that Francis had taken occasionally to filching one of the keys to use for whatever he did.

Those had been happy times, working with Mr Kennedy. Or had she ever been happy? She later learned that Mr Kennedy had had a stroke and the police had come down to help the Post Office officials hastily clear out the place.

All gone, the two other shops and the pub too, some years later. No one had troubled to redecorate the fronts or to clear the interiors. The butcher's and baker's were close to each other, on opposite sides of the narrow road that ran through the village and on which all the buildings were clustered, and their windows still contained the display trays that had been there the day they closed, simultaneously, some seven years before. At least the window of the grocer's, just around the slight bend at the heart of the village, had been boarded up. The frontage of the pub was boarded too, the old swinging sign dragged down by youngsters for the fun of it a couple of years back. Mr Kennedy's post office stood where it had always been – rumour had it he was still in the nursing home, but for all Bridget knew he might well already be dead – the proud sign, cream on red, faded now, the old Post Office logos long superseded. She could remember turning up at the place at eight in the morning, ready for work, keen to get started. It had not been much, but it had been something.

The little library that had provided most of her reading closed down shortly afterwards. Now she was reliant on the van that came from Newry every three weeks and which, if Mrs Bryce was driving it, pulled up briefly at the cottage before going on to the village square.

No one had thought of buying any of these premises, and so it was with the little terraced houses as their occupants grew old and passed away. Carrickcloghan itself was largely derelict and dying; the only discussion to be had was over who to blame. The overwhelming local view, encouraged by the councillors, was that this was the result of the occupying power's choice to starve the border counties. Bridget doubted whether, even if the British government had been more benignly minded, Carrickcloghan would have prospered, but it was certainly invisible from Westminster.

Over all this, like a malevolent warrior god, the Troubles had loured. This was what became normal as she grew up, a police station bombed in Newry, an ambush in Forkhill, the boy who'd worked on the petrol pump in Silverbridge shot dead, the soldiers and the police tramping through the village, in full combat gear, guns swinging round and levelled in your face, the helicopters, army checkpoints sprouting all over the place at no notice, latterly the towers. They'd not been present in her *Swallows and Amazons* or her *Famous Five*, or later her *Pride and Prejudice*, but then fiction was fantasy, was it not?

Real life was insignificance, fear, the constant sense of being malignly observed from all sides, and finally death.

It was nothing, this place where she lived. And here she was, flying thousands of feet above the ocean.

She remembered the day when Francis first appeared in the village. He'd been leaning against a wall by the pub, smoking and smirking at her. He was not like the boys in the village. It was clear he was from the big city, the question was: Dublin or Belfast? And this was answered as soon as he spoke.

'A good afternoon to you,' he'd said, his smile broadening.

She looked at him.

He looked around him, as if she might be staring at something behind him. He said, 'Sorry. Have I upset you?'

Her eyes widened. 'Oh. Oh. No, I . . .' she said.

'I'm awful sorry if I have. I'm new here. I wouldn't want to upset you. Not someone like you.' The smile turned into something warmer. 'I could do with being shown around here. You local?' he said.

And so it had begun.

Francis O'Neill did not consider himself a bad man. Far from it. He knew he could evoke fear, in his neighbour's child or a fellow with whom he shared the counter of a bar. A catch of the eye, a gruff tone or an unusually swift movement was all it normally took. His reputation played the largest part in it, an occupational hazard, no more. Fear was the small change of his currency; violence and death its larger denominations. He was good at hurting people, in various ways, that was the long and the short of it. Technically good, and he had the stomach for it; he didn't particularly enjoy it. He did it for the cause, and that explained and excused everything.

But here at 30,000 feet he was no one and that was a good feeling. No one knew him except the missus, who sat beside him, in and out of sleep. To be sure, he could ginger up the flight attendant a little with a glare or a snarl, but beyond that he was just Joe Public. Flight attendant. Fecking air hostess was what she was.

The announcement came that they would shortly be landing. He nudged Bridget and she looked at him, momentarily fearful before realizing where they were. She gathered herself, taking the crushed beer cans from his tray table and holding them in her lap until the rubbish bag passed by. He watched the air hostess as she fixed him with a bland smile, painted like her make-up on that bland face on its bland head with its blonde highlights piled neatly on top. She knows what I'm thinking, he thought. She'll be glad when the flight's over. Get her feet up, let down her hair and be glad to be rid of that unnerving man in row 47.

Finally the aircraft lumbered to the ground at Changi airport, next to where the Second World War prisoner of war camp had been, the place his grandfather, fighting for the English, had died in 1944. The story had acquired the status of myth in the family: his mother's father, once an IRA gunrunner, stunning everyone by volunteering for the British Army in 1941; his posting to the Far East; his capture by the Japanese; and his lingering death reported by fellow prisoners, from malnutrition and typhus. 'A foolish, foolish man,' Sean O'Neill would reflect sadly. 'Thought he was a man of principle, fighting fascism. He was a dupe of the English. A lesson to us all.' It had been a matter of shame to the family. It was only when he was looking at their itinerary that Francis had realized they would be landing at this place, so close to where his grandfather had perished.

When eventually they were freed from their seats, the first thing Francis noticed was the sticky, musky heat on still air in a grey overcast dawn. It almost overwhelmed him. He should feel pleasure at this adventure, he knew; for weeks beforehand he'd felt a childlike sense of anticipation. But he'd been inoculated against excitement and felt the weight of home even here. Then, in the terminal, it was the noise, the busyness of all these purposeful people. Their village, even anxious Belfast, to which he returned every so often on business, seemed in slow-motion black-and-white compared with the bright frenzy of this place.

They collected their luggage from the carousel and trudged through the passport checks. From here onwards it was all-found, from the transport to the hotel, to their accommodation and food and drink throughout the wedding celebrations. Pocket money's all you'll need, Cheryl had told Bridget on that buzzing telephone call two months earlier. The rest is sorted.

Among the press of diminutive men holding placards Francis could see a card across which, in large neat letters, was printed 'O'NEILL'. So much for anonymity, he thought.

Cheryl had been Bridget's best friend throughout secondary school. By the time they were teenagers Tony was invariably in tow, moping after Cheryl. The three of them had been inseparable, slipping off to smoke in the field behind school or nicking Cheryl's mum's sherry, so Bridget had liked to tell Francis. They would invent lives for themselves that contained sunlit college days, successful careers and families of their own – anything that would take them away from Carrickcloghan.

Then Francis had pitched up and changed Bridget's life at a stroke. He'd opened up a different future for her, he'd known it: the thrill of the boy from the big city and what he did, of which everyone was aware. He was a romantic figure, with his dark good looks and that mischievous smile, and he played on it consciously as he romanced her. It was natural that the four of them should spend a lot of time together, during which Francis and Tony became firm friends. They would all

25

get drunk at parties, then split into pairs to fumble in dark corners.

Before they knew it – they were so immersed in each other – their friends had gone off to university and things were never the same. Cheryl and Tony would come back during the holidays and talk incessantly about student life. They still had the same dreams, but Francis and Bridget had different ones. It did not destroy their friendship but a distance had opened up that was small then but had widened since. During Cheryl's occasional trips home now, they called across the chasm that remained, finding only trace elements of the connection between the four of them that they'd thought unbreakable.

Cheryl and Tony moved into financial services – whatever that was – in London, later joining the same brokers and getting jobs in Singapore. Francis had no idea what they did that was so valuable as to warrant their spectacular salaries, but he envied them neither the money nor the lifestyle. Over the years the distance, and his occupation, had opened up that chasm, which until recently he would have regarded as unbridgeable. When the wedding invitation had arrived, though Bridget was so enthusiastic in her reticent way he'd immediately dismissed the notion. They had no money, the RA wouldn't let him go, and besides, why should he travel so far to some sweaty hole to watch Tony and Cheryl, who'd abandoned Ireland for money, get hitched? But then he'd got to thinking: he felt so weary, so worn down by it all. The look of that dirty-blonde woman in that car park in Calais had got to him somehow, and it shouldn't have. So he'd decided to go, and had persuaded Joe, even if he wasn't entirely frank about his motives. Joe, he thought, must have recognized his underlying fatigue and must have made a calculated decision to permit him to have this moment outside himself. Francis had decided he needed it. He wasn't so sure now.

The little Chinese man greeted them with a small bow and a 'Welcome to Singapore' in broken English. He led them wordlessly through the crowds, insisting on carrying their bags. Freed of the anchor of his suitcase, Francis swayed slightly. The tiredness, the jet lag, the realization they were here and the upshot of numberless beers drunk in the darkness: all of them conspired. Bridget laid her hand on his shoulder, but he shook it off irritably. He was glad to make the car, where, cocooned in silence and leather upholstery, he swooned between sleep and wakefulness as the suburbs and then the city skidded by.

The room was luxury beyond their imagination. During his travels in Europe Francis stayed in the cheapest available hotels, generally the most unremitting bare neon-lit modern anonymities at the edge of autobahns or autoroutes or the nastiest cold rooms over city estaminets in mean districts. There would be threadbare sheets, noisy plumbing and minimal hot water. But this was something else: plumped pillows and brilliant white smooth satin bedlinen, the hum of efficient air conditioning, a spotless marble bathroom with fluffy white bathrobes, an imposing television boasting dozens of channels, and a breathtaking view over the city, waking from the fug of night as sun began to break through the mist.

They did not speak for some minutes.

Then Bridget said, unnerved, guilty, 'God, Francis. Will you look at this room?'

'Aye,' he said simply, and examined the minibar.

'I'll unpack our things.'

'Aye,' he said again.

He switched on the television and tuned into a music channel. Black girls gyrated on the screen to a crushing beat. This detained his tired gaze but only for a moment. He noticed an envelope on the desk.

'What's it say, Francis?'

'Give me a minute, will you?'

He opened the envelope. At the bottom of a typewritten letter was a scrawled note from Cheryl. 'Welcome to Singapore!' it said. 'Join us for the reception in the bar this evening. So looking forward to catching up! And by the way, everything's taken care of. Cheryl & Tony x' The rest of the letter consisted of a guide to proceedings over the next few days: the reception in the Champagne Bar that evening, the dinner, the optional tours the next two days, the stag and hen parties and the day of the ceremony itself. Francis grunted and put the letter down.

'Going to get some shut-eye,' he said. He pulled off his shoes and trousers and lay in his underpants on the silk counterpane.

She lay down beside him for a moment. He snored as if he were blameless. She was too tired to sleep, too tired almost to think. This was what the end of the world felt like, she thought. Or at least the end of life. A point where it is simply too exhausting to continue. But there was no escape for her in sleep.

The smell of beer exuded almost visibly from his greasy pores. She looked down at her husband with an expression that she intended to convey fondness. Indeed she did feel something close to affection for him. He was a big man in the village. Not that she cared for status. But what it ensured more than anything else was that people did not bother her. Apart from the other volunteers' women, they would ignore her gaze and scurry along the street. She was connected with Francis O'Neill and that meant trouble. People kept their distance, which these days suited her well.

He'd been brazen, smiling while he chatted her up in front of the neighbours. Francis is the name, he'd said, Francis O'Neill. We'll be getting to know each other for sure. It was only later that he'd told her he was on the run. OTR, he'd said,

28

laughing as if it were the result of a small misunderstanding in his home city. Occasionally he'd had to jump across the border when the RUC or army came calling. But it was infrequent. While they could have their incursions with their armoured vehicles and their helmets and their guns pointing every which way and twitching nervously, they were not in control. People would know of their coming, be perfectly civil with them and wait them out. Soon they would be on their way and life could go back to normal. But less so as the years went by. The mobile checkpoints had changed things and now the watchtowers were going up everywhere. The English were strengthening their grip.

Where had the depth of their love, if love was what it had been, disappeared? When they'd first met, Francis had been so smitten he'd said he'd be giving up the fight.

'I've done me bit, Bridget,' he said. 'What's it all for? We're getting nowhere. And now I've met you. We can settle down, you and me. It's easy for those feckers, handing out their orders. I'm out. I'm going to tell them.'

Francis could make her do things she would never have imagined before. She would climb out of her bedroom window at the back of the house and slide down the roof of the little lean-to kitchen, dropping into the safety of his arms. He owned a Ford Transit van back then and had flung a mattress in the back. They would drive, where, she did not know or care; and she would undress in the back while he watched, make love for ever, it seemed, and wake as the dawn broke through the mud-flecked windscreen.

Once he thought he heard something outside the van. He pulled out a pistol from somewhere and lay on top of her to protect her. 'Just lie there until it's over, then don't say nothing,' he said in a matter-of-fact voice. She could smell his sweat and feel his heart pounding, never more alive than at the moment of his death. But they realized it was some animal or other and afterwards they'd relaxed, giggling uncontrollably.

At first when she arrived home after those nights she would creep up the stairs. Later she simply walked into the kitchen, said 'Good morning' and tacitly challenged her mother to say something. The sheer doing of it was a thrill. She'd never been so bold, to disobey and flaunt it so brazenly, before.

For Francis O'Neill she gave up all lingering thoughts of studying. He, rather than dusty libraries or dry tutorials, represented her escape from the mundane. A volunteer in the footsteps of all those brave boys through the centuries, a masked marauder, glamorous and charismatic. Or so she'd thought. Even if his life were that thrilling she knew nothing of it. He said so little about what he did and she could not live her life by proxy. She was installed in the run-down little cottage away from the village where Francis could come and go without anyone seeing him, to wait for him during his absences, at first with a jumpy anxiety, later a bored resignation, to endure his mood swings or, which she at first found worse still, his ignoring her as he brooded. Increasingly she wished for him to ignore her and padded round mouse-like when he was about. But she found she could not altogether evade the sharpness of his glare or the edge of his tongue.

She'd so looked forward to their wedding, in 1981, in a small ceremony in Dundalk. She was already pregnant but they'd planned the day long before that happened. She wasn't yet showing and they hadn't told anyone about the pregnancy, not even her parents, which turned out to be wise.

But now she recalled the day without fondness. Francis, to give him his due, had tried to make the occasion special for them both, but circumstances conspired against them. Mr and Mrs O'Neill were little less than openly hostile. Liam, then twelve years old, was ostentatiously bored, yawning loudly through the ensuing lunch. It seemed he was only vocalizing his parents' feelings and the meal ended earlier than planned. The guests were few. Francis couldn't invite most of the boys he knew and who would form the nucleus of their social circle, such as it became, owing to their notoriety, and big Paddy, the older brother who was later killed by the Brits, was OTR; but they were more than compensated for by the police presence, taking photographs almost brazenly, which in turn annoyed her parents. She'd been tempted to offer the Garda watchers a drink.

Bridget's parents, in their wedding finery, had looked on aghast. Her mother had bought a new dress and a hat and her father wore a suit uncomfortably. Marie O'Neill, in her denim skirt, sniggered at the hat, Sean's grubby trousers didn't match his jacket and his tie was loose round the neck of the fraying collar of his shirt. He bestowed his beery breath and the rasp of his stubble on all the womenfolk he tried to embrace.

Her mother had had aspirations for her, if not of a university education and a career then of a sensible marriage to a man with prospects and an escape, most likely to a comfortable existence in a trouble-free town in the South. Instead they watched Sean and Marie bicker and swear, and Francis flash his gangster smile. At least their elder daughter had done as she should.

Francis's plans to leave the Provos never materialized. At first he explained that he would have to approach the subject with care. 'I need to speak to the right boys,' he said. 'I need to take it slow. Careful.' Later he stopped talking about it altogether and was around the house less.

Once he was fully re-engaged it was as if he'd been snared by an addiction. He was rarely at the cottage and when he was his monotone dealt only with the transactional. He would sit through the night in the sitting room morosely drinking beer or whisky.

Her mother had once asked her why they remained child-less. She'd shrugged.

'Is it him or you? Or don't you know?'

She'd shrugged again.

'Him,' said her mother. 'I thought as much. Men like him, flash and bossy and angry. They're the type.'

She shrugged again, her mother glared, and it was over.

The child. The poor wee child. It always came back to that. Little did her mother know there had, once, been a child.

It had been a month or so after the wedding. Fortuitously Francis was at home when she doubled up with the stomach cramps.

'What is it, love?' Francis had asked, though he probably suspected.

'I don't know,' she'd said, though she did know, for certain.

He helped her upstairs and into the bathroom. Already blood was trickling down the inside of her thighs and she was terrified. He led her to the toilet and sat her down, gently pulling her bloody knickers off. She could feel the dragging inside her and the gush and the agony. Despite what he was, he could not hide his expression of horror. He stared helplessly into her eyes and then the pain hit again like an explosion and everything but her core became distant and unreal.

Afterwards he filled the bath, testing its warmth with his elbow, and, having removed her clothes carefully, as if their contact with her body might harm her, he carried her the couple of paces and laid her in the water. He turned back to the toilet. She could see him standing there, looking down into the bowl for what seemed an age before pressing the flush. Then the sound of the churn began and life, such as it now was, started again.

He called the doctor and carried her to the bed. They lay together as they waited but did not say a word. Perhaps it was at that moment it had begun to unravel. There was nothing the doctor could do, other than recommend rest, prescribe painkillers and tell her to go to the hospital if the bleeding became profuse again. He referred her to a specialist who could not say with any certainty what had caused the miscarriage but confirmed that any subsequent pregnancy could be high-risk and that they might have difficulty conceiving anyway. His matter-of-fact demeanour did not add to the pain, she was already numb. Another pregnancy was at that moment unthinkable and the idea later became irrelevant. Bridget and Francis did not discuss what had happened and it felt as if he blamed her. The deficiency of her body had killed his child, so it seemed to her, and he did nothing to reduce her guilt. Nor did he say it would be all right and that one day they would have kids.

Her child haunted her now. She did not even know its sex. Francis had flushed it away, whatever it had been. And now, however irrationally, Bridget O'Neill still desperately wanted a child, though she knew she would never have one. She wanted, beyond reason, a wee one to care for and to live for, on whom she could bestow the love she stored so assiduously in her heart. She longed to observe her baby as he or she grew and became gradually sentient, to shape and nurture this small being the right way, to teach the child as best she could. But not in this life, it was not to be; and here her child would have had to share not only her life but also her burden – her fear of the police, the army, the Protestants, even her own people, her fear that this whole place might explode or implode, taking her and her lovely child with it.

Eventually he'd been caught. Did his stint in the H-Blocks. Took part in the Dirty Protest. Grew his beard and long hair. She waited for him, quietly.

He was stopped at an RUC roadblock in possession of an

old Lee-Enfield rifle. It was enough in front of a bastard Diplock judge to sentence him to two years, but he'd been lucky. He was supposed to be carrying Semtex and a resupply of sub-machine guns, so Aidan Murphy had whispered in the pub one night, but the quartermaster had had other ideas for them. The change of plan had enabled the Provos to isolate the source of the information, an ill-advised telephone call to the QM from one of his lieutenants that had seen the lieutenant disciplined and drummed out of the RA.

She visited him regularly there, running the gauntlet of the hard-eyed wardens, feeling occasionally the warm wet slap of saliva on the back of her neck, absorbing the undiluted hatred of the place. Francis's eyes begged her but his words were resentful, as if she'd put him there. The stench might have made her gag, had she not been determined to be loyal, or at the very least to appear loyal.

There were what they called support structures in place. Stevie Shaw, one of the local boys, brought Francis's weekly volunteer's wage, along with occasional small bonuses or food parcels. Father Dunstan, the priest from Forkhill, paid the odd awkward visit. Legal help was on offer. The man from the council called to say that they would understand if she fell behind with their payments.

But mainly it was the girls, the wives and partners of other volunteers in the area, who had converged on her to offer embraces and tea and numberless half-pints of lager down the pub.

'You're not alone,' Cathy Murphy would say. 'Any time you need company, you just give one of us a call. We know what it's like. We're family.'

So she would smile and sit there as the empties collected on the table, quietly playing the role she thought was required as the vacuous banter circulated, unheard by her as she thought of Francis, poor, vulnerable, frightened Francis, who needed her, and she wished she could be left on her own in the cottage to wait for her man to return, to serve her own punishment for whatever crimes he'd committed.

The girls' embrace concealed, unsubtly, their surveillance of her. They checked constantly how she was, always probing, monitoring her soundness, waiting for her to fall apart. She assumed they must be observing each other in the same way, but it seemed as if their attention was devoted solely to her. From time to time she wondered what would happen if she failed their tests. But at least they understood, partly, some of it.

He was out after eighteen months, shaven and shorn, eager, bright-eyed with the righteous religiosity of the struggle, more driven than ever. Only a fool would contend that the H-Blocks were a place to find reconciliation and rehabilitation. Francis emerged a bitter and ever more closed automaton. She was only thankful that he did not return to Belfast and leave her. It seemed he was still required in South Armagh.

Were these things of which she could ever talk to Cheryl? Of course not.

She didn't allow herself to think further, instead climbing wearily from the bed. She looked at him lying lost and vulnerable on the counterpane. A child, like all men. He was the centre of her existence and assumed that role as if by right. She did not even have to ask whether she was the centre of his life. But the answer to the question did not perturb her. This was the way of the world, her world at least. She felt no resentment; she supposed what she felt must be love or something like it.

She went into the bathroom and sniffed the contents of the little plastic bottles of colourful, viscous liquids that proclaimed to consist of peach blossom and raspberry essence, or avocado and lime. Selecting one and carefully retaining enough in the bottle for the duration of their stay, she poured some into the bath and watched as the cascade of water foamed it up to a decadent and dangerous volume. She pulled off her clothes, laden with the sweat of the journey, left them on the floor and climbed into the silky warmth of the water. It felt more self-indulgent than anything she had afforded herself in her life, and serenely joyful. She looked at the shining beige of the tiles and dozed.

Later, she dressed in a clean pair of shorts and a T-shirt and washed her knickers in the sink, leaving them to dry on the towel rail. Francis was still asleep. She took her key card from its little folder and, trying to minimize the click of the closing door, left the room and went to the lift.

The public areas of the hotel elicited awe: high ceilings with ornate cornices; polished marble pillars and floors strewn with thick, sumptuous rugs patterned in pastel swirls; sofas and armchairs gathered around gilt-legged coffee tables on which lay glossy magazines as well as the world's newspapers. A hushed bustle around the massive wood check-in desks that ran the whole length of one of the walls, behind which young men and women ministered with practised smiles to arriving and departing guests. The café, where Chinese waiters in bow ties, white jackets and white gloves served high tea, delivering tiered plates laden with dainty cakes, deftly serving tiny sandwiches with spoon and fork, solicitously pouring tea.

As Bridget approached, a uniformed commissionaire opened one of the glass doors for her with a broad smile and a touch of his hat. She stepped outside. Immediately it hit her: the temperature. The humidity took her breath away. She consulted her map and submitted to the heat and the noise and the smell of spices, garlic and drying exotic dampness. By the time she had reached the first intersection she was lost and anonymous in the rush of people. It was enthralling. She stopped to look at her map again and heard tuts as people walked around her. She was an obstacle, an unhelpful island in this stream.

The exhaustion had returned like a blow to the head that drained her instantly of energy or will. It was the heat, she thought. Her T-shirt was drenched with sweat. She concentrated carefully and retraced her steps.

Back in the room Francis had woken.

'Where you been?' he said.

'I just thought . . . You were asleep.'

'Just don't go anywhere without me. Right?'

She looked at the floor.

'Right?'

'Right, Francis,' she said.

'It's a strange country. You don't know what might happen. You just do what I say.'

'All right, Francis.'

Bridget had been surprised when Francis agreed that they should attend the wedding. Since Cheryl had moved abroad she'd been back to Ireland every two or three years to see her parents and these were the only times they'd seen each other. They'd generally met for a stilted drink in the pub and it was always clear that Cheryl could not wait to be away from her parochial past and return to her cosmopolitan present.

'Everything's just the same,' Cheryl would sigh, 'only smaller.'

'Is it?' Bridget would reply.

'Well, yes. Bits and pieces change. Places close. The security force stuff. There's more of that. But really it's all the same. Only it's . . .'

'Dying?'

'I don't mean it like that. But there's a whole world out there. Don't you ever want to get away?'

She understood so little.

'No,' Bridget lied.

The invitation had come out of the blue. The only correspondence she normally received from Cheryl was the annual rushed letter in January apologizing for not having sent a Christmas card and replying to Bridget's card. Cheryl's letters were always sparse on detail but full of good intentions, never fulfilled, to do better and write more comprehensively when she had more time. But here they now were. From somewhere Francis had found the money for the two airfares – that in itself was a mystery to her.

Now she felt cold fear at the prospect of meeting all these strangers and the big ceremony. At the same time, this was a once-in-a-lifetime opportunity. This was a life she could have led. After all, she'd not been that different from Cheryl: brighter probably, though less outgoing. Or possibly that was no more than a delusion that sustained her for a moment.

'You wearing that?' he asked.

'No, Francis.'

'Better hurry up, then. The drinks thing starts in twenty minutes.'

He was wearing his best shirt and his trousers were neatly pressed. He had shaved and applied copious amounts of aftershave. She thought he looked great, as attractive as that first evening back in the village.

'Well, get a move on,' he said.

She rushed to the shower, put on the plastic cap to protect her hair and immersed herself in the high-pressure stream. What luxury, to have a long bath and then a shower not an hour later. At home they had a stained enamel bath and the shower attachment emitted no more than a dribble of water that the dodgy immersion heated to just about lukewarm. She put on the only dress she had with her, her only good dress in fact, bought in Grafton Street seven years previously in the sales. She had fretted over wearing the same dress for this reception and later for the wedding itself, but had no choice.

The function room on the mezzanine floor was brightly lit. A chandelier sparkled. A white-suited waiter offered them champagne as they entered. Francis scanned the room while Bridget watched him.

Eventually, with relief she saw Cheryl and nudged Francis. He strode towards Bridget's friend and enveloped her in an enthusiastic hug. Bridget contented herself with a more hesitant peck on the cheek.

'You're looking lovely,' she told Cheryl.

'I'll say,' said Francis. 'You look fantastic, woman. Now where's your ugly other half?'

Cheryl summoned Tony from a nearby scrum of men while Bridget observed her. She was the same person with whom she had shared her secrets as a girl at St Mary's but more polished. Cheryl's complexion was immaculate, make-up expertly applied to convey an impression of health and naturalness. Her hair was coloured with subtle highlights that turned its natural mousiness into a blended sheen of mid-brown and blonde and cut cleverly so that it flowed over her shoulders. Bridget had been to the hairdresser's in Armagh before travelling but her coiffure now felt amateurish, as if achieved with rulers, set squares and shears.

Tony was detached from the crowd and ambled towards them, beaming.

'Now then, me old mucker,' he said to Francis, and embraced him. Normally Francis would not have tolerated this bodily contact from another man. 'How the devil are ye doing? Looking good.'

He turned to Bridget and swept her up in his arms, almost hurting her with the ferocity of his hug. 'And how are you, Bridget, darling? You're looking just great too.' He beamed at her.

'Fine, Tony. Just fine,' she said, as she was supposed to, with a small smile.

He turned to Francis. 'Well, mate. Been too damn long.'

'Sure has,' said Francis.

Bridget was aware that they were the centre of attention, people regarding them, smiling.

'Let's catch up,' said Tony, putting his arm around Francis's shoulders, ushering him gently to a corner of the room.

Cheryl had disappeared somewhere into the throng. Bridget followed the two men, eyes down.

'Great to see you both,' he said, but his voice was wary and he was looking at Francis.

'I'm not going to piss on your parade,' said Francis with a smile.

'Thank Christ for that,' said Tony, and led him away into a crowd near the bar, leaving Bridget to drink her champagne on her own. She felt tired.

Cheryl returned. She wore a short cocktail dress on which sequins sparkled and she towered in her high heels.

'How're you, then, Bridge?'

'All right. We're OK.'

'Good.'

'What a life you have here. And this . . . It's wonderful.'

'Thanks. Means a lot. And Francis? How's he?'

'Oh, you know. Not so bad. Things aren't so bad.'

'That's great.'

'I like your hair. And that dress suits you.'

'Thanks, Bridge. It's good to see you. Hard to imagine you here, but I'm so glad you made it.'

'Yes,' said Bridget.

'Look, I have to do my perfect hostess bit. There'll be plenty of time to catch up later. Let's make sure we have a good long chat.'

'All right.'

Bridget didn't know what she should have expected. Not, certainly, to fall back immediately into that old intimacy, to be able to share the confidences of their teens and early twenties. But perhaps to connect in some way.

It was just like Cheryl. They had met on their first day in secondary school. While Bridget had been stand-offish and shy, Cheryl had been welcoming and confident. She'd reached out and grasped Bridget's hand at lunchtime, saying, 'Let's go and see what there is.'

Now Cheryl flitted between people as she had always done, smiling and seemingly fascinated until her attention was taken by the next person she spied. Bridget was left standing, an empty glass in her hand.

Forty-five minutes later she judged she could safely leave and return to the room. Cheryl would not notice her absence. Nor would Tony. Francis certainly wouldn't.

Francis laughed at her when he returned to the room. He noticed her knickers drying in the bathroom and said, 'Don't you realize Tony's paying for everything? They clean your clothes for you here. All you do is put your things in a bag and leave them in the room. Tony'll sort the bill.'

'Sorry, Francis,' she said in a small voice.

'Don't apologize to me.' With that he began to undress.

He lay down on the bed in his underpants and began flicking through the television channels. This was the way of it, she supposed. Life. Whatever the glossy magazines might say that lay neatly splayed on the glass-topped coffee table next to the bowl of tropical fruit and the sharply folded copy of the *Straits Times*.

3

The next morning he was again snoring as she used the bathroom quietly and dressed. She moved the lamp while searching in the darkness for her key card on the bedside table and he was instantly awake.

'Fuck you doing? What time is it?'

'Seven thirty.'

'I thought we were on holiday.'

'I was just on me way to breakfast, Francis. The girls are supposed to be meeting at eight thirty to go shopping.'

'Don't expect me to be getting up at this hour.'

'I wasn't. I thought you might want to sleep on.'

'I'll have my breakfast up here. Later on. Then I'm off with the boys to do some sightseeing. You'll be all right?'

'Sure I'll be all right, Francis. Cheryl has it all organized. I'll see you here later?'

'Yeah. Enjoy yourself.'

'You too.'

She took the lift down from the fifteenth floor and joined the bustle at the buffet with the besuited and purposeful businessmen and the glamorous women. She felt dowdy, she knew she was dowdy; with her drab clothes cut straight and cheap, completely unsuitable for the climate, her sensible shoes and her straight dark hair.

Taking a bowl of cereal and asking the waiter for a cup of tea, she sat at a table as far away from the dazzling central hum of conversation and glittering teeth as she could. She ate in small mouthfuls, watching. It appeared to her that she was watching a television show, live, each participant playing his or her role to perfection, lines learned from other shows over the years. She had a sense that between her and these people there was an invisible but inviolable glass wall. She was tempted to approach the wall, if she could locate it, just to touch it and with no hope of penetration; but this thought made her fearful. She had imagined this trip would take her somewhere different and help her understand her life. Perhaps it had, but it had also reinforced her sense of how alone she was.

After breakfast she waited patiently in the lobby, on a sofa that was far too well plumped with cushions to be comfortable, for the rest of the women to appear. For fear of waking Francis again, she didn't return to the room. Nor was she sure she wanted to see him at the moment.

By and by they appeared, individually and in small groups, to gather around the fountain in the centre of the reception area, chatting excitedly. Bridget recognized several of them from the night before but she doubted any of them would have known her again. Finally Cheryl arrived and with her the moment that Bridget could no longer put off. She stirred inwardly to move, and then again. At any moment she would find the courage, stand up and head towards them with the best smile she could muster. But not just yet. She knew she would not be able to buy anything, even the smallest, cheapest trinket that would demonstrate her relative poverty. But that was not the true reason for her immobility. She shifted her torso a millimetre or so. This was it. No, it wasn't. She found herself seated still and her stomach muscles relaxed slightly, only to tense again in readiness for her next attempt to stand and join them, only fifteen feet or so from her. Now they were moving and it was too late. There were no frowns or discussions about missing persons. They simply walked, giggling, self-absorbed and evidently enraptured by the prospect of the day ahead. Still Bridget sat and watched. The sliding glass doors closed and she could see the women climbing into a small bus parked outside, which promptly pulled away. Well, she thought, there's always tomorrow. Sightseeing's more up my street anyway. But she doubted she would be here in the lobby the next day, waiting.

It was over a half hour later that she saw her husband coming out of the lift. She didn't know how she had spent the intervening time. Sitting, thinking into open space, she imagined, looking gormless, mind spinning. She had been doing more of this recently.

Francis did not see her but marched over to a stocky, diminutive man in a blue pinstriped suit, a loud tie and a pink shirt. The two men greeted each other effusively and walked out of the hotel together. Francis seemed to have recovered from his evening's carousing and looked well. She felt glad.

Now she was free to return to the room. She sat and watched American television for a while. At lunchtime she allowed herself an extravagance, ordering a sandwich from room service which she ate absent-mindedly. She dozed a little on the huge bed but was wakened by a sharp rap at the door. She rose quickly and felt mildly nauseous. The knock came again and a voice called, 'Housekeeping!'

The term meant nothing to Bridget and she opened the door carefully. The chambermaid with her trolley stood there looking cross. She said, 'I sorry. I come back later.'

Bridget stared at her for a moment before saying, 'No, no. I'll go.' Francis would want the room tidy when he returned and this lady needed to do her job. She collected her handbag and left the chambermaid to her work.

In the lobby Bridget decided she needed air and stepped outside into a hot breeze that was far from refreshing, under a heavy overcast sky of gunmetal grey. It remained oppressively warm and she regretted her decision. She decided to walk a small distance nevertheless and wished she had changed into her T-shirt and shorts before leaving the room.

She had taken no more than forty paces when she saw a woman in a dark business suit stumble. Her briefcase fell to the ground and a few papers spilled from it. 'Bugger,' Bridget heard her say in an English accent. No one stopped to help the woman or shared eye contact with her.

Bridget had drawn abreast with her. 'Here, let me give you a hand,' she said.

The woman turned and looked at her with curiosity. 'Thanks.'

Bridget began gathering the papers.

'Thank you,' said the woman again. 'A friendly face in this bloody city. And even better, an Irish voice. Reminds me of home. Thanks.' She smiled, and Bridget smiled back, automatically. The comment about the Irish voice was confusing.

'I think I've broken the heel of my shoe,' said the woman.

'Oh dear,' said Bridget.

'No,' she said, checking, 'it's all right. Small mercies.' She looked around. 'Don't suppose you happen to know anywhere I could have a quick sit-down, do you? Inside, out of this heat? I may have sprained my ankle.'

'Why, I don't, no,' said Bridget, then reconsidered. 'What am I saying? My hotel's just back there.'

'Oh good. You couldn't possibly lend me a hand, could you? We could have a cup of tea if you like. On me. Or something stronger if you prefer.'

Bridget carried the papers as they made their slow progress back to the hotel. They sat at a table in the corner of the lobby and the woman rubbed her ankle while looking closely at the heel of her shoe. Bridget placed the papers on the table.

'Thanks,' she said. 'I'm Sarah by the way.'

Bridget looked at her properly for the first time. She was about her age, roughly her height, slightly overweight, ill-at-ease in her smart suit and dark stockings, it seemed to Bridget. Her hair had been carefully blow-dried and Bridget thought that her make-up was perhaps slightly overdone.

'Bridget.'

'Pleased to meet you, Bridget. It's lovely to meet someone helpful in this city. Everyone's so busy. They don't mean to be unfriendly of course. It's just the way of the city. It runs on 24/7 business. Now, what would you like?'

'Tea would be nice.'

'Me too. Now I must get to the loo to clean up. I'll track down a waiter on my way.'

Sarah winced slightly as she stood and limped towards the toilets. Bridget was left on her own. She glanced idly at the papers. They appeared to relate to some kind of business meeting in Singapore but she understood it would be improper and discourteous to look at them longer.

Bridget watched as Sarah returned. She'd brushed her hair and walked more normally. For some reason she liked this woman instinctively.

'It's eased off,' said Sarah. 'Thank goodness for that. It's an important week for me.'

'Are you here for work?'

'Yes. It's the first time I've been abroad for the job. I've just got this promotion and the boss said I should come here for this meeting. So if I go back hobbling and unable to deliver the goods, then . . . Anyway.' She smiled.

Bridget looked at her, quizzically polite.

'Anyway,' continued Sarah, 'let's not talk about my work. The least said about the engineering of small electroplated widgets the better in my view. You here on business too?'

'No, a wedding.'

'Ooh, nice. Beats what I'm doing. Though I am planning on taking tomorrow off to see the sights.'

'You're Irish?' said Bridget.

Sarah looked at her quizzically.

'Only you said. An Irish voice . . .'

'Oh yes. Of course. I like to think of myself as Irish. I could get an Irish passport, I suppose. My parents went over to England in their teens.'

'They're Irish?'

'Yes. They eloped when they were kids. It sounds romantic but it was because my dad's Protestant and my mum Catholic. Neither set of parents approved.'

'That still makes you Irish. If you want to be.'

'I'm not sure I want to be anything in particular. I'm proud of my heritage – not that I see much of my relatives – but I've seen all the problems divisions can bring. I suppose I'm English when it comes down to it.'

'Where did you grow up?'

'A small village near Manchester. My father got a job in a brewery. They struggled to make a living. It certainly wasn't an advantage, being Irish. So I had to be English in all things, my mother said, a sweet little English girl. I went to college and then a group of us went over to Dublin for the weekend and I fell in love with it. I hadn't really thought about Ireland before, but since I've got to know it more I do like to think of it as home, in a way. You're lucky to be Irish.'

'I don't know about that.'

'But you are. I know, the Troubles and all that. But look beyond that . . .'

The tea arrived and Sarah fussed over serving it for a few minutes.

'I don't know why they promoted me, really,' she said. 'It's a terrible thing to confess but I'm not at all ambitious.'

'Why terrible?' asked Bridget.

'Oh, I don't know. It's expected of you I suppose. Even more of women. There are all those men there just waiting for you to trip up. Oh, ha ha ha.'

Bridget was puzzled for a moment by Sarah's cackling laugh, then smiled. 'Oh yes,' she said. 'I see.'

'Seems I've proved their point for them. Thankfully only you to witness it. You won't tell, will you?'

'Tell? Of course not.'

'Thanks. Listen. This tea's lovely. But I do fancy something a little stronger. How about a little G and T?'

'What about your meeting?'

'I've got loads of time. And I'll probably do better on the back of a stiff drink. How about it?'

'All right, then.'

It was in fact three gins and tonic later before Sarah left. Bridget returned to the hotel room feeling more than a little drunk. She found she had agreed to meet Sarah the next morning. The room had been cleaned and she resumed her place on the bed, the television switched on to drown the air conditioning and provide comforting noise. She slept a while and woke at eight, groggy. The humid fog outside the window had closed in with the approach of night and the room was half dark. She took out her book and, to the crashing tones of the music channel and its strobing lights, read for a while. Eventually it became apparent that Francis was not about to return for dinner. She ordered again from room service, feeling as alone on this earth as she could. But somehow not despondent.

She waited until midnight before going to bed. She fell asleep quickly and slept deeply, to be disturbed only vaguely by Francis's arrival at five in the morning. He crashed around a while and then she felt the bounce as his body landed on the bed. She smelt cigarette smoke and spirits on his breath and sensed no more until she awoke at eight.

The Russians had a term for it, he knew from his studies in the H-Blocks. Most of the boys stuck to obvious subjects like politics or sociology. He had decided on a module in Russian literature. For no particular reason he could remember, possibly for the hell of it. A bit like those bastards on *Mastermind* who mugged up on a certain subject just to show they could. Except for him it was a module in a degree course. And he'd passed with flying colours. And like those *Mastermind* bastards he'd forgotten it all now. Almost all of it anyway.

He hadn't forgotten about prison, though. Beforehand, even on remand, he'd been sanguine about the prospect. It was just a rite of passage. A spell in the Maze was a badge of honour. To describe his arrival there as a shock did not begin to convey the shaking of his beliefs and his being, the more profound because he'd thought he could cope, eat shit and do the time quietly.

But the squalor. The cruelty, the sheer condensed, concentrated cruelty of the screws. The grind of routine. The stench and the filth. The beatings. The physical bars and the fences and the locks and the figurative but more real ones entrapping his soul.

For sure, it was an especially tough time to be there. The dispute over Special Category status became the Dirty Protest while he was in. He too smeared his shit over the walls and refused to be cleaned. He too went on the blanket, refusing to wear prison uniform and huddling inside the filthy wool, clinging on for dear life in a cell plastered with his foul excrement, fresh and wet smeared over dried and faded, all this for the elusive ethereal political status. Whatever doubts he and his fellow inmates had, they could not utter them but instead followed military discipline, a lesson that had served him on the outside ever since. Tolstoy, Gogol and above all Dostoevsky had sustained him, somewhat, but mainly it was his hatred that carried him through.

He'd have been on hunger strike himself had he not been released a week or so before the first of them began. All that suffering and death and then that fucker Thatcher made the concessions anyway.

By that time all doubts had been erased. The H-Blocks had educated him and he had emerged with a new vigour and hardened commitment.

Zapoi. That was it. A continuous binge. He groaned with the memory.

He'd met up with Alfie, that cocky little sod from London with the spiky blond hair, in the morning and Alfie had taken him straight to his club in a high-rise. The place was done up like an imagining of one of those gentlemen's clubs in London. They started off on champagne and pretty quickly moved on to Black Velvet in honour of his being Irish. Then to the hard stuff, trying the range of Irish whiskeys. By this time several of Alfie's pals had joined them and the porters in the club had begun to look askance at them. Someone had a word in someone's ear and before he knew it they were out in the heat again. It must have been about eleven. Alfie was buoyant. His tie had disappeared and his shirt was soaked in sweat or alcohol, Francis didn't know which.

One of the crowd had an idea and soon they were in three taxis heading towards the harbour and a completely different kind of drinking club near the docks. Music pounded and girls cavorted in front of them, neither of which interested him, and there was hard liquor, which did. They spilled out into the thin daylight mid-afternoon, blinking, and began what Alfie called the millionaires' pub crawl, with a hit list of the swankiest five-star hotel bars, beginning, of course, with Raffles. The rule was that you didn't move on until security had been called and asked you to leave. Though Francis itched for a bundle with these muscle-bound nonentities, a remnant of inner prudence prevailed. At some point Tony had appeared and they were dancing like two fifteen-year-old girls in some nightclub to Soft Cell. Just as quickly Tony faded away.

Francis could recall Alfie hectoring him in the middle of the night. In drink his demotic London accent came out even more strongly.

'Fucking shit place, Ireland. Fucking shit place the UK altogether, come to think of it. But you Micks. Ireland, it's the arsehole of the universe. Get out is what I say. Look at old Tony. He's done all right, hasn't he? Come and set up here. He'd see you right. Or I would. See, I like you. Whassyourname again?'

'Francis.'

'Thass right. I like you. You don't want to live there no more. Don't get me wrong. I'm as patriotic as the next man. Rule Britannia and all that. No Surrender. Fuck the IRA. But it's all going to shit. Can't stand to be there. Get out while you can. Before one of those IRA bastards has you. Ditch the wife. I do all right, I can tell you.'

Francis was calm. 'What if I told you . . .'

'What? Told me what, Francis?'

'Nothing. It's just not as easy as you think.'

'Of course it's not easy. Nothing's easy. Then again, nothing's difficult. Just do it. Ain't that what they say? Just fucking do it, man.'

Instead of following his instinct and taking out the smug little Brit there and then, Francis had smiled at him and ordered another round of tequila slammers.

Now he felt as bad physically as he could. He turned over

in bed and looked at the clock. Ten fifteen. Bridget had gone, wherever. Francis didn't care. Probably on that tour thing with the girls.

There was no point dwelling. He'd been out and done jobs feeling as bad as this. Perhaps not quite as bad as this. But despite his promise to meet Alfie in the lobby at eleven thirty, he was not about to spend the whole of this day with him too. He might just make the stag night, for a brief appearance. Maybe a little longer than that.

He forced himself out of the bed and went into the bathroom, defecating profusely and painfully. He stood in the shower with the water as hot and as fast as he could bear it. He drained the litre bottle of water that stood in the refrigerator in the room. He dressed in shorts and T-shirt.

In the lobby, he spoke to the concierge about day trips. Johor Bahru was mentioned and, without thinking or precisely understanding what was being said, he found himself being signed up for a trip.

Francis left the hotel comfortably in time to avoid Alfie. He could not bear another day with the English and nor did he want to spend it in an alcoholic haze. He was slowing down with age and wanted some time on his own.

He dozed as the coach wended its way through the streets and jams, leaving the glittering centre, passing through rather more shabby and authentic suburbs, before leaving urban Singapore altogether.

They stopped at the border and while the formalities were completed he disembarked with the other passengers. They were on a rise and looked over the causeway towards a city that seemed to Francis identical to the one they had left.

They were dropped eventually in the middle of an anonymous shopping mall, where they would be picked up again in four hours. This was not what he had expected at all and within fifteen minutes Francis was bored. He spent the rest of his time wandering aimlessly between the air-conditioned stores, stopping every so often at one of the food halls for a coffee or a Coke. He would rather have gone on another bender with Alfie and his pals. At least, he supposed, in the bustle and noise and garish glare of this place he could find some time for reflection. His conclusions were cold. His commitment to the movement, all his achievements, they were as nothing. How much closer to a united Ireland were they? How close were the English to surrendering? When would the Prods recognize them as human beings, let alone equals? It had been futile, his suffering. He was no less able than Tony and he too could be leading this empty but affluent life. Perhaps that's what he was doing here. Showing himself what might have been.

Or alternatively this musing was the penalty for distance, he told himself, for dislocation from reality. The sensation of floating unreality was unnerving and he must find solid ground before he unravelled entirely. This whole trip was probably a mistake; possibly it was just a symptom of the loosening of his ties. Too much theorizing, he told himself. He was not a dreamer. It was all much more basic. Hangover and dehydration, they were the causes of this. Get yourself together, man.

By the time the bus turned back towards the border Francis was ready for the stag night. The passengers were asked to leave the coach to have their papers checked as they entered Singapore. At the desk his mind was on how much he might permit himself to drink tonight when he looked up to see two small men in immaculate blue uniforms and peaked caps staring at him. One held his passport.

'Mr O'Neill. Would you please come with us?' he said.

4

They met at the Botanical Gardens and entered by the Tanglin Gate.

Sarah said, 'It's a bit like bunking off school. Delicious but at the same time you feel guilty.'

'I never truanted,' said Bridget, then sensed she might seem self-righteous. 'But I'd have liked to.'

'The more distant you are from work, the less relevant it seems. All of those things you worry about back there seem so petty.'

'I suppose so,' said Bridget.

'Don't you agree?'

'You have to go back to them sometime.'

'You're right of course. Things can look simpler and less bleak, though. Just for a while. Shall we?'

They walked, heading for the lake first of all. The sun was unremitting and the air was again humid.

'Orchids,' said Sarah. 'That's what I want to see.'

At the National Orchid Garden they paid their entrance fee and negotiated the steep incline to Burkill Hall, the colonial plantation bungalow built in 1886. They wandered on, inhaling the impossibly sweet scents among the sultry wet tang.

'Wonderful, isn't it?' said Sarah.

'Yes.'

They sat on a bench. Rain was beginning to fall in a fine, warm mist. Neither woman moved.

'All that . . . stuff going on out there. You wouldn't believe there was a world, it's so quiet.'

'Yes.'

In truth the intermittent gaggles of tourists making their way through the gardens created their own noise. But it was quite different from the constant mechanical grind and bustle of the city, and Bridget could hear birdsong too. They stood.

'Shall we carry on?' said Bridget.

'Yes. Let's.'

There were few people around them as they walked slowly.

'Are you married?' asked Sarah.

'Yes. Are you?'

'Was. It didn't work out. His career. My job. That's the way he saw it. And put it. But now my job's turned into a proper career. Who'd have thought it? Children?'

'No.'

'Me neither. Never got round to it. Unlikely now. How do you feel about it?'

'I don't think about it most of the time. No, that's not true.' She was silent for a moment.

'Sorry. That was very rude of me,' said Sarah. 'Intrusive. I'm afraid that's me. If I take to someone I just talk about anything. It puts a lot of people off. I'm not a frivolous person, though. Honestly.'

'It's all right,' said Bridget. 'I'm just not used to talking. Especially about myself. To anyone. I try not to think about it too much, but I've always wanted children. That's the truth of it. It's not just that it's expected of you. I love children.'

'Then why not?'

'It just hasn't happened.'

'Doesn't your husband want kids?'

'We've never talked about it as such.'

'It's difficult, I know. It was one of the things that led to my marriage breaking up.'

'It's not that we're about to . . .'

'Sorry. No. I didn't mean that. It's just really difficult.'

'Yes.'

The expectations on her were immense, though not from Francis himself. Ever since the miscarriage – something that she was not about to mention to this virtual stranger – it had been tacit between them that there would be no children. And this made it harder. It might have been easier if he'd shouted at her and she'd eventually submitted to whatever his will was. But the conversation, like so many, was evidently off limits and always would be, she suspected. Meanwhile, apart from her mother's occasionally caustic badgering, it was the other girls, looking sidelong at her as they talked about their own children, checking her reaction in sympathy rather than condemnation, or so she could only hope. She would never tell them about her child and would withdraw still further into herself. But that was not an option either. Denying the support and camaraderie of this close-knit group would have been regarded as a hostile act. She let it simply be assumed that she and Francis could not have children and allowed them to feel sorry for her. Poor Bridget.

They ate lunch at a small café near a lake. Sarah billed it to her expense account.

'I don't much enjoy this business stuff,' said Sarah over coffee. 'Long days and endless meetings with strangers. I often want to just shout out, or laugh. Sometimes I fantasize about doing something worthwhile. Teaching or something. Sometimes I wish I'd never got into it. I envy you the life you must have.'

Bridget looked at her in amazement. 'I don't think there's much in my life to be envied.'

'Come on. The simple life. Out there in that lovely countryside. Without the clamour of all these . . . people. No schedules to keep. Not having to talk to arseholes all the time. Count your blessings, Bridget.'

'There are some, I suppose,' she replied reflectively. 'We get by. But it's hard. Very hard at times.'

'In what way? If I'm not prying.'

'They're difficult times. Francis isn't the easiest of men to live with.'

'Why not?'

'He's under a lot of pressure. A lot. It must be difficult for him.'

'But for you too.'

'Aye. At times.'

'Is it money? What does he do for a living?'

'He's a mechanic,' she said hastily. 'No, it's not money. I mean, we don't have any, but that's not it. We're used to that, where we come from. We have sufficient, which means enough to put food on the table. Most days, anyway.'

'What, then? The Troubles?'

'I can't explain. It's just hard. I spend a lot of time on my own.'

'What do you do?'

'I read. I've been through most of the books in the library. Good and bad. Trash and the classics. I know what I like, but I'll read anything. You know, when I was a child I really wanted to do something.'

'Do something?'

'Yes. Not necessarily leave Ireland or even the village, but do something I could feel proud of. I don't know what. I could have joined the Sisters, I suppose.' She allowed herself a brief smile.

'But?' said Sarah.

'That wasn't about to happen. I think I always knew I lacked the faith. And now . . . Now I don't think I believe in God at all. Goodness gracious, that's a big confession to make.'

'I know. I was brought up in my mother's faith. It took me years to realize that most of us don't actually believe. Hardly any priests do, I imagine. Isn't that a scandalous thing to say? But the ritual never leaves you. Or . . .'

'The guilt.'

'Exactly.'

'I know everybody says it but it's true,' said Bridget. 'I feel wrong about what I do and think and worry how to put it right and then realize I can't and worry some more. I feel . . . lacking in the eyes of others and of this God that I don't believe in. I worry about perdition at the same time as I believe there's no such thing.'

As she spoke she wondered why she was being so candid with this stranger and had found such a strong connection with her.

'I'm not so sure it's a purely Catholic thing,' said Sarah. 'We're better at it for sure. But people need to feel guilt. Those who have a moral consciousness, anyway.'

'A moral consciousness?'

'Yes. I'm not sure I know what I mean, myself.'

'Anyway, along came Francis and that was that.'

'A lightning bolt.'

'Something like that. It was just right, straight away.'

'And?'

'Well, we got married and . . . shall we go back?'

They spent the afternoon together, walking through the bustle of Orchard Road, stopping for a coffee on the way. They each took refuge in their respective hotel rooms before dinner at a restaurant that had been recommended to Sarah. As she left the room, it came to Bridget that she had barely thought of the wedding or of Francis during the day. She wondered where he might be. Off on a binge again, she supposed; the stag do had probably begun mid-afternoon. She herself was grateful to dodge the hen party and was sure her absence would only be noticed, if at all, by Cheryl. She'd have to say she was jet-lagged if it came to it.

She fretted about the wedding.

'I've only brought one dress with me,' she said. 'This one.

It's my best dress. I wore it for the party and I'll have to wear it again tomorrow. I'll look so drab and they'll all be glammed up.'

'What size are you?'

'A 12.'

'I'm a 14. When I knew I was coming I thought I needed to get something in case there was a function. So I went out and got this cocktail dress in the sales. It's a 12. I managed to fit into it in the changing rooms but who am I kidding? I tried it on in my room. It makes me look like, well, like an overweight woman, size 14 going on 16, trying to wear a size 12. You can borrow it if you like.'

'I couldn't.'

'Of course you could. I'm not going to wear it. Give it back to me afterwards.'

'But we're getting changed straight after and flying back.'

'Well, I'm sure we'll meet up again. Give it back some other time. Or not at all. I'm under no illusions I'm ever going to fit into the damn thing.'

'But what will Francis say?'

'Will he notice? Really?'

'I suppose not.'

They went back to Sarah's hotel, where Bridget tried on the dress. 'I love it,' she said. 'It's gorgeous.' It came to her that this was the last she would see of her new friend. The next day would be taken up with the wedding and they were booked on the midnight flight out of Singapore. Before she knew it she would be back home.

Sarah suggested they swap telephone numbers, but Bridget said, 'I'm not sure. Francis can be funny.'

'Funny? In what way?'

'Just funny. He's very protective of me.'

'Well, he doesn't need to know, does he? I can always phone you from work. Let me know the good times during the day to call. And if I end up speaking to Francis I'll pretend it's a wrong number or I'm someone from the bank or something.' She giggled, then said, 'But keep my number safe. It may be better for you to learn it by heart if you're concerned about what Francis might say. Can I have your number too?'

'I . . . I suppose so.'

'Thanks. Look on me as a friend. I am, you know. It's odd how you meet someone and get on so well. I am a friend. Truly. I'm there if anything happens. I'll do my best to help if things get bad. You mustn't let him . . .' She looked at Bridget seriously and placed one hand on top of hers, then smiled. 'And besides, you have to return the dress sometime.'

Walking back to her hotel, Bridget felt she had been rash. She was certainly not the kind of person to start up new relationships from nothing. Maintaining distance was a necessary protection. So why this? Probably because she was so far from home, scared and intoxicated at the same time. Possibly, just possibly, because Sarah was not so very unlike herself.

Police offices were much the same the world over. The neon-lit corridors as you were ushered along by your elbow. The conversing cops who stopped talking and looked as you passed by, as if you were some unsavoury specimen of pond life. The way they seemed to will your undoing, the way things seemed to be rushing by far too quickly, the squeak of rubber-soled boots on the ground, the fear, the fear.

But despite its similarities, Singapore was a step up. The floors were covered in light grey rubberized flooring that gleamed under the lights. The escorting officers were scrupulously polite, the watching cops stood upright rather than slouching against the wall looking tired beyond endurance, the walls were white-clean. This was not Castlereagh, though the fear was still there.

He was taken into a room with which he was familiar: again, less shabby to be sure, but still windowless and stuffy, the fetid air of numberless interrogations – or interviews, as they would put it – hanging in the air. A room built to lower the spirits. Bare government-issue furniture – a single desk and two chairs – bolted to the floor to prevent violence on the part of the interviewee.

He was surprised to see his adversary already sitting on one of the chairs. Normally he might have expected to be flung into the room to stew for a few minutes or longer, to sweat over what they might or might not have on him and what they might be about to do with him. Normally he might have expected to be given time to think back to the H-Blocks and the beatings for each minor misdemeanour and more often than not for no reason at all. Normally he might have expected at his leisure to reflect on Paddy, prompted by the hissed whispers on the way in: 'You'll be next.'

Paddy was his older brother. Had been. Patrick Shane O'Neill. A big shambles of a boy grown into a big shambles of a man. Dark curly hair just like his ma. Tall and broad, unkempt, always with a ready smile, but fierce. Fierce when roused, that is, which was whenever he smelt the English nearby. 'Fee-fi-fo-fum,' he'd say with vicious glee when they went out on jobs.

Paddy was straight out of school and into the RA, some four years before Francis. Never a leader, always a willing follower. Somehow, unlike Francis, he'd never been one of Joe Geraghty's boys, but he was brave as a lion. He didn't shine in the same way as Francis, that was all. He cheerfully admitted he was brawn, not brain. And this had been reflected through their childhood. Francis had been favoured by their parents, burnished for the future, but Paddy seemed not to hold a grudge. Sean and Marie had high hopes for Francis, fewer for Paddy, though he was loved, and none at all for the runt of the litter, Liam. But Paddy was a useful enough piece of muscle for the boys, a brave heart. The two brothers ran together in West Belfast occasionally and they laughed when they went out and laughed even more when they came back home from jobs.

It was in 1986 that it happened. Paddy had been called off to a job somewhere and it was Thursday night when Marie took the call. Francis was summoned to see Joe Geraghty, who gave him a privileged briefing at midnight, out of respect, so he said, for the O'Neill family.

'Ambush by the SAS,' said Joe, looking grey-faced. 'Never had a chance.'

Francis asked about the mission.

'The RUC station the other side of Tyrone. You know the one, it's always been a sitting duck. Maybe it was the tethered goat after all. Your Paddy and six others. All mown down. Paddy was driving the digger with the device. He died a hero, if that's any consolation. You'll take a measure?'

Joe always drank Scotch rather than Irish whiskey. 'Jameson's! Not lining those Prod bastards' pockets,' he'd said. Francis had never pointed out the obvious inconsistency, that most Scottish distilleries had been founded by men from the same stock. With Joe, it was always best not to point to any flaw in his logic. Francis had followed suit with the whisky. But not now. He declined.

Joe said, 'They obviously knew well in advance. We'll work out how. We'll find the bastard.'

Joe had been one of the pall-bearers, had wiped back tears as he consoled Marie with a decorous hug, had shared a few sombre words with Sean, had had a small one with the mourners before Kenny coughed and whisked him back to the high command.

They never did find the tout.

Francis needed no prompting, no vile whispers, to recall

that night in complete clarity. He had the words in his head anyway as he entered the interview room: 'You'll be next.'

The mild-looking man in a crumpled suit raised his eyes from his papers as if unexpectedly interrupted.

'Hello, Mr O'Neill,' he said with a polite smile, waving towards the empty chair. 'It's nice to meet you after such a long time. My name's Richard.'

Francis sat. Did he sense a slight quiver in that patrician English tone?

'I'm so sorry we have to meet under such circumstances. I've been trying to catch up with you in more, um, conducive surroundings since you arrived. But sadly this is what we're left with, seeing you'll be fully occupied tomorrow.'

Francis looked at the floor. He was hot, he knew his neck was flushing and he could feel the rhythm of his left leg pumping up and down on the floor. He tried to stop it but within a few moments there it was again.

'This must seem very much like some of the interviews you've had before in similar rooms,' said the man. 'But it's nothing like them. I'm not the police, for starters. Don't suppose I remotely look like a policeman anyway.' He smiled as if he had made some kind of joke.

Spook, then, thought Francis.

'So I'm not under arrest?' he said.

'No, not at all. Let's just –'

'I'll be on me way, then.'

He stood, and the guard shifted from his post by the door.

'No, no,' said the man. 'No need for that. You can go just as soon as we've had a quick chat. Completely off the record. I've taken great pains to ensure that no one knows you're here. Which is part of the reason I've had to wait so long. You've been having a good time. Been to every bar in sight, by the looks of it. Enjoyed yourself?'

Francis thought for a moment before sitting down again. Sit this one out. Could be worse.

'Must be good to get away from it all. All that stress. Like a bloody pressure cooker. Let your hair down a bit. And then this happens.'

He looked at Francis expectantly before continuing cheerfully, as if he'd not noticed Francis's insistent silence. 'Now then,' he said. 'I'll be as quick as I can. You'll want to get back to the festivities. You're on the late flight home tomorrow, I see. Good day in Malaysia? Seen a lot?'

Francis looked down again.

'First day you've spent on your own. Chance to really get away from it all, eh?'

Francis shrugged. He would give no more.

'Just sightseeing, were you? Or did you have an appointment over there?'

Francis looked up. How wrong could these bastards be? A grin formed in the corners of his mouth.

'No,' said the man. 'Didn't think so. Just had to discount the possibility. So I can say I dotted the Is and crossed the Ts when I get back. This meeting –'

Francis snorted.

'This meeting is very much to your advantage.' The man paused again. 'I don't want to insult your intelligence. You're a clever man. You know the attrition rate of volunteers. You're no longer a spring chicken. You'll be thinking of what happens to you afterwards. If there is an afterwards, that is . . .'

Francis looked at him questioningly.

'You'll be thinking of your family. Your wife. You'll want a bit of financial security. You'll not want to end up . . .'

'Are youse threatening to kill me? Is that what you're doing? If I don't help you?' His eyes were wide. He radiated hostility. He shifted in his seat. His fear was not feigned.

'No, no, 100 per cent no. That's not the way we work –'

'Because you can fecking forget it. Now, can I go or not?'

'Soon, soon. Soon.' The third time he uttered it, he spoke the word slowly, soothingly. 'What I'm trying to say is that I can offer you a way out of all of this.'

'In a coffin you mean.'

'No. A good way out. With money. A place of safety. Where you could begin a new life, a normal life. An end to it all. That's what you want, isn't it?'

Francis looked down again and heard the rhythmic thud of his left foot on the linoleum.

'I want to help you.'

Francis laughed caustically. 'You want to help. Yeah, right.'

'Let's do this sensibly. Talk it through like reasonable human beings.'

Francis was grinning now. But not talking.

'You've come to the stage where you don't want to do it any more. But you're trapped. There's no way you can get out of it without help. My help. Sooner or later it's going to be over anyway. You know that. And then your people will leave you high and dry. I won't. I'll take care of you. Alternatively, you'll get caught along the way and end up doing a stretch. I know,' he said, waving his hand, 'you're a big man. You can do your time. But it'll be for longer. You're good at what you do. But they'll catch you. I know it; you know it. Your bosses will want you to do bigger and better things. You're cannon fodder to them. You will be caught eventually and they'll throw away the key. You know this to be true.'

Francis shrugged again.

'You don't have to like me. I don't expect you to. I expect you to like what I represent even less. But together we can find a way out. I know you're not a bad man at heart. You're caught in the trap. You want to do the right thing, for your people, for your country. At least you thought you were doing the right thing, but by now you're having doubts. This is your big chance. Take it, because you may not have another one like it.'

Francis stared at the floor.

'Not speaking? We can play that game together. We can sit here while you think about what's best for you and come to that what's best for your people. Let's take a few moments of quiet time.'

Francis looked straight at Richard, or whatever he called himself. He saw a man younger than himself, but not in such good shape. His complexion was pale and flesh hung from his cheeks. He sagged somewhat in his seat and appeared exhausted. Simply to look at him was oddly tiring. His hair was too long to be described as tidy and periodically hung before his eyes. Every so often he pulled the strands back behind his left ear as he feigned to read his notes.

Francis was accustomed to counting the seconds in interrogation rooms. It was good displacement activity as they shouted in your face, spittle spraying in your eyes, or gave you a few sly nudges in the kidneys. Piece of piss, just sitting here in the air-conditioned quiet. They sat for two minutes thirty-two seconds approximately before Francis looked at his hands. A further six and a half minutes more or less elapsed before the man looked at his watch. Nine minutes is a very long time if spent immobile and in silence in a locked room with your sworn enemy.

'Well, then,' said the man, sighing. 'You'd better be getting back, I suppose.'

He reached into his pocket and placed a card on the table between them. He straightened it before Francis.

'Perhaps this isn't your only chance,' he said. 'If you should change your mind this is my number.'

He placed his index finger on the card. Francis looked up

and into his eyes. After a few moments his gaze drifted to the card. It was blank apart from a handwritten number.

'You're welcome to take the card if you want. But I'd advise against it. Best to memorize the number. Call me any time.'

'Are we done?' asked Francis.

'Oh no. I don't think so, do you? Not by a long chalk. But you may, of course, go. In fact I'd suggest you do if you don't want to be missed.'

Francis stood.

'Before you go,' said the man, 'I wouldn't plan on telling your bosses if I were you. I know your standing instructions say you must, but experience shows it's generally not the best course. The cloud of suspicion. You know the realities of the situation as well as I do. Better, probably.'

He nodded to the guard, who opened the door and with a gesture of politeness, as if he were a hotel doorman and Francis were a guest, ushered him out.

Richard Mercer remained seated. His notes, previously neatly arranged, were forgotten, now somehow strewn haphazardly before him. Even his spectacles looked untidy on the table. He ran his hands through his hair. Disgusting. He'd not had time to get it cut before leaving London three days earlier; today he hadn't even been able to shower before the urgent call to the hotel informing him that Francis O'Neill was on the move. And alone. He'd been waiting a good five hours for O'Neill to reappear at the crossing.

He put his arms on the table across the papers and laid down his head. Despite the chill of the air conditioning he was sweating. He thought he might be sickening for something. His glasses fell to the floor but he didn't pick them up. Instead he moaned. He might easily fall asleep here. Perhaps then this would all go away.

A young man going places, that was how they considered him, an assessment that brought out jealousy in Charles.

'I was once the rising star myself,' Charles had said sourly in his office a few weeks back as he conducted Richard's annual appraisal interview. 'A word of advice. Don't listen to the siren songs. They'll draw you to the rocks.'

He'd been sent on a wild-goose chase – Charles's description – and didn't feel up to the job. As confident as he was, uncertainty and inadequacy flooded his thoughts, along with the inevitable jet lag.

Charles had rung him in his office in Lisburn on the Sunday. He'd been catching up on some paperwork.

'Get your arse over here,' Charles said. 'Apparently our friend Francis O'Neill is off on his travels. Singapore of all places. Bring your warm-weather gear and plenty of it. You may be a while. Brief you when you get here.'

He dashed home to pack, caught the first shuttle to London and spent the evening reading the file. The next morning he met Charles and listened to his plan of action.

'Hopeless, of course. You don't stand a chance of getting him on board. The man is a fanatic. The legal issues don't bear thinking about. He's in up to his neck. But the powers that be insist that if these blighters pop their heads above the parapet we have to have a go. Wherever it is. You know the mantra. Well, have a good time. If you need to take anyone with you as backup, OK. But only one.'

Should this thing be done obliquely, bewitching O'Neill with subterfuge, or should it be full-frontal with a figurative – or actual – suitcase full of used fivers?

Charles waved the question away. 'Up to you, old man. Fuck knows why we bother with this after-you-Claude nonsense at all. Fuck knows why we don't just string the bastards up. Still, one day sense may prevail. I shall be one of the first to say I told you so. Good Lord, is that the time?'

Events, as it transpired, determined what happened.

Having heard Charles out, Richard had the whole day to devise his own plan. He was less pessimistic about the venture than Charles, but it was difficult to be more pessimistic than Charles on any subject, from the England cricket team's chances to the prospects for world peace. He spoke to people, booked the tickets and then knocked at Charles's door again, holding his operational proposal.

'No need, old chap,' said Charles, 'I'm sure you have it all in hand.'

So Richard took the Tube to the airport.

The Singaporeans had been watching Francis O'Neill for the best part of three days, waiting for a moment when he was on his own. And now after fifteen minutes, much of it spent in uncompanionable silence, it was over.

Christ, the double jet lag, the paperwork, thought Richard. Christ, the cross-questioning from Charles that would inevitably come.

'You mean, you didn't have a go while he was out carousing?'

'Insecure. He was never on his own.'

'You didn't suborn any of the wedding guests? Still better, these friends of theirs? They'd have helped you.' Suborn was a Charles word.

'I didn't think it would be right.'

'Not right? So it's right that this blighter can get away with whatever he likes?'

'That's not what I said.'

'What did you say, then? Am I being dense? Did you achieve anything? Did you tell the bastard in no uncertain terms that the SAS would come knocking on the door if he didn't play ball?'

'No. Of course bloody not. I didn't realize that was in the training manual.'

'Training manual? No. You're a field officer. Supposed to show initiative. Not leaf through the training manual.'

'I was being facetious.'

'Damn right you were being facetious.'

'Facetious rather than tell you where you can stuff your job.'

But of course the conversation would not take this course. Instead, Richard would say, equably, offering a crumb, 'We did make some progress, Charles.'

'Damn little from where I'm sitting.'

Richard groaned as he pictured it and sat upright again, gathering his glasses and swiping his hair back from his brow. He felt grease on his hand. The state of me, he thought.

Word came from the team watching O'Neill that evidently he had been strongly affected by the meeting. He was going around in circles muttering to himself and looking desperate. He seemed to be gasping for air. Someone might need to guide him gently on to the last bus back to the city. Out of character for him. He was known as a cool customer too. Poor bastard. Richard had seen that Francis O'Neill's terror had not been feigned when he'd asked whether Richard intended having him killed. Possibly if the likes of Charles had their way his fears would not have been so misplaced. Sodding mess, thought Richard.

It was all over bar the shouting, most of which would take place in London. The Singapore Special Investigations senior officer with impeccable grooming, impeccable diction and impeccable manners would simply shake Richard's hand, murmur some soothing platitudes and hand him a branded souvenir of the force, then he would be on his way.

He wandered around the crossing point for a number of minutes, looking backwards, glaring at anyone who took an interest. He felt unbearably hot and wanted to tear his clothes off. He was conscious of just how peculiar he must look, but it was some time before he began to care about it. Then, bit by bit, he started to control his breathing and quieten the screaming in his head. The throbbing diminished. At the same time he was aware that he might still be in danger. Who knew what this man might do to him? Some accident or other? A bus crash? A fall from a height? No one here would ask any questions. The island of Ireland would mean very little here.

Get a grip, he told himself, he can't do anything. He did not believe anything the man said, but common sense told him that they couldn't just do away with him. Surely not. Not here.

Just at that moment a polite Singaporean lady approached him and told him with an obsequious smile that the next bus back to the city was about to leave.

By the time he was let out near his hotel he still could not think for all the noise in his head. He knew this was panic, had heard these voices in the past and been able to quell them. Not so easily this time. He was not delivering a car full of explosives to an RUC station in Antrim. He was not lying in the cold, wet undergrowth of County Fermanagh armed with a Kalashnikov. He was not undergoing interrogation at Bessbrook Barracks. He was on his own in a strange and dangerous place. He must think, think, not least what he would say when he reached home. Nothing, he concluded immediately, unless he wanted to sign his own death warrant. Your man was right about that, at least.

He decided he must have a drink and subsided into a dark corner of a nearby bar with a large whisky. The burn at the back of his throat both awakened and calmed him. It cauterized something. Or that was how he felt. His hand still shook, but reason was returning.

He decided to walk for a while from bar to bar in the dusk, to use his training to gauge the size of things. It was a hopeless task. He would not be able to spot their men behind him in this swirl of colour, smell and humanity. This was their ground. But each drink made him feel a little better. Finally he decided it was time to return to the hotel. He would make no secret of what he planned to do next. He asked the concierge to check whether any seats could be found on flights that night. It was as well to leave as soon as possible. There were seats, but they came at a hefty surcharge, so he left it that they would fly out as scheduled on the midnight Lufthansa flight the next evening.

He took the lift back up to the room. It was empty: Bridget would be at the hen night. He had forgotten all about the stag party but had even less appetite for it than he did for the wedding itself. He drank three beers from the minibar before falling asleep fully clothed.

The next morning, she was already up, dressed to the nines.

'We're not going,' he said.

'What do you mean, Francis?'

'We're not fecking going. We're going home.'

'But we've come all this way.'

'You think I don't know that? Anyways, I thought you didn't want to come.'

'That's different, Francis. We're here now and we have to go.'

'No, we don't. Not if I say so.'

'But why, Francis? Why?'

'Because I don't feel like it. All right?'

She did not reply, did not push him. For which he was moderately grateful. 'Look,' he said. 'I don't feel well. I just want to get home as soon as I can.'

'What is it, Francis? Should I fetch a doctor to you?'

'No. Stop fussing over me. I'll just stay in bed for a while. Will you just be telling them I'm not well?'

He watched as, sitting on the edge of the bed and biting her lip, she contemplated what she would say. She picked up the phone.

'And while you're at it you'd better say you're sick too. I don't want you to be going either.'

'But I thought if one of us –'

'Don't you be worrying about thinking. Just tell them.'

She made the call while Francis watched her intently.

They remained in their room, he sullen and she nervous, both silent, until the evening, when it was time to take the rapid transit to the airport. They checked in early for their flight. It took off on time, almost at midnight, and twenty hours later they arrived at a cold and misty Dublin at eleven forty-five in the morning. By the time they reached home it was almost four in the afternoon. Bridget lit the fire and began to unpack while Francis went out in the car on some unspecified errand. The adventure was over. No longer could she imagine herself as a strong, independent woman like Cheryl or Sarah, even in a distant dream. No doubt Sarah would forget to keep in touch, or had never intended to, and that would be the end of that. The end of it all.

1991

5

Richard Mercer had that feeling of inferiority he always experienced when entering military premises. Not absolute, but momentary and distracting, the sense of being a less developed life form when coming into this world of order, control and discipline where everything had its place. As did everyone.

In fact Mercer outranked all of them in this office according to the tables that codify such things, drawing cross-government lines between colonels and assistant chief constables and deputy PUSs, and between WO2s and third secretaries and HEOs. But he still felt less than them, with his reliance on feel and doubt rather than process and certainty.

The majors came and went, young, thrusting and enthusiastic when they began, all darting eyes and relief when they left eighteen months later. Provided, that is, there were no debacles in the interim. If there was a disaster they would be short-toured immediately and an old salt put in place to steady the ship until the next bright-eyed youngster came off the production line. This posting was a rite of passage before moving on to bigger and better things: perhaps a spell in MOD Main Building or as staff officer to a brigadier before a taste of real command. For some reason, being in charge of this covert unit was regarded as important, or at least formative for the military soul. Its criticality, though, was in not dropping a bollock, rather than making real headway. Everyone knew progress was impossible: until something dramatic happened politically the army, like everyone else, was stuck. But it seemed that none of these eager young men had been told. Each was determined to make his mark. Until after a year or so it all sunk in.

David Pope-Norton was no different. Bland aside from his punctilious military sharpness, he used language that was carefully strained and filtered to convey nothing other than an unshakeable certitude and positivity. This was what they taught them at Camberley these days. It passed for leadership. Thank goodness he hadn't followed the advice of the careers adviser at university, thought Richard.

Pope-Norton was one of a modest dynasty of army officers. His uncle had been a full colonel, his father only half. That must have made for fun fraternal relations. At least it would have provided young David with his aiming point. He was a nice enough man, though, and the times they were a-changing. No doubt he would have been briefed by his superiors in MOD Main Building to do his best to clear out the stables, put a calm hand on the tiller, keep his head below the parapet and the rest of those military clichés. Whether he was up to even beginning to shovel away the shit of decades and jettison the multitudinous hulks of five-tour mammoths like Freddie Spencer was open to question. But he was a nice enough young fellow.

Richard was shown in by a uniformed non-com with a snap in his step. Four government-issue seats were arrayed around the coffee table. Easy chairs they might have been called had they offered any semblance of comfort. David Pope-Norton, the only one of the three in uniform, sat in one; Freddie Spencer, the retired emeritus operational adviser who answered to a captain's rank but no longer wore military uniform, occupied the second; and in the third, in his jeans and Shetland sweater, was Geordie Smith, the senior warrant officer who had been cycled through Northern Ireland three or four times on successive roulements and who actually knew the job. Richard knew that it was the warrant officers, with whom he felt marginally more comfortable, who kept the ship of state in the source unit afloat.

A glance at Geordie told him that this was going to be one of those meetings.

'Richard,' said Pope-Norton with a broad smile. 'How goes it?'

'David,' he said. 'Well, thanks. And you?'

'Never better. Extraordinarily well, as a matter of fact.'

David Pope-Norton was around thirty-two, fresh-faced and with a shock of dark brown hair. He'd want to be on his way onwards and upwards before too long.

Richard said, 'Freddie. Geordie.'

'Richard,' said Freddie Spencer, blinking slowly and flattening his brilliantined hair with a greasy palm, smiling his plumply complacent smile. A lurid flaming-red polka-dot handkerchief sprouted profusely from the pocket of his sharkskin double-breaster. Freddie had risen from the ranks – without trace, it seemed to Richard – and his tenure as an officer had been studded with gossip of narrow escapes and foolish ventures from which he was saved only by his own men. Freddie wasn't, though, one of the officer class by birth and destiny. His nasal tones and ill-at-ease demeanour betrayed that he was not the product of some terrible and terrifying public-school upbringing and that his origins must be closer to Richard's own than was comfortable. They did not, however, occupy the same philosophical space. Freddie, by his own lights, had *arrived*, and Richard doubted he ever would. Freddie strove to identify with these people; Richard could not. Yet something in each of them nodded at the other in contemptuous recognition.

'Sir,' said Geordie Smith.

They waited for tea to be brought in by a nervous squaddie, the standard-issue stainless-steel pot polished to within an inch of its life and the thick china crockery that would not break when dropped from clumsy, podgy fingers. Predictably the tea came nuclear strength and red as the young man's cheeks, requiring several spoonfuls of sugar to make it palatable. David Pope-Norton served, as if to demonstrate that this was an egalitarian show.

'Congratulations, by the way, on the new job.'

'Thanks.'

'Charles moving somewhere interesting?'

'Oh, you know. Bigger and better things.'

'Good, good. And when do you leave us?'

'I think I've got about six weeks.'

'And counting?'

'Not at all. I've thoroughly enjoyed my time.' This was what Richard was supposed to say and it had the advantage of being mostly true.

'Plenty of time to bury the old skeletons, then?'

'Something like that.' Richard smiled politely.

'Well,' said Pope-Norton, 'got a good one here. Particularly wanted to talk it over with you. Hope you'll have time to give it the once-over before you're off to London. Be good to have your view. I'm sure your successor will be a perfectly good man, but . . .'

'I know what you mean. I've been round the course a few times. And my successor's a woman.'

'Oh really?' This stalled the conversation for a few moments as Pope-Norton strove to compute. Eventually he continued: 'You must introduce us when she's in town. Anyway, this case. Don't know if you'll be excited by it. Rather hope you will be.'

Richard tried to look suitably attentive, unable to remember the last time he'd been excited by anything in the province. Terrified, yes. Bored, certainly. 'Yes?' he said.

'O'Neill,' said Pope-Norton.

'O'Neill?'

'That's right. Ex of Belfast. Now living in South Armagh.'

'O'Neill as in he of the continental campaign,' said Freddie Spencer drily. 'As in crack operator. As in public enemy number one, if memory serves. Place him?'

'You've recruited Francis O'Neill? I'm impressed.' Richard thought he could see Geordie grin minutely. Freddie Spencer sighed but gazed on implacably.

'No, no,' said Pope-Norton. 'I think we'd be putting newspaper down our trousers in expectation of the inevitable caning if we'd had a pop at Francis O'Neill. He's a bit out of our league.'

'Or so your masters would say,' interjected Spencer.

'The brother,' said Geordie softly. 'Liam.'

'Ah,' said Richard. 'A lot younger, isn't he?'

'He's a bit wet behind the ears, yes. But we think he has potential, don't we, gents?'

'Yes,' said Spencer.

'Yes, sir,' said Geordie.

'What's he like as a person?' Richard addressed himself to Geordie.

'As the major says, sir, a bit immature. Headstrong if you like.'

'I don't particularly. Headstrong's not good. And how's he ended up talking to you people?'

'Phoned up the main switchboard, bold as brass,' said Spencer. Richard raised his eyebrows. 'Yes, we thought that. Took all the necessary precautions. Every care. It's been all right so far.'

'Hmm,' said Richard. 'RUC in the know? Everything all square with them?'

'Of course, Richard,' said Pope-Norton. 'We've learned

from our mistakes. Of course we've told our friends all about it. Everything's tickety-boo as far as they're concerned.'

Richard glanced at Freddie Spencer, one of the key practitioners, while he was serving, of the it'll-be-all-right-on-the-night-what-they-don't-know-won't-trouble-them school of operations. Freddie's own proximity to certain of the Loyalist paramilitaries had also been, at best, questionable. Spencer was expressionless.

'And they're relaxed? Don't want a piece of the action?'

'Let's put it like this. They've given us the all clear. I can show you the note if you like,' said Pope-Norton.

'There's no need.'

'To be frank, I think there's a little jealousy there,' said Pope-Norton.

'Understandable,' said Richard, and Geordie shifted slightly in his seat.

'But they'll let us get on with our stuff.'

'Hmm. Good.' He looked up at the three men.

'The thing is,' said Pope-Norton, 'we wondered whether you might want to look at our bright young thing. Before you head off to your new job. Evaluate him. Value your input.'

'It's probably better to let you get on with it, don't you think? Geordie knows his onions. Develop him. See in six months where we are?'

'We were thinking, Freddie and I,' continued Pope-Norton, as if Richard had not spoken, 'that with his access he might even make the grade to your exalted ranks.'

'Well, David, I'd feel very uneasy about poaching your joes. It's not something I like doing.'

'I quite understand. And I'm appreciative. But for the greater good? Queen and country? We understand, don't we, chaps?'

'Yes,' chanted Freddie Spencer and Geordie Smith in unison.

Richard, too, understood. The incentives had altered within the military. They'd got the idea that it was good for them to nurture new people for the high table. That there could be potential for their street informants to become real spies, and that they would gain kudos as a result. He must be polite.

'Look, here's what I'll do. I'll give it a bit of a ponder. Don't suppose you could send the papers over sometime?'

'Of course, of course. We'll get them over to your office quick sharp.'

'Excellent. Give me a couple of days to mull and I'll get back to you.'

He knew the conversation with Charles the next time he was in head office would be difficult.

'Take my advice, Richard. Humour them,' said Charles.

Easy for him, sitting in London, just seeing out his time. Richard was the one in Belfast.

'This is going nowhere, Charles. Liam O'Neill has spent the whole of his short life doing as little as possible. He doesn't associate with Republicans, he's been disciplined by them for petty crime, he's nine years younger than his brother and they're not close. Plus, he'll have his own agenda.'

'Don't we all have our own agendas, Richard?'

Richard looked at him.

'The thing is, Richard, we need to maintain good relations with the military. They're not such a bad lot when all's said and done. They have a difficult job.'

The moment when Charles became emollient was the moment to feel concerned.

'Don't we all, Charles?'

'Indeed. Look, I know Freddie Spencer gets a bad press. But in the end our job is to defeat these people.'

'Is it?'

'All these rumours about Freddie, they're wildly exaggerated, I'm sure.'

'Rumours? Such as?'

'You know. His proximity to some of the Loyalist factions. Ill-advised certainly, at least for it to be quite so blatant. But is there really so much wrong with reaching out to those of a similar mind? Even if they're a tad overenthusiastic.'

'A tad overenthusiastic?'

'Whatever our mealy-mouthed politicians – or our mealy-mouthed bosses, for that matter – may say, the job is about crushing these bastards, by fair means or foul in my book. Strange bedfellows and all that. It's easy for us to be prissy. Real life doesn't have to intervene for us.'

'Or real death, so it would seem.'

'Pardon?'

'Never mind. These good relations. Can you describe relations based on dishonesty as good?'

It was Charles's turn to widen his eyes. 'I find your naivety wholly endearing, Richard. Always have. I admire your youthful enthusiasm –'

'I'm hardly a youth, Charles.'

'You damn well are in comparison with me. You've never served in the forces, have you?'

'You know I haven't, Charles,' said Richard, ready for the inevitable lecture that drew on Charles's experience in a Guards regiment.

'The army is a different universe.'

'Like the past?'

'Eh?'

'They do things differently there.'

'Well, as I was saying . . . well, yes. Indeed. They do. Do things differently, I mean. You'd imagine the army was a place for straight talking? Well, it isn't, not by a long chalk. Give an officer less than an A box marking at appraisal time and you might as well be signing his dismissal papers. This is the same. We say anything even mildly disobliging and the major gits it.'

He smiled, evidently impressed by his cowboy accent.

'So?'

'So go and see this character. Say some nice things in the debrief. Write them a letter saying don't phone us we'll phone you. Kick the can down the road. They will then do whatever they want with him. Or alternatively take him on yourself. See if it's possible to make a silk purse out of a sow's ear. Waste of time from my point of view, but it may satisfy your bleeding-heart sensibilities for him to be safely sidelined. If you're so set on giving them the bum's rush you can do it when you're in my chair.'

Richard could understand why Charles was being moved on. But why so gently?

'There's no point kicking against it,' said Geordie as they sat in the car in darkness. The radio sputtered into the earpieces they were wearing under their woollen hats. It was a test message. 'The gaffer's determined this is his big triumph. If you don't take it on he'll see that as a green light for us to plough ahead ourselves.'

'What do you think?'

'Not paid to think.'

'You're not paid to breathe, Geordie.'

'Well, whatever I think is irrelevant.'

'Not to me.'

'Aye. That's as mebbe. What I think is, there's no point kicking when you're on a loser. We both know the score. It's already decided. By my bosses and like as not by yours.'

'We'll see. I'll be in charge on my side soon.'

'And what? Everything's going to change?'

'You sound world-weary, Geordie.'

'Wouldn't you be? A succession of Tim Nice-But-Dims who see this as a stepping stone and fucking Freddie Spencer with his handkerchiefs sticking out his pocket like some conjuror with a rabbit up his arse. This fucking mess. Ireland was a mess before I got here. Has been all the time I've been here. Always will be. In my lifetime anyway. Why we can't just clear out and leave them to fight it out is beyond me.'

'How long to go?'

Geordie consulted his watch. 'Six,' he said and they were silent for a moment.

'What do you make of the boy?'

'Hopeless, but I didn't tell you that. You'll work it out for yourself soon enough. Complete gobshite. Won't listen for a second. Reckons he's going to be in an ASU any minute. On his brother's coat-tails. Bit of the old stardust, he keeps saying. And then he winks. Flaky as hell. But the major's convinced this is the one.'

The boy looked little different now under the harsh neon light than when he'd first seen him, thin and bent against the misty rain, hood up, smoking a cigarette as Geordie drove past him prior to the pick-up.

Goodness knows where they were. After the boy had climbed into the back seat the military cavalcade moved away, turning off the bypass quickly and negotiating the country roads, this way and that, hedgerows flashing by in the headlights. It could scarcely have been less obvious had they put up posters in advance advertising the carnival. But that was just Richard's opinion. Eventually they pulled off into a long driveway.

And now here they were. In this safe house, wherever it was. It was quiet but for the sound of water dripping off the boy's jacket on to the linoleum floor as he sat on a plastic chair, cigarette between finger and thumb, bowed down, legs apart, as he drew the last of the nicotine from the burning stub. A kitchen of some kind, cheaply equipped, harshly strip-lit. Not the sort of place where confidences could easily be elicited.

'Bit wet out, Liam,' said Geordie.

'Aye,' said the boy, still looking down. 'You don't say.'

'Liam, this is the boss I was talking about.'

He glanced up and then looked down again.

'Hello, Liam. I'm Richard.' To Geordie, 'Is there somewhere more comfortable we could sit?'

Geordie looked over Liam's bowed shoulder and shook his head. Richard sighed. Liam showed no sign of having heard. Richard drew up a chair opposite him. Geordie switched on the kettle and delved for tea bags and mugs.

'Do you want to take your coat off? Let me hang it up for you,' said Richard.

'Cold,' said the boy.

'You'll soon warm up. Heating's on. I can feel the radiator. Best dry your coat off.'

Geordie flicked the tea bags into the sink, splashed some milk into the mugs and brought them over, gripping the handles in one large hand. 'Get that down you,' he said.

Liam raised his head and looked at them in turn. 'Checking me out?' he said to Richard, attempting a wry smile.

'I wanted to meet you. I thought it was right, now.' He bided his time.

'I was saying to Mr Smith, I know all kinds of stuff. About the RA, about my brother. Ask me anything. What I don't know I can find out. I can go down to Francis's place. Any time. I can get inside. Bit of Francis's old stardust. All youse got to do is tell me what youse want.' He winked.

'That's very good. I'm very interested. But shall we take things one step at a time?'

87

Richard looked at him. He was so young. A kid. Perhaps they were like policemen, joes. The older you got, the younger they looked. He knew from the file that Liam O'Neill was twenty-two years old but he looked like a child, gaunt and gawky, lank-haired, permanently suspecting and suspect, ill-at-ease and defiant.

'Well, then, Liam. Shall we get going? What made you phone our people in the first place?'

'I've got those things you asked for,' said Liam, addressing himself to Geordie. 'And I can't be long. I'm expected back.'

'Never mind what I asked you for,' said Geordie, taking a seat. 'This is important. I thought you said you had all evening.'

'Yeah, well. I forgot. I'm meant to be seeing Gary down the pub.'

'Not exactly vital, is it? Not like you're missing your own heart transplant operation, is it? I told you you needed to find time for this. All right?'

'I suppose so.' He shot a glance at Richard and looked at Geordie. 'Yes, Mr Smith.'

'There we are, then,' said Richard. 'Why are you seeing your friend Gary this evening? Anything we'd be interested in?'

'No, he's just a mate.'

'And?'

'Um, I'm seeing him about a microwave he might be able to sell me for me ma.'

'Well, let's talk later about what you might be able to say to him, shall we?'

'I suppose so.' He looked again, before adding, 'Sir.'

'Richard'll do fine, Liam. Now then, shall we get down to business?'

'If you like.'

'I do like,' said Richard without aggression. 'So, what prompted you to pick up the phone? In your own time.'

'I was sick of it all. Ireland's going down the pan. All this trouble. And Francis is up to his neck in it. I thought I might be able to protect him.'

'I see. So you think the IRA is a bad thing?'

'Fuck yes. Don't you?'

'What I think is rather by the by, Liam. I'm interested in your thoughts. So you want to help stop the IRA doing all those nasty things it gets up to?'

'If you like.'

'Don't let me put words into your mouth, Liam, please. I'm just trying to get a picture of what you feel. That's all. No problem. There are no wrong or right answers. Say what you think.' He smiled in encouragement.

'Well, you've probably got it just about right.'

'Good. Ever been in trouble with the RA?'

'What do you mean?'

'You know they like to think they're the law in West Belfast. Judge, jury and so on. Have they ever had you in to discuss your behaviour?'

Liam O'Neill looked at Richard, calculating. He looked back, implacably amiable.

'There was one or two things when I was a kid. Nothing serious.'

'I know. We all get up to things when we're teenagers. Anyone in particular you dealt with?'

'It'd be Martin Dempsey who spoke to me.'

'Verbal warning, would it have been?'

'A bit more. Nothing too bad.'

'I see. And what did you do after that?'

'Spoke to Francis about it when I saw him.'

'Spoke to Francis. And what did he do?'

Liam shrugged. 'Couldn't do nothing. Told me the Belfast Brigade was in charge of its own business and he couldn't interfere. He wasn't there no more.'

'And when would this be?'

'Three or four years back.'

'I see. He must have known this Martin . . . what was it?'

'Dempsey. Yeah, he knew him well enough.'

'But he wouldn't have a quiet word. Did you feel angry at that? Just a bit?'

'No. He'll have had his reasons.'

'So you're not doing this out of grudge?'

'No. I just think . . .'

'Hmm,' said Richard. 'But of course we couldn't let you do this and be out of pocket, could we?'

Liam looked more directly and his face lightened.

'I'm not in this for the money,' he said.

'No. I can see that. Though we would insist on paying you generously for your commitment. If, that is, we can come to an arrangement over how we play things. I'm curious. Doesn't it worry you at all, coming to us?'

'Not particularly. Should it? You'll look after me, won't you?'

'Yes, of course. But I'm wondering why you seem so relaxed with it. It's a big step and I can imagine people in your position feeling pretty concerned.'

'Worried they might be putting me up to it?' He grinned.

'Not at all. And of course it's a good thing that you can handle the pressure.'

'There you are, then.' That petulant little grin was back.

Richard attempted to keep his sigh inward and inaudible. 'Yes. There we are. Good. Shall we talk about how you might help?'

'There's all kinds I can do. I can spend more time with Francis. He can get me in in Belfast.'

'I thought he didn't interfere?'

'Well, I'm on all fours with Martin Dempsey now anyway. He'll find me something to do for the boys. Run guns or something. Or I could spend more time down there with Francis. Find out what he's doing.'

'Very interesting. I didn't know that's how it worked. I thought you had to prove yourself with boring little tasks to begin with. I didn't realize you could just step in and take things on like that. Or that Francis would be forthcoming to you.'

'You'd be surprised at what I can do for you.'

'We've talked about this, Liam,' said Geordie. 'We need to take things steady. Gradual. Can't afford to take risks.'

'I know. But I can do this. I can look after me own self.'

'I'm sure you can,' said Richard.

The conversation continued, spinning on in its strange circular fashion. Concealing his despair, eventually Richard said, 'Much food for thought, Liam. It's been a real pleasure meeting you. Anyway, you must get back to your . . . microwave, was it?'

He was patient through the debrief. The full team attended the first part and they were taken through all the preliminaries of the meetings. The military cannot be faulted for lacking thoroughness, he thought. By the time they filed out and left the officers to it, it was past midnight. David Pope-Norton, who was there both in Richard's honour and in expectation, took a bottle of whiskey from his briefcase.

Geordie went through the practical details. Liam O'Neill had improved his tradecraft: the pick-up had gone more smoothly than last time. His employment situation had not changed. He was still living with his mother and father. His spirits were good and he remained enthusiastic about his informant role. He'd split up with his girlfriend, suspecting her of infidelity. He thought she might be pregnant. It might be Liam's child. They had agreed to meet again in the same place the following week, with the same cover story, that Liam was considering buying a second-hand car and had agreed with Geordie, the putative seller, to meet in the lay-by on the bypass.

'So,' said Pope-Norton eventually, and turned to look at Richard, who also had Freddie Spencer's attention. Geordie looked away.

'Very interesting. An interesting young man. There's a lot going on there.' Richard ventured a faint smile.

'And?' said Freddie.

'And I think you've done a tremendous job bringing him on board. Geordie in particular of course.'

'You don't need to spare our feelings, Richard,' said Pope-Norton. 'What did you make of him?'

'Well.' Richard coughed and took another slug of air. 'As I said, he's an interesting young man. Ultimately, though, I think you should cut your losses and disengage.'

Pope-Norton looked dismayed. Freddie Spencer glared.

'And why might that be?' asked Pope-Norton.

'I think you've better things to do with your time. He has no access. We know from reporting that the IRA has disciplined him for crime. He has barely any relationship with his brother. Yet he seems to believe that in a few weeks he'll be leading active service units and telling you exactly what's in Francis's mind.'

'He may be ambitious, talking a good fight. We all know it'll take time to wheedle his way into an ASU. But somehow I like that. It's our job to keep it in check. Stop him overreaching himself. Isn't it, Geordie?'

'Yes, sir.'

'Of course it's entirely up to you what you choose to do, David. But I see a young man who's not sufficiently amenable to anyone's influence. I'm troubled by what motivates him and

92

I think he's immature and foolhardy. He's little or no sense of the danger he's placing himself in. We're not looking for panickers but he seems to be in a world of his own. If he had real access or I could see a way for him to gain that access I might feel differently. I don't think we'd want to take him on.'

'Is that what Charles would say? Or his boss?'

'I don't know what Charles would say. But it'd be on my conscience if I didn't tell you exactly how I felt. It's up to you what you do, though.'

In fact Richard knew precisely what Charles would say, and he did so, with alacrity. Richard shrugged, wrote it up, sent Pope-Norton a polite but unambiguous letter and assumed it was the end of the matter. It was time, anyway, for him to pack up and get back to London.

Whether they persisted with Liam O'Neill was up to them. He'd fulfilled his obligations, duly protected his own and his organization's back and it was no longer his concern. This place eroded scruples, the inclination to foresee the consequences of one's actions and any sense of personal responsibility. It was all too awful and if you began to think too much you'd never get anything done. Placing one foot blindly before the other was all you could do in these trenches.

6

It was a damp Tuesday morning when Sarah rang. It was an event in itself when the telephone rang, so she almost knew it would be her. She'd called each month since Singapore.

'I'm glad I caught you,' said Sarah.

'I'm just in from the shops,' said Bridget. 'Can you wait a moment, please?'

'Of course.'

Bridget took off her wet raincoat and hung it carefully on the hook in the hallway. Water dripped on to the linoleum. She folded her headscarf in two before draping it over the banister. She mussed her hair and picked up the telephone again.

'I'm sorry. It's wet outside. I had to take my coat off.'

'That's all right. It's raining here in Birmingham too.'

'Only, you're calling from England . . .'

'It's all right. I'm phoning from the office. They'll never know,' she said in a conspiratorial whisper. 'How are you, then, Bridget?'

'I'm fine, Sarah.'

'Am I disturbing you? Francis around?'

'No.'

'Are you all right?'

'Yes, thank you, Sarah. I'm fine. It's nice to speak again. How are you?'

'Wonderful. What's going on with you?'

'Just the normal stuff. Summer'll be here soon enough. I'm starting me spring cleaning. The blossom's starting to show on the trees.'

'I can just imagine it. Sitting there in your cosy little cottage in the middle of nowhere . . .'

'It's not that idyllic,' insisted Bridget.

'I'm sure it's not,' said Sarah.

'What are you up to?'

'Oh, busy busy busy. God, meetings, whoever invented them? But I'm blathering again.'

'No you're not.' She was, but it was pleasant to hear her talking.

'You're far too polite, Bridget. It's good to talk to you though. Listen, I've had this crazy idea.'

'Yes?'

'I'd really like to see you. I've been given a bonus. Much bigger than I dared expect. Anyway, I was planning a long weekend away on my ill-gotten gains with one of my old girlfriends from uni. South of France. She's just cried off, though. I'm quite relieved. I'd much rather go away with you. All my friends, they have complications with kids and they talk about them constantly when they're away from them. Please say yes. Otherwise I'll have to cancel and lose my deposit. Are you up for it?'

'Excuse me?'

'South of France. Charles Trenet on the car radio. Ricard at the café watching the chic set go by?'

'Me?'

'Yes, you.'

'I'm not sure. When were you thinking?'

'Didn't I say? It would be this weekend. Is that a problem? Will your husband not let you?'

'He won't be back until next week.'

'Well. There you are, then.'

'I can't just up and go like that.'

'Why not?'

'People. People would know.'

'And that matters?'

'Of course. If only you knew.'

'I can well imagine.'

'Maybe you can't. Anyway, I'm not like you.'

'Yes, you are. You know you are.'

'I don't do things like this. I don't just get up and go on impulse. How would I get there for a start?'

'That's another thing I forgot to mention. I've got a provisional booking on a cheap flight from Dublin to Marseille. Call it an early birthday present. Aer Lingus is waiting for me to call back with the passenger details. All you have to do is turn up at the airport with your passport and away you go.'

'All I have to do. You don't realize how difficult for me that would be.'

'I do. I know it's hard.'

'People round here know everything about me. They know what I'm doing. They check up on me.'

'Check up?'

'Not in a horrible way. There are people who see me all the time. They'd ask where I'd been.'

'Right.'

'And people round here don't just up and go to France for the weekend. We don't up and go anywhere.'

'How about this? Could you say you'd been to see your sister?'

'I could, I suppose. I don't see her often, though.'

'Well, say she's ill, or going through some crisis. Would anyone check with her?'

'I don't think so.'

'Could you ask her to cover for you if they did?'

'I suppose. She'd probably think I had a man . . .'

'Well, is that so bad? All right, then, phone her and tell her it's to do with some medical condition that you don't want to worry your husband about. So she needs to cover for you.'

'He wouldn't speak to her anyway.'

'All right. But just in case. Don't say anything more. Don't make anything up or talk about the condition. She can fill that in for herself.'

'It sounds like you've done this sort of thing before. Assignations and so forth.'

'Ha. You could say that. In this day and age you're lucky if you haven't had to engage in the odd act of subterfuge, if only for a friend. Are you happy with that plan?'

'I . . . I suppose so,' said Bridget meekly, feeling she was being carried along.

'Great. When you get to Dublin just go to the desk and pick up your ticket. Don't feel the need to explain yourself to anyone.'

'And if I meet anyone I know?'

'We'll cross that bridge if we come to it.'

When she put the phone down Bridget felt a mixture of emotions: fear of discovery, anxiety about explaining her absence, but at the same time a certain lightness of heart.

They were off the motorway now, so she could wind down the window and inhale. Lavender and a mixture of other fragrances she did not recognize – herbs, maybe – intermingled on the mild breeze. She could feel the warmth on her skin, let it imbue her, seduce her. She closed her eyes in pleasure.

She hoped she'd been sufficiently hesitant before accepting the invitation. Francis was away, she had no idea where, and would be back in his own good time. It would not be before next week, though, she was sure; and if it was she would, for once, take her chances. The thought of her rashness thrilled her with a mixture of excitement and fear. This weekend was a turning point, she knew it. She was not inclined to melo-drama, but it seemed like that to her.

It was all so unnerving. The very process of getting here had been daunting, so much so that she'd thought several times of turning round and going home. But the desk that Sarah had said would be there at Dublin airport magically had been and a woman with shimmering lipgloss handed Bridget her ticket with little interest when she recited the jumble of letters and numbers that Sarah had given her. She'd looked at it, bemused, for a moment until, with a glance at the queue behind her, the woman had dismissed her.

And then to check-in. She'd handed in her ticket and pass-port and her bag and had been seriously considering backing out when she realized she couldn't any more. Her bag was wobbling away on the conveyor belt and she was checked in.

She'd flown to Singapore with Francis but that had been dif-ferent. He'd taken control of everything. This morning, though, she'd wandered through the controls and the shops as if she'd just woken and was full of sleep. She'd taken her seat at what they called the gate and eventually the passengers had been called forward to the aircraft. At each stage she'd expected it, somehow, to end, but she was now in France.

And there Sarah had been at Marseille, with a broad smile and outstretched arms, and it felt suddenly all right. She'd allowed herself to be guided to the car park and, as Sarah fum-bled for change, she looked around. It was real, then, this wide blue sky, the kerosene tang of the airport, all those signs and adverts in French, with its acutes and graves and circumflexes, and the liquid elegance of its sounds that she recalled from school. She'd enjoyed languages, but it was all forgotten. The snatches of conversation she picked up were somehow famil-iar but incomprehensible.

Sarah drove confidently but cautiously, quite unlike Francis, with his garrulous manoeuvring of their old Ford round country lane corners and his complaints about its suspension and handling. Their progress was fast enough, then again slow enough for her to take in this new and so far magical world with its beneficent sunlight. They passed through small towns and Sarah concentrated as she followed the route and as mopeds ridden by helmetless young boys wearing shorts and sandals buzzed between the flow of cars. They spoke very little; for Bridget it was enough to breathe. She did not allow herself to consider what the next few days would bring, only that it might be pleasurable.

They stopped in a small village. 'Bread,' said Sarah, and walked towards the baker's. After a moment Bridget too stepped out of the car and stretched her arms, basking briefly in the sunshine.

The small square was deserted and silent. She could smell oily-smoky diesel, the sweet, yeasty doughiness of fresh-baked bread, and the odour of the open drain nearby. The sun was not beating down but beaming on her. She squinted in the bright light. An old man came out of the nearby café, smiled at her, climbed on to an ancient bicycle and pedalled off. Sitting on the ancient yellow stone of the small fountain in the centre of the square and dipping her hand into the clear water, she looked at the war memorial.

It still had that ring of utter but benign unreality, so tranquil, so distant. France: this was actually France. She was glad to be away from home and from him, free for a moment to confess her feelings to herself: terror when he was in the house and hatred when he was not, bound up in despair. These were the things that she could never say to the other wives and nor, yet, to Sarah. She surprised herself at the vehemence of her sentiments, then brought herself back to the pleasure of the present.

Sarah came out of the baker's waving a baguette.

'You should have come in with me,' she said. 'What fantastic bread. And loads of superb croissanty things. I thought you must be tired after the flight.'

'No, I feel fine,' said Bridget. 'Really I do. By the way, who's Charles Trenet?'

They arrived at the villa at around midday. The grey-blue wooden shutters were closed to keep the heat out and together they walked around the house, opening those on the ground floor. Inside, it was cool, quiet, rustic and ordered. The kitchen was long and tiled, with a rough-hewn farmhouse table, its surface smoothed by generations of use, set at one end near an open hearth, and the range, sink and other units at the opposite end. There was a formal dining room which they would not use, with a musty smell and chairs lined up with precision at the table seemingly to denote absent guests, and a large lounge with French doors at either end leading out to the two main parts of the garden. Three old sofas that looked shabbily comfortable surrounded the massive limestone hearth, smoke-stained from centuries of use, and at the other end of the room were two tub chairs near floor-to-ceiling bookshelves containing hardback and paperback books, mainly fiction, some biography; all, Bridget noted, in English.

Upstairs Sarah showed her her room and its bathroom with blue Delft tiles, shower and claw-foot bath, stained and chipped. Together they worked their way around the other upstairs rooms, opening the shutters, welcoming in the light. Sarah had the second-largest bedroom, at the opposite end of the house.

They unpacked the bread, found cheese in the fridge and tomatoes in a bowl on the table, misshapen and partly green. Sarah said she'd picked them in the garden that morning before she left for Marseille.

They took their food outside, crunching across the gravel drive, and climbing the short flight of steps to the large grass area at the back of the house next to the swimming pool. A routine had commenced.

Sarah spoke less than Bridget had expected. It seemed she had less need for volubility.

'You seem more relaxed,' said Bridget.

'Less talkative you mean,' replied Sarah. 'When you come somewhere like this you realize life doesn't have to be led at a hundred miles an hour. And you don't have to talk all the time.'

'I don't exactly live my life at a hundred miles an hour. I suppose I'm not much given to talking either these days.'

'You must have your stresses. Life's never simple. I'm sure even here people have tough lives though it doesn't seem like it. There's something to be said for being taken out of your life. Out of yourself in a way.'

They cleared the table and went upstairs to change into their swimming costumes. When they emerged Sarah said, 'My God, Bridget. You look amazing! Your hair when you let it down, it's lovely.'

She reached out and touched it, brushing Bridget's shoulder as she did so. Her hand remained there for the slightest moment and they smiled at each other. Bridget was embarrassed by the compliment.

'Thank you,' she said.

They sat by the pool reading, then swam together for a while, before reclining on their chairs to dry in the sun. Then they opened their books once more and remained until a chill began to take hold.

The first evening they went to a restaurant to eat, but subsequently they decided to remain at the house in the evenings. The day's end was then not punctuated by a rush to dress before getting into the car and finding the restaurant, and there was not the peering through the impenetrable country night to find their way back to the house. Instead, they ate lunch in a town they decided to visit and returned home to while away the afternoon in the sun.

Three nights was all they had but it was surprising to Bridget just how easily they had settled into a domestic pattern that resembled permanence. A suspension of reality, she thought, but Ireland and Francis nagged at her and conscious effort was required to push them into the background just for the moment. She knew, however, that this trip concerned how her very real life might unfold.

This was not like a dream, Bridget felt. Over the years she had dreamt frequently of other possible lives, usually while asleep, often while fully awake, hanging out the washing or shifting the venerable cylinder vacuum cleaner over resistant, bobbled carpets, or walking in the rain to the village to buy food. But this was better than a dream, this alternative reality out of reach but not entirely absurd, a distance but a measurable one from the place where every action, innocent and guilty alike, was prone to condemnation, where blind certainty was everything, where in the midst of apparent normality even the most innocent of people could be seconds from a brutal death.

She felt for Sarah a warmth she continued to try to suppress, a bond that had, however, become undeniable.

It was on the third evening that they spoke of it. She'd packed her bag, leaving out only her toiletries and a change of clothing for the morning. They would need to be up and out of the house early, Sarah had said.

In the afternoon she had walked down the hall, cool in contrast to the terrace's fierce heat, and caught sight of her reflection in the mirror. I'm pretty, she thought, or at least attractive, and was surprised and at the same time pleased. She wondered whether Francis would notice she had a tan. She would not know how to explain it; but Francis hardly looked at her these days, and besides it would almost certainly have faded by the time he returned to the cottage.

Back on the terrace, she resumed her reading. They swam at some unremembered point and prepared *citrons pressés* so bitter they pursed their lips. It seemed as if the day would last for ever. Bridget tried to read again but could not concentrate. She looked up and saw that Sarah was, it appeared, focused completely on the paperback in her hands. She set down her book and saw Sarah looking at her, suddenly serious.

'We have to talk,' said Sarah.

'I know,' she replied.

'I've been psyching myself up to say something. We both know what's going on.'

Bridget nodded.

'When did you work it out?'

'I'm not sure there was a moment. It gradually dawned on me. Even then I couldn't be certain.'

'Well, you are now.'

'Yes.'

'You're an intelligent woman, Bridget. Did you not have an inkling when we were in Singapore?'

'No. It was odd that a stranger should show an interest in me. I suppose I thought that that kind of thing happens to other people all the time. So why not me for once?'

'I'm sorry. The subterfuge . . .'

'No. Before you say anything, I can understand. In a way. You had to . . .'

'Find a way. Yes. If I'd come out with it straight away you'd have . . .'

'I'd have run a mile. I still don't . . .'

'We'll come to that later,' said Sarah hastily. 'You're not angry with me, then?'

'No.'

'Because I've not – until now – been honest with you. Don't think I've enjoyed being deceitful –'

'I thought that was it. I thought you people did enjoy it.'

'No. Not me, anyway. It was just the only way.'

'Not angry, no. More . . .'

'Yes?'

'Worried. Do you realize just how dangerous this is for me? I have to be so careful.'

'I know. That's why we did things in this way. I've done everything I possibly could. There's no chance your husband knows.'

'Who does know?'

'I'd be treating you like a fool if I pretended it was just me. We need a number of people precisely in order to protect you. But it's genuinely only those who need to know.'

'Put a number on it.'

'Seven people,' said Sarah without hesitation. 'I know precisely because I keep a very careful track of it.'

'Seven people. Seven people who have my life in their hands and whom I don't know. And that's if I believe you.'

'And do you?'

'It's irrelevant, isn't it? What is, is. But yes,' said Bridget with a sigh, 'I suppose I do believe you.'

'It seems a large number. But these people are completely trustworthy. They're colleagues and I would – I do – put my own life in their hands.'

'No police, then?'

'No.'

'You're sure?'

'Yes.'

Bridget considered for a moment before saying, 'It's cold. Let's get inside.'

It was artificial, she knew, to postpone the conversation. But it required instalments; she was not certain she could cope with everything all at once. Sarah seemed to welcome the fact.

Should she feel resentful at having been taken for a fool? Sarah had taken advantage of her gullibility and actively duped her. Why had she talked to her in the first place? Why had she, uncharacteristically, sat down with her? Drunk those gins and tonic? Gone to the Orchid Garden? Borrowed that dress? What had been the turning point? When, really, had she known?

The truth was, there probably had been no turning point. A gradual realization was what it had been. Sarah's story, now she considered it, had been extremely thin, almost preposterous. Deliberately so, possibly. Francis, if he came to hear of this, would be scornful. That, though, would be the least of her worries.

They ate quietly and it was Sarah who resumed the conversation.

'I had to,' she said. 'I hope you can see.'

'I can. But it doesn't make it any easier.'

'We know each other now, Bridget. I like you. I really do want to do the best for you.'

Bridget drank long and slow. 'It'll be Francis you want to know about.' There was some comfort in stating the obvious. It made things somehow graspable. But, she thought, not really.

'Whatever you think of him, and I can understand your loyalty, he's involved in things I'm sure you don't like.'

Bridget looked at Sarah. 'I know my husband. I know what Francis is.'

'I'm sure you do. For all I know, he may not want to be involved. He may just be in too deep. These are the kinds of things I need to know.'

'Why don't you just talk to him? He can tell you what he's thinking.'

'I know you're not that naive, Bridget. I'm talking to you because I can talk to you.'

'I don't know what he does.'

'But you can help me understand him. To know what's going on inside his head.'

'You're wrong if you think I have any idea. But why do you imagine I'd want to tell you if I did know?'

'The fact that you're here?'

'That means nothing. You said yourself you tricked me into coming. What is it you're wanting to know anyway?'

'Anything and everything. The state of his mind. How he feels about the cause. Is he disillusioned? Who does he trust? Who doesn't he trust? What are his plans, his movements?'

'You've really no idea, do you? You think I know any of this?'

'Well, let's just start with the small stuff. Any small detail.'

'You're desperate, aren't you?'

'Yes.'

'And why do you need to know all this?'

'It's my job to stop the people Francis is working for. As part of stopping it all.'

'Stopping it all. And I'm supposed to believe that? Don't you mean win? Beat us?'

'No, I don't. And you either believe me or you don't. That's up to you.'

'And if I choose not to?' Bridget wished she hadn't asked the question. She dreaded the answer.

'That's up to you too. You go home and that'll be the end of it. I won't harass you.'

'How do I know you won't use what I tell you to get the SAS or the Prods to kill Francis?'

'You don't. But that's what I'm saying. You can pass it all off as words if you like. I'm not going to have Francis killed. But sooner or later he's going to end up in big trouble. You know that as well as I do, probably better. He'll be lucky if it's a long jail sentence. To his bosses he's just another soldier.'

'So you will have him killed, just like Paddy?'

'No, I won't. The only person likely to get Francis killed is Francis himself.'

'But you want to put him in prison?'

'If necessary, yes.'

'That's a bit blunt.'

'I'll not pretend. It's important you know how things are. You want me to be honest, I'll be honest. But be honest with yourself at the same time. Francis is involved in things that make my stomach turn. I'm guessing you feel the same way. Nothing's going to change that or put right what he's already done. I'm determined to stop him and see him prosecuted. I'll not try to sugar the pill. But I won't try to have him killed. He's the one most likely to achieve that. There are no good choices. It won't go away. All you have are terrible choices and slightly less terrible ones.'

'And me? What happens to me?'

'Let me ask you a couple of questions first. Do you believe, even remotely, in what Francis and his people are doing?'

'I believe in a united Ireland, that's for sure. And the Provos are just defending their people. The only way they can.'

'But things are changing. It's not the only way. Francis and people like him don't change, though. With them doing what they do the violence will carry on for ever. I'm not offering to wave a magic wand but I am offering you a means of escape before it's too late. We'll take you away, to lead a new life of your own choosing, away from all this.'

'Sometime in the future.'

'Better than no hope at all.'

'Meanwhile I take all the risks. Do you know just how dangerous this is for me?'

'I think so. I'll do everything I can to keep you safe.'

'I'm expected to believe that?'

'You're not *expected* to. It's a matter of your faith in me. I've been doing this a long time. I'm good at it.'

'Do you have any idea of what they'd do to me? Any idea how many people are looking at me all the time, thinking: is she sound? Not just Francis and the boys. The other girls. Cathy, Anne-Marie, Patricia. How would I face them?'

'I do know. And you'll face them because you can. Because unless I'm wrong you're an incredibly strong, resourceful human being.'

'You may well be wrong on that.'

'I don't think so. You've hung on in there until now.'

'If you're saying I've already agreed . . .'

'I'm not. And if you decide you don't want to help we'll not do anything that could harm you. But you need to say nothing to anyone else. Francis included.'

'I'm not that foolish.'

'I'm sure you're not. And I don't think you're foolish enough to have come here without having a fair idea of what this was all about.'

7

Training. In the naughty corner. The incident in Bruges had been unfortunate. Very unfortunate. Nothing more. It was a setback to be sure; but they had to realize that accidents happen. No omelettes without breaking eggs etc. Not that the hierarchy had seen it that way. 'You idiot, what came over you? Thank Christ they weren't Americans,' Aidan Murphy, nominally his commanding officer, had said. 'Think what the big men are going to say. I'm going to be shat on from a great height. You don't know what's going on, fair play, but the timing of it.'

Francis had seen the press, both sides of the border. 'Atrocity' – *Irish Times*. 'Inexcusable' – *Irish Independent*. 'Get These Scum' – *Sun*. 'Betraying Their Cause' – *Guardian* leader. *An Phoblacht* had offered nothing. There was little to be said in their defence, he supposed.

It was all Brian's fault, and now Brian was in custody in Germany. The lawyers reckoned he'd soon be released. Nothing to hold him on. Brian had spotted them up. Was up in Rheindahlen first thing in the morning. Saw the green Opel, four up, leaving the barracks and followed it along the motorway. John Boy and Francis were waiting up in the house, not sure how the day would go. Got the call from a breathless Brian from a service station near the border. Rushed on up there and phoned in to Dublin, where Brian had left a message. Bruges, it was. Targets on the canals. Get a move on.

Except Brian had got his green Opels mixed up. God knows where the one with the soldiers in it went. Francis and John

Boy caught up with him at a café in Bruges in sight of the Opel. Piece of piss. Just wait for the targets – two guys, two women in tow – to return and Bob's your uncle. Easy-peasy, and they did return, at about four p.m. No one in the vicinity to cloud the issue, quick march up, Brian watching his back. Pop, pop, both men down. One of the girls decides to get feisty but a quick slap puts her down. And away. Job done.

Or so he had thought. He'd not known that they were Canadians. What on earth had possessed them to have the same car as some British servicemen? Admittedly it had been easier in the days the British forces' cars were clearly identified. But Brian, what were you thinking?

When they'd heard about it in the car on the way to the airport Brian had gone into a blind funk. He got it into his head they were being followed and took his handgun out, releasing the safety catch. He told John Boy to speed up, but John Boy demurred. Brian began gesturing at other vehicles and they'd had to leave the motorway so that Francis could drag him out of the back of the car, disarm him and slap him into something resembling composure. Francis and John Boy looked across the roof at each other. It was likely if not inevitable that when they left Brian would do something stupid and get picked up. Each evidently allowed the same unpleasant thought to cross his mind, but in the end they decided not to let this enterprise spin even further out of control. Brian was allowed to live and Francis and John Boy took the next flight out of Düsseldorf to Ireland, crossing their fingers. Brian was arrested just outside Essen, having in his panic evidently forgotten the place they'd selected for torching the car. Thankfully it happened after the car was in flames, though they only discovered this later. They'd sweated for weeks over whether some forensic trace had been left to be detected. As it was, Brian could only be prosecuted for stealing the car and torching it. Francis had had the foresight to throw their hand-guns into the Rhine before they entered Düsseldorf rather than let Brian store them. A waste of two good weapons, but that was how it went.

Now Joe Geraghty was trying to sort things out. He could shut Aidan up with one glare. Joe took special care of Francis. He'd been one of Joe's boys.

Gentleman Joe had a light touch mostly. He had been Francis's first brigade commander. He'd eased him – though eased was palpably not the right word – into the RA. Francis had all the right credentials of course. Joe had been his mentor. Despite his amiable demeanour he was a hard man when required. He was tough on his boys, brutal with some, and Francis had been no exception. His admiration was leavened with a measure of naked fear. Terror, more like, when sometimes he looked back. All those years ago, Joe had insisted Francis move to South Armagh. He had long-term plans and needed Francis's particular aptitudes. He could not be wasted taking potshots at the RUC in Belfast, so Joe told him.

Joe was among the eight most influential individuals in the movement. Member of the Army Council. In charge of security among other things. Three weeks ago he had come to see Francis at the house near Roscommon where the boys had put him and John Boy for a couple of weeks.

'I know, I know,' Joe had said, gesturing with flat palms for him to calm down, before Francis had uttered a word. 'Not your fault. What was your man thinking of, I wonder? If he wasn't sure, he should have told you. And he didn't?'

'He didn't, Joe. Not a hint.'

Joe shook his head thoughtfully. With his neatly cut grey hair and his well-fitting suit and elegant tie, he resembled a lawyer rather than one of the leadership cadre. Like most on both sides of the divide, Francis knew Joe Geraghty as a man of accomplishment. You didn't get to his position by being a slouch. With his quiet voice, his anodyne words and his gentle, self-doubting manner he cast fear into the hearts of volunteers who transgressed.

'Sure we'll do our best for the boy,' he said. 'We're setting up the support straight away. The German brief thinks there's nothing to hold him on. Can't even pin the car theft on him now. Setting fire to the car is a bit more of a problem. He'll be bailed for a later court appearance. But that's not your concern, is it now, Francis?'

'No, Joe.'

'We'll look after Brian. I wanted to drop by to say you boys did your job properly. There's no recrimination from me or anyone else who matters. We know how it is. We've all been there. It's a shame but we have to take the broader view.'

'But Aidan –'

'Aidan's a hothead. You and I know the score. We see the bigger picture. I'll look after Aidan, don't you worry. Now, just for the moment we think we'd better pull you off the front line. Let it blow over. There's whole legions of young lads who need bringing on and we want you to help.'

'Training kids?'

'If you like. We need the best people to be bringing the next generation on. They're our future after all. They'll look up to you, Francis. And see it this way: it'll only be for a short while.'

'How long?'

'Don't press me on the detail. A short while. How long's a piece of string? I can guarantee you that you won't be doing this for any longer than is necessary. I'll look after you. You'll trust me on that, won't you, Francis?'

'I will. But don't ask me to be happy.'

'I don't expect you to be, boy,' said Joe soothingly. 'I expect you to want to get straight back at it. That's the measure of the man, I said to them. But we think it's wiser. Let things cool down a bit. You know what I mean?'

'I suppose so.'

'Well, there you are, then. Why don't you get yourself back home to your little house and your little wife for a week or so? Then you'll be expected up in Donegal to help with the new boys. How does that sound to you?'

They'd organized a meal at the pub in Silverbridge to welcome him back, although Aidan was obviously off with him. He seemed cheerful enough despite what had happened. Not that he spoke to her about it, not that she could ask. She'd pieced it together from the press reports, his absence and the sympathetic looks from the other girls. Four tourists with no involvement or interest in Ireland, so the papers said. No doubt Francis would say different.

It was steak and chips and Spanish red wine. The bosses had sent some boys down to guard the pub, six of them, four posted on the corners outside looking for strange cars and strange men, checking prospective customers and peering out with baleful nervousness. The other two sat in a car, just in case. Inside Francis was greeted like a film star and she travelled in his slipstream. They sat initially man–wife–man–wife, but after the meal the men got down to some serious drinking and the girls bunched up at the table.

'It was just bad luck, that Belgium thing,' said Anne-Marie Shaw. A glance from Cathy, Aidan's wife, shut her up.

'Did you hear about poor Jackie Sullivan?' said Patricia, from Forkhill. 'Taken in for questioning.'

'No,' said Cathy. 'Really? I didn't know.'

'Yes. A group of us went down the police station, but they'd sent her on to Castlereagh already.'

'What charge?'

'None. Just questioning. They must have thought she knew where Mikey was.'

'She'll have give as good as she got,' said Anne-Marie. 'Bastards.'

'Doesn't even know where Mikey is. Hasn't seen him in seven months. Anyway, the brief went straight up there. She come out this morning, so I heard.'

'They'll never find Mikey. The boys'll look after him.'

'He's OTR in the South too. Some post office raid. The Guards down in Dundalk were telling Aidan's brother.'

'They won't find him.'

'Hear about that tout they got up in Derry?' said one of the other girls, Bridget didn't know who.

'Yeah,' said Anne-Marie, 'may they ever make an example out of him.'

'Oh, they will for certain, Anne-Marie,' said Cathy. 'Joe Geraghty's boys are on to it, Aidan says. They'll tear the bastard limb from limb.'

'It's his wife I feel sorry for,' said Patricia.

'Your problem is you're too soft, Patricia,' said Cathy with a laugh. 'Anyways, the way I hear it, it was her turned him in. She'll be all right. No sympathy for that bastard, though.'

'Anyone need a drink?' said Bridget, and she took a moment at the bar to breathe deep and slow.

When the party broke up Francis and Bridget were driven home in one of the cars sent down from Belfast, another following behind. They swung round bends at speed, plunging into the night.

'No hurry, boys,' said Francis with garrulous drunken loudness. 'No one following.'

The driver said nothing.

'They know where I live sure enough anyways.'

★

So here he was, lying in a field with these impressionable young volunteers. Two boys and a girl. Nineteen or twenty, he'd guess. He didn't know their names, though one of the boys' accents was noticeably Derry. The other boy came from somewhere in the Six Counties, but Francis could not place it precisely. The girl was from the South: if pressed he'd say from the Midlands, but he wasn't so clever on Free State accents. They'd each been allocated code names – Alice, Brendan and Colin. Stupid games, Francis thought.

And they did look up to him. Officially they knew him as Dave. But they were obviously in awe of him. It did not matter to him: one of this holding pattern's small consolations was that he could, momentarily, bask in the hero's glow.

He rode them hard, harder than they were ever likely to experience in the real glare of an active service unit on the ground. There, there would be complete vigilance but slack cut so that each member could gather himself or herself for the task at hand. Here, on the other hand, it was relentless, from six in the morning until nine at night and they were on full operational alert twenty-four hours a day. If things started to go wrong in the real world they needed to have the stamina, physical and mental. Drink was not allowed on active service training, though Francis had tested this by taking them to the pub one evening, where they had all ordered soft drinks. Francis was not sure he would have passed this test himself at their age, but training back then had involved no more than going out after last orders, borrowing an old Lee-Enfield and having a potshot at some soldiers in an armoured car from some convenient ditch.

Their quarters were in an old stable block in a secluded farm near Buncrana, in the Republic, which had been fitted out with basic washing facilities and a row of camp beds, each with its own sleeping bag ingrained with the grime and sweat of previous volunteers. It was on the farm that most of the weapons training took place, while a local helper looked out for the Gardai or other inquisitive interest. They did most of their anti-surveillance training on the rural roads of County Donegal, but had some exercises over the border in Derry City itself. They had been working for ten days now and Francis could sense the kids' exhaustion. He found against his better judgement that he enjoyed this and was raring to go each morning, rising quietly at five thirty to get the rudiments of breakfast together and after close of play ensuring that the packing away had been efficiently done.

Tonight was a live weapons exercise over the border in the North. The task was to service a notional weapons cache, retrieving an imaginary load of Semtex and weapons to take back to their base in the farm. They were armed because Francis wanted them to experience the tension of carrying their loaded guns, and because it was standard operating practice in the North not to operate without defensive weapons. The chances of a real engagement were minimal; the greater risks were posed by one of the volunteers misfiring his or her weapon. But they were good, diligent kids, obviously committed, far too serious, and Francis had few fears on this score. Soon they would be launched.

Brendan was counting down their timing, while Francis monitored discreetly. He was playing the role of a member of the ASU. Alice was the leader of the team and shortly she would send Colin out to recce the ground.

It was cool lying next to the hedge, though not as bitter as it would have been in midwinter. Francis felt damp seeping through his camouflage trousers but this was a minor privation. It was a pitch-dark night, with a cover of dense cloud and without a sound save the rustle of small animals making their way through the undergrowth. The four of them lay in the small ditch, almost touching.

Francis could just make out the small hand signal from Brendan to Alice. It could have been still more unobtrusive and Francis made a mental note. Alice touched Colin gently on the shoulder and he began to move. Smoothly, thought Francis approvingly; starts and finishes were generally where you made yourself obvious. Colin had done well and was making his way noiselessly forward to the opposite end of the field. Colin was the country boy and he would be all right on this task.

They waited, and the wet made a greater incursion up Francis's leg, nearing his crotch. He would need to wear his other set of fatigues the next, final day. He could hear his own breathing but not the others'. He peered and could just distinguish the motionless shapes of Alice and Brendan. He could only see them because he knew exactly where they were. So far, so good.

On his earphone Francis heard the single click from the radio that denoted that all was clear along the route to the corner of the next field. He watched Alice as she gave him and Brendan the signal to move off. They walked slowly in single file, Brendan in front, Alice in the middle and Francis taking up the rear, scanning behind for potential threats. He felt the buzz: this was real but not real and it was strange once again to be the back marker on a job rather than its leader. He could hear the steady swish of the grass as they walked in time with each other.

At the edge of the field Francis noticed Colin standing in front of them. Terrible: he would be marked down for this. Readily visible against the skyline even in this dark. Then he heard two crackles on his earphone. He stopped still.

'Yorkie, that you?' came a man's voice from the figure he

had thought was Colin. An unmistakably English accent, Midlands probably. The two figures in front of Francis stopped still in their hunched positions. Francis said wearily, 'Yeah, mate,' and began to stand slowly, coughing and releasing the safety catch on his weapon. He fired as soon as he levelled it, from the hip and with less control than he would have liked, but over the heads of Alice and Brendan. He hoped Colin was safely tucked away somewhere. His semi-automatic spat and the bullets sprayed. 'Fuck,' came the elongated groan of the Englishman, and he went down, silent.

'What the fuck?' came another voice from the right, maybe fifty feet away, and Armageddon began.

Francis dived to the floor and crawled quickly to Alice and Brendan. He could see the spits from the soldiers' weapons as they fired in panic. They must have traversed the field diagonally before encountering Francis and his trainees.

'OK, going to have to return fire,' he said quietly, hoping the Brits would not hear his voice in the clamour they were creating. 'Where's Colin?'

'Here, boss,' came the boy's whispered voice.

They had the advantages of being together as a unit and of knowing where the enemy was, approximately.

A more authoritative English voice cut through the firing. 'Cease fire. Now.'

A silence fell on the field and Francis could hear rustling as the Brits presumably reassembled and gathered for what was to come. He and his team of three lay motionless, huddled.

Nearby, he heard a whisper: 'Sarge, are they gone?'

'Quiet,' came the terse reply. 'Not sure. Let's flush these bastards out.'

They were closer than the Brits realized. He thought he could see a hand moving, signalling. He knew he had only seconds, and a small number of them, to make his decision.

There was no point just lying there. There was no point attempting to retreat without firing. They would be sitting, or running, ducks. Then he caught sight to his left of the outline of the bulky torso of a kneeling man. He tapped Alice on the shoulder and pointed. She nodded in acknowledgement. He touched Brendan on the thigh and gestured with a sweeping hand where he wanted him to concentrate his fire. Colin was already looking at him for cues, he could see. He drew his hand across to denote the ambit of his firing. The team were all obedient, attentive, waiting. So far the training had worked. Now they would discover just how far it had stuck.

He tensed his body and saw the others do likewise. He held up his hand displaying three fingers. Then two. Then one.

They stood in unison. Alice fired at the crouching figure on semi-automatic. Colin took the area to her left, spraying bullets perhaps as blindly as the Brits but under greater control. Brendan and Francis himself fired into the darkness to Alice's right. They heard several of their shots thudding into surfaces and heard groans, but Francis could not be sure whether they were hitting their targets. In normal circumstances it would be a hugely wasteful use of resources, showing precisely where they were. But the situation wasn't conventional, even in combat terms, and evidently they had taken the Brits by surprise. Their fire was not initially returned.

A ten-second burst and they ceased fire, without the requirement for a command, as abruptly as the firing had started. They began running, initially towards their training objective and away from where they had left the car. Francis knew the topography of the field and hoped that if the Brits chased them they could trace a wide circle and come back to the relative safety of their vehicle. Maybe if these hadn't been novices he might have split them and divided the soldiers' forces.

He heard voices. They would be summoning up helicopters

and armoured vehicles, so he and the others had little time. There was another spurt of fire, aiming at an area of the hedge well behind them, which was welcome. The sergeant gave the command to withdraw. Francis held up his hand and his unit halted immediately. They could see nothing but heard the sound of running feet receding.

They waited for a moment, and Francis was aware of the sound of his own breathing. When they could hear the Brits no more he gathered his team together and whispered, 'Back to the car as quick as we can. Now.'

They moved fast, retracing their steps. As they reached the point where the fighting had begun, Francis heard a moan.

'Yorkie, that you?'

It was the soldier he had shot first. He approached him and knelt, checking carefully for weapons. But this man was beyond the use of weapons. He lay without moving, looking up with the terror of a trapped animal. 'Fuck,' he said.

He could only be about eighteen or nineteen, Francis thought. Downy, light facial hair. Brown eyes. In his face was fear, distilled.

The blood seeped mainly through his midriff, though Francis could see that his right arm, splayed unnaturally just above the wrist, had been broken too. He would be in shock. Francis felt in the compartments of the soldier's fatigues and found what he wanted. With shaking fingers he tore open the field dressing and placed it on the largest entry hole, pressing. The boy convulsed and gripped Francis's right arm with his left hand.

'Ssh. Now, now,' said Francis soothingly. 'Press this to yourself, hard. Hard as you can. Hold it there.'

The boy gasped and said, 'Don't leave me here. Stay with me.'

Francis looked down on him and said, 'They'll be back for you soon, son. Won't be long.' But he waited a moment, his hand holding the boy's and pressing down into the warm wet-ness of the wound. It was unlikely the dressing would serve any purpose other than possibly providing the boy with some comfort in these last moments.

'Francis,' said Brendan behind him.

'That's Dave to you, boy,' he replied, though he knew it would not matter. Gently he withdrew his hand from the boy's and wiped it on the long wet grass. He turned back to the young soldier, whose eyes had closed, then led them back to the car.

Francis drove, with no lights. He knew these back roads. They heard helicopters in the distance, then closer as he crashed the gears, trying to urge speed from the vehicle that was just not there. No one spoke and Francis was grateful. They needed the focus. They dared not cross the border at Strabane, where there would be a checkpoint, so they headed down the Urney Road towards Clady. If they saw trouble there, they would have to head still further south, towards Castlederg or even Killeter, hurtling down narrow lanes. That would be desperate. But Clady was asleep and Francis slowed the car to a crawl, the engine ticking over as it crept to safety. They crossed the River Finn and were in the Republic. Francis knew the British army or the RUC would not now dare to chase them, even in hot pursuit.

Finally someone spoke. 'Alice's been hit, boss,' said Colin. He had been silent as they were making their way to safety, but all the while he'd been cradling her in his arms. Francis stopped the car and they examined her in the back seat. She was still conscious but blood spread like spilt black ink from the wound in her upper chest, near the shoulder. He cursed himself for not having taken the Brit's remaining dressings – he would not be needing them – and stuffed a handkerchief into the fleshy hollow where the bullet had penetrated. Alice screamed.

At the next village they found a telephone kiosk and Francis rang his local contact. A doctor would be raised. Stop outside the main post office in Letterkenny.

There was a car there when they arrived, a portly middle-aged man with a full beard standing beside it. Francis drew up alongside him and wound down the window.

'Will you be following me, then,' said the man tersely, and climbed into his Volvo.

Francis followed him to a rather grand house on the outskirts of the town. The man opened the garage and gestured for Francis to park inside. They carried Alice into the kitchen and laid her on a large farmhouse table over which plastic sheeting had been carefully placed.

'I run my practice from here,' explained the doctor. 'But my consulting room's not big enough to deal with operations. From time to time we have to use the kitchen for emergencies. Now what will we be calling the darling young lady?'

'Alice,' said Colin.

'Aye. Alice it is, then. What have we here?'

Francis and his two companions were the doctor's assistants as he sedated Alice, cleaned the entry and exit wounds, stitched up the holes in her chest and back and gave her a tetanus shot.

'She'll be all right,' he said to Francis afterwards, 'though it'll be a long old road, I shouldn't wonder. Let's get her off to bed for a few hours and you and your boys go off yourselves. Alice is in safe hands. Your friends will get her into a hospital discreetly down south somewhere in a few days' time, where she can recover properly.'

They were told to lie low at the farm until further notice. The training was abandoned and they played cards all day. He learned that the boys were Bobby and Kieran. They were interested in his stories but he told them none. In the evenings the farmer's wife brought them hot meals and beer. The alcohol embargo was not worth maintaining and at least there was the opportunity to sleep.

After four days a small saloon car pulled up at the farm. Francis could not see who emerged but told the boys to be alert. They took out their weapons.

The farmer was sent over to fetch Francis, and him alone. In the farmhouse kitchen a fire was blazing in the hearth, emitting the delicious sulphurous smell of burning peat, and Gentleman Joe sat daintily at the table sipping a cup of tea.

'Thanks now, Harry,' said Joe, and the farmer left the house.

'His wife's off running errands,' explained Joe. 'Kenny's in the car looking out. So we'll not be disturbed.'

He sat for a moment looking at his teacup. 'The thing is, Francis –'

'If it's about the fuck-up we didn't have no option. It was just bad luck.'

'No, no,' said Joe. 'It's not about that. That was a success, if we can set aside poor young Alice's injury for a moment. She's fine, by the way. Tucked away in Killarney for the time being. Two soldiers dead, one critically ill. Three out of five is good going, I'd reckon. You boys did magnificent. We're proud of you.' He sipped his tea. 'Do you want a cup by the way? There's still some in the pot.'

'No thanks,' said Francis.

'No. It's not about that at all. I need to ask you a few questions.'

Francis waited. Joe's mild demeanour and his courteous manners aroused an alertness in him.

'Now then, Francis,' said Joe. 'Have you had much to do with the security forces just recently?'

'To do with?' said Francis.

'That's right,' said Joe patiently, looking mildly at him.

Francis thought of the man Richard and the encounter

almost two years before in Singapore, and he tried to push the thought away. He had not disclosed anything about the pull and the conversation with Richard. On this, he agreed with him: to do so would be suicide.

Joe was well versed in sniffing out the shadow of a lie. If Francis could successfully persuade himself that he had never been approached, then he would be better placed to conceal it from Joe. But what if, despite the spook's promise, something had crept out, from some corrupt cop or by some terrible coincidence? What, indeed, if that bastard spook had decided to leak something deliberately? There would be photographs, recordings, and despite the fact that he had rebuffed him he would be tortured and killed. He had no choice but to brazen it out.

'Nothing,' he said. 'Not had any contact at all with them.'

'Nothing on your travels?' said Joe. 'No one sidling up to you while you were in Germany or France?'

'No. I don't think I'd be killing British soldiers if that was the case.'

Joe looked at him and gave it fair consideration. 'No,' he said, 'I suppose not. But then again they are devious bastards, aren't they?'

'The answer's still no, Joe. We've not been rumbled. Ask any of the lads out there with me. It'd all have been closed down. Is this about Brian?'

'No. Brian's sound as a pound as far as I know. His judgement's maybe off, but I don't think he's been talking out of turn. Do you think maybe he has?'

'No. And nor have I, Joe. Not over there, not here.'

'And Singapore?'

'Singapore?'

Joe looked at him steadily, without expression. 'Yes. Singapore. The trip we agreed never happened.' He waited for Francis to reply.

'No. Nothing happened.'

'Nothing?'

'That's right. Nothing.' He looked Gentleman Joe in the eye.

'No pull on the way in?'

'No.'

'Or the way out?'

'No. I'd have had to report it if there had been. I know the standing instructions.'

Joe chuckled and murmured, 'Of course you do, Francis. No suspicious individuals cosying up to you at the bar? I know you like the sauce.'

'No, Joe.'

'No shady offers of timeshares? No fancy women with their pimps showing you the full-colour pictures after the event? No charming Englishmen? You know you can tell me. You know you have to.'

'No. What do you think of me, Joe?'

Joe smiled. This was it. I think you and me need to go off for a couple of days with some of the boys to chat this through, he'd say.

Instead Joe said, 'I have to ask these questions, you understand. I can't be seen to be doing any favours for my boys. I have a job to do. You do understand?' He was almost deferential.

'Of course.'

'Now, then. Have you heard from your wee brother recently?'

'Liam? No.'

Francis was confused. Liam lived at home with his parents in Belfast. He spent most of the time in bed listening to music, it seemed, and the time he was out of his pit he was involved in petty crime. He'd been warned by Martin Dempsey more than once. Even been slapped by some of Martin's boys. Surely Gentleman Joe hadn't graced him with his ethereal presence just to tell him to keep his brother under control?

'Is he in trouble again?'

'Well, yes and no,' said Joe, looking vexed. 'He may be in a spot of bother, but it's not the usual. I may as well tell you the whole thing. But I have to ask you one or two things first.'

'Fire away.'

'Thanks, Francis. Now, do you see much of young Liam?'

'No. Christmas maybe if I'm at me ma and da's.'

'Could you put a figure on it for me for the past two years?'

'Say, three or four times.'

Joe looked at him expectantly.

'Oh. Let me see. I saw him at Christmas in 1989. When I got back from that job in Calais.' Joe nodded. 'He was there at me ma's and then went out on Christmas Day. We went back home the next day. Then, must have been September last year I bumped into him in McLaughlin's when I was up in Belfast on some business.'

'All right. Do you talk about business with him?'

'Shit, no.'

'And?'

'Not seen him recently. Why are you asking?'

'We'll come to that in a bit. What do you know about him getting involved with the boys?'

'He's not. Is he? He never used to be interested. Used to drive me ma and da mad.'

'Interesting. Would it surprise you to find out he'd offered his services to Martin for the Belfast Brigade?'

'I'll say. He'd be a liability. He hasn't the backbone for it. Even if he had the commitment. Do you want me to speak to Martin?'

'No, no. All I'm doing is a bit of due diligence here. Just sorting out the detail. Best if this is between the two of us.'

'Fair enough.'

'Young Liam's not been in touch with you recently?'

'Nope.'

'Not phoned you or had a message sent?'

'No. He's not interested in family.'

Joe nodded. 'Now, would you do me a favour, Francis?'

'Of course.'

'If your brother does get in touch, just let me know, will you? As soon as. By the normal channels. Confidential. We should keep this between us. We don't want anyone putting two and two together and making five now, do we?'

Before Joe left, Francis said, 'You were going to tell me what this was all about.'

'So I was,' said Joe with a smile. 'Slipped my mind. Well, you know, something and nothing. That's all I ever seem to deal with, something and nothing. Usually nothing. Some nonsense. A couple of the boys happened on Liam –'

'Happened on him?'

'Yes, let's not dwell on that, shall we? Liam seems to have become passionate about the struggle. And flush with money. Anyways, my boys saw him meeting someone in a car park. Just something that needs clearing up. You'll see why I'm duty-bound to take an interest. Just some iffy deal, probably.'

Francis was silent.

'I have to look into it. As I say, something and nothing. Don't go mentioning this to anyone.' He patted Francis on the shoulder.

1992

8

Word came that Liam O'Neill had disappeared.

Before the formal FLASH telegram arrived that was sent to every official entity that could possibly have relevant information, requesting details of Liam's whereabouts urgently, Geordie rang Richard.

'Liam O'Neill's gone missing. Any ideas?'

'Missing?'

'Missing presumed snatched. Missing presumed shot in the fucking head. Clear enough?'

'Don't get hoity-toity with me, Geordie. You were at the same meeting as I was.'

'Yeah, I know. Anyway, the major's gone into a panic. That's his promotion up the swanny. Freddie went white and he's not been seen since. Not even necking gin in the mess. And I don't think he's mounting a one-man rescue mission. So buggerlugs here is trying to pick up the pieces. You heard anything?'

'If I had I'd have told you straight away.'

'I know. But when everybody's abandoned ship and the captain's running round shouting, "Don't panic," you begin to wonder. You'll put the word about?'

'Of course.'

'Discreetly?'

'Yes.'

'It's going to be a field day for the I-told-you-so merchants. When the cops get to hear . . .'

'Not from me, Geordie. Not from us.'

'It's that poor fucker I feel sorry for.'

'I know. What were they doing with him?'

'What do you mean?'

'His tasking. Might give us an idea how they got on to him.'

Geordie sighed. 'Just routine stuff.'

'That all?'

After a while Geordie said, 'What you getting at?'

'You know. Francis.'

'The major was keen for him to show his worth, that's all.'

'And Freddie's still got his old contacts?'

'Not going there.'

'Not sure I want to know anyway. Thought you lot had learned your lesson.'

'Just because we're mates doesn't mean we're friends. I'm not going to commit suicide for the sake of your fucking curiosity.'

'Professional suicide, you mean.'

'You heard. It's not as if what the kid knew was worth the risk. Now Gentleman Joe's boys'll be all over him. Or if he's lucky they'll have finished.'

'Are you sure about it?'

'What? That they've got him? Who else? Fucking aliens from outer space?'

'He could have gone to ground for a couple of days.'

'I don't think so, Richard. I've got that sick feeling. Poor bastard. Let me know if you hear something. Anything.'

In the middle of it all.

It was just at this time that things began to shift. Not imperceptibly, but not especially noticeably either. Liam's disappearance coincided with Richard's introduction to what Charles called the Inner Circle. Richard would not have been surprised to learn that his initiation involved rolling up his trouser legs, chanting new mantras and learning new handshakes.

It was more formally, though sotto voce, known as the

Channel. Richard had been dispatched to rooms to receive secret briefings and to sign his life away on forms that swore him to eternal silence. Charles chaperoned him, as the point man until now. Then Richard had taken the baton. Something about a safe pair of hands.

Whether there was something in the air, or in the water, in the late 1980s and early 1990s Richard saw as debatable. Whether the reunification of Germany, the thaw in East–West relations and the release from prison of Nelson Mandela created a context was one for the birds. But it seemed to Richard that at almost the same moment each of the principal players in the tragic drama that was the Troubles had some impetus to put an end to it.

In the middle of its latest act – Richard could not later recall the specifics – Liam O'Neill disappeared.

They gave him water at last, though he found it difficult to swallow. He spluttered and retched, bending double. He raised his head again to see the light bulb above him swinging slightly in the breeze that permeated this building, this shed.

He had told them everything he could remember. Dates. Places. Names. Telephone numbers. Meeting instructions and drills. Car descriptions. Who and what he'd reported on. What they were interested in. Ideas about other touts. He knew it would do him no good but the fear had just made it spill out of him, like the liquid shit from his body, trapped in his underpants, that smeared him with each move he made. He could smell himself but was beyond caring. Beyond anything. It seemed just to be part of the business for them too.

Three of them. They'd worn balaclavas throughout, which was something. It must have been hard labour too, as they took turns to hold him and hit him with the end of the snooker cue, across his head, his torso. Kicked him, in the crotch, up the arse, in his midriff as he lay there. Held his hand carefully across the work bench as they broke his fingers, one by one, using a claw hammer. Panting, perspiring; if it hadn't been for the stink of his own excrement, he might have been able to smell their sweat.

They could have made it easier on themselves. Asked nicely. He'd have given it all up. A grim smile formed but he coughed again, pain spiking in his chest, swelling through his throat and spilling out again as bloody slobber on his chin. He must look a sight. He tasted metal.

But they seemed to take a professional pride in it. Maybe it was an article of faith that a confession wrought without the use of violence had no value. Maybe they felt they must earn their volunteers' wages. Maybe they just enjoyed it.

This was an interlude. They'd been at it for hours. Seized off the quiet street corner where he'd been waiting for Francis. They must have followed him there. Thrown into the back of a van. God knows how many hours hurtling around the roads. Then parked somewhere. Silence. Involuntary sleep like a shutter across his soul. Sudden shudder as the van started again. More bruises as he was shaken from side to side. Then silence again. Doors opened. Darkness. A hand reaching in and grabbing him by the collar. Dragged out, tumbling to the ground. Smell of grass. A courtyard somewhere. Stumbling to his feet, finding his hands were tied. When had that happened? Pushed and dragged. Here. The world had changed to a continuous dark smudge of pain and fear.

'Hey,' said one of the voices. Harsh, West Belfast. He probably knew the man, but it wasn't Martin Dempsey or anyone else he recognized. 'Pay attention.'

Someone grabbed his hair and jerked his head up.

'Now then,' said a softer voice, and he struggled to gain focus, and hope. He was shifted on to a broken-spindled kitchen chair that held his weight, but only just. He looked up to see a thin face, but kindly, looking down at him with concern.

'Now then,' the man repeated. 'Been through the mill, haven't ye, young Liam?' The man wore a suit and tie. He could be his saviour.

The other men stood in the background, arms folded.

'You must see that these boys had their work to do, right enough?'

He found himself nodding, agreeing with anything this man might say.

'Well, it's all over now, I can tell you that.' The man took a handkerchief from his pocket and blew his nose carefully, delicately. He had bony white fingers, like a piano player's. 'It's all over now. My name's Joe Geraghty and you can see my face true as day. Look at me, Liam.'

He complied and moved as if to stand. He could see the men in balaclavas tense, ready to step forward. But he lacked the strength anyway and slumped back down.

Joe Geraghty said, with a tenderness that caused tears to form in Liam's eyes, 'You know where we've got to, Liam. It's a pretty pass, but we're here now. Your chance to find solace.'

'Mr Geraghty, sir, I'm sorry . . .'

'Shush, shush, there. No need, boy. We're beyond that. What's done is done and we all have to live with the consequences. You've no need to explain to me, or to plead. I know how you ended up here. What's important is to find peace. No need for words. In a few minutes it'll all be over.'

Liam looked into those reassuring eyes. There was yet hope. Joe Geraghty touched his face with the palm of his left hand and smiled tenderly. His face reached forward and Liam felt him kiss his cheek.

'I wasn't being quite literal when I said a few minutes,' said Joe Geraghty, his gaze steady and warm.

Liam O'Neill had not noticed the revolver Geraghty had nimbly taken from his pocket and now it was at his temple. He continued to look into Joe Geraghty's eyes, and felt safe.

Bridget was hanging out the washing on a breezy morning when the car with two men stopped outside the cottage. One remained in the car while the second, an older, quite distinguished-looking man with grey hair climbed carefully out of the passenger seat.

'Sure I'm getting no younger in me old age,' he said, laughing. 'Would you be Mrs O'Neill by any chance?'

She considered him for a moment, her arms folded across her chest, concealing her anxiety, and said, 'That's right.'

'And would your good man be around the house?'

'I'm sure I wouldn't know. Would you like me to go and check?'

'That'd be kind.' He grinned at her knowingly.

'Who should I say it is?'

'Name's Joe. Joe Geraghty, Mrs O'Neill.'

She held her face impassive. Joe Geraghty, she knew the name and the reputation. Big man in the movement. Never seen him, not in the flesh, not in a photograph. She could see why they called him Gentleman Joe. Fastidious, with his smart suit and silver hair. Mannered, too.

'Well, Mr Geraghty, I'll just go and see for you.'

'It's good of you. And it's Joe.' He looked at her kindly.

As she approached the front door Francis came out of the house.

'Joe,' he said.

'Francis. Beautiful day.'

'You come down from Belfast this morning?'

'It's a lovely spot. The solitude. It must do wonders for the soul. It's good not to be having to skulk about the place. The peelers all the time, trying to harass me in the city.'

'They can't quite do that round here, Joe. Almost, but not quite, yet.'

'Aye,' said Joe, 'those towers.'

'Would you like a cup of tea now, Mr Geraghty?' said Bridget.

'It's Joe. Certainly I would, if it's not too much trouble. Thank you kindly.'

'Will you come inside now?'

She brought the tea through to the sitting room and said, 'I'll leave you to it, then. I'll be in the kitchen if you need anything.'

'Mrs O'Neill,' said Joe as she turned. 'You're a few miles from town here. It must take you a while to do your shopping.'

'Oh, I manage. I walk down to the village and I can get the bus to the supermarket once a week.'

'Would that be the Superquinn over in Dundalk?'

'That's right,' she answered. 'We try to shop over there when we can. We avoid the British shops.' She glanced at Francis, who was not looking at her.

'That's grand. Listen. My boy Kenny is outside in the car. He could run you over to Dundalk to do a bit of shopping now. He'll only be sitting there waiting for me otherwise. And me and Francis here, we could be a little while.'

'No, Joe, I couldn't ask you to do that.'

'It's really not a problem,' said Joe with a smile, and Francis flicked her a glance.

'Well, then. I'll just get me bag and me coat.'

As she left the house she heard the car start up. She had done the week's shopping the day before. She would, instead, find somewhere to have a cup of tea.

*

137

'Well, Francis. You'll know why I'm here. We've had a long drive of it from Donegal. Or Kenny did. It was all right for me. I could doze in the back. Stopped for a good breakfast in Belturbet. But still. You'll know why I'm here.'

'Yes.'

'The boys did their job properly, Francis. There's no mistake. He told them everything. Name of his handler, what he told them, everything. All the details checked out. He held nothing back. I'd have loved to take him back home to your da's and tell him not to be so stupid. Or better still, wind the clock back. But . . .'

He shrugged. Francis looked at him.

'You know as well as I do that I couldn't let it pass, much as I'd like to. It's not something we can tolerate or turn a blind eye to.'

'No.'

'We have to do these things. I know how cracked up you must be but you'd do the same if it was my brother.'

'I would, Joe. I understand. I have no issue with it. It was Liam's own stupid fault.'

'Not entirely true. It's the British who killed him. They led him up the garden path. But I'll tell you this, Francis. It was me who fired the shot. I looked him in the eyes and pulled the trigger. I felt sorry as I did it but I felt it was right. I thought that was what you would want.'

'Fair play to you, Joe. What should I say to me ma and da?'

'Nothing at all. This is between you and me. And no stain attaches to them or to you. I want you to be clear on that.'

'Thank you, Joe.'

'This'll take some time to get over, I know. Let me know when you're ready. We'll talk then.'

'Now would be good, Joe.'

'No, it'll keep. I've told the boys that you'll sit the next one out. You're stood down for the time being.'

'No, Joe,' said Francis firmly. 'I need to get back doing stuff. And it'll take my mind off Liam.'

Joe looked at him dubiously. 'Well, if you're sure. It's England.'

Bridget was finishing her pot of tea when Kenny beckoned her through the window. Kenny was solicitous enough but uncommunicative. He looked shattered too.

'Time to get you back, Mrs O'Neill,' he said.

'I thought it was going to be longer,' she said.

'Got a call,' he said, holding up a mobile phone to her with what looked like self-satisfaction. It was a tiny device, held in the palm of his hand.

Back at the house, Joe Geraghty said a hasty goodbye and got into the car.

Francis sat on the sofa in the sitting room. He looked spent, barely recognizable.

'What's the matter, Francis?' she said. 'What did Mr Geraghty say?'

He looked up at her sharply. 'What?'

'You just looked worried.' She had spoken rashly. Francis discouraged her from asking questions.

'Aye. Well, it's just –'

'Yes?'

'Nothing,' he said. 'Nothing for you to worry about. Will you be getting us a cup of tea now?'

He sat on the sofa all afternoon watching the horse-racing on the television and drinking beer. It was unlike him. From the duty-free pack that he'd acquired on one of his European adventures and stowed in the back of the wardrobe to give to his father, he took a pack of cigarettes and smoked them one after the other.

'I thought you'd given up the smoking, Francis,' said Bridget.

'Sure I had. And now I've started again,' he said. 'Anything wrong with that?'

'Of course not,' she said in reply to his glare, and left him to it.

Apart from the frenetic commentary that she could just hear from the television, its sound turned down low, and the occasional creak of the sofa as Francis reached for another can, there was no noise in the house as she went about her chores. She looked in on him every so often. He stared glassily at the screen, not watching, lifting his hand mechanically to pour beer into his mouth. He did not acknowledge her presence.

Later she saw tears rolling down his face, his expression and pose unchanged. She knelt next to the sofa and touched his cheek with the back of her hand. He showed no sign of noticing.

'Francis, love? What is it?'

The tears turned into a shrugging sob which he tried to suppress with a grimace, but in vain. His shoulders heaved and he turned to her. He looked desperate.

'I'm a rabbit in the fucking snare, Bridget,' he said.

'Don't worry, Francis,' she said. 'It's all right.'

'What do you know about it? It's not,' he said with vehemence, and buried his face in her shoulder.

Finally he seemed to regain some composure but lost it immediately. She put her arms around him and he submitted.

'It's Liam,' he said.

'What about Liam?'

'Me own brother. Me own fecking brother.'

'What's Liam done?'

He gathered himself briefly and said, 'Nothing. Nothing.' She waited.

'The stupid fucker,' he said eventually.

'What is it, Francis?'

'Stupid bastard. He should never have . . .'

'Should never have what?'

'Why, in God's name?'

'Francis, it'll be all right. Whatever he's done, you can sort it out. We can sort it out. It'll be all right.'

'No, it won't.'

So he told her. How Liam had become a tout for the Brits. Had tried to sell him out. Had been found out by the boys. He told her Joe Geraghty had become involved. Had spoken with him about it. Asked whether he knew anything of it. He told her he'd denied all knowledge. Which was true. He'd disowned his brother. He'd agreed with Joe to say if Liam got in touch. And Liam had. Francis had told Joe. Had arranged to meet Liam but hadn't turned up.

And now Joe had reported what had happened to Liam. Liam was gone, dead and dumped somewhere in County Donegal. Joe had told Francis to look at the bigger picture. This was part of the struggle. This was their burden.

'God,' said Bridget. 'And you, Francis. Does he think you . . . ?'

'He said there's no stain on me. Liam was doing this on his own. He made that clear before . . . I can't say nothing to my ma and da.'

'It's probably better that way.'

'And he wants me to get back to . . .'

'To what, Francis?'

'To what I do.'

'And do you want to?'

'I don't know. If I don't, they may think I'm not sound.'

'And why would they do that now?'

'You don't know them, Bridget. You don't know how it works. If you don't follow orders, they get to thinking. Especially if there's something against your name.'

'But I thought Joe said –'

'I know what he said well enough. He has to. And I have to say, yes, Joe, I believe you. I'm 110 per cent with you.'

'But if your heart's not in it.'

'Oh, my heart's in it right enough. But I'm afraid, Bridget.'

'Then we must find a way out.'

'There is no way out.'

'There must be. There's always something. However bad things seem.'

'What? The darkest hour is just before dawn?' he said. 'Shows how much you fecking know. You should try being me.'

'I know it sounds stupid. What'll you do, Francis?'

He was silent for the moment. He did not look at her, but seemed somewhere else entirely, in his head perhaps but not with her.

'Christ knows. I just have to carry on, do what the boys say until I can think of something better. Maybe after the next job I can ask Joe if I can jack it in.'

'I'm here, Francis. It's all right. You can rely on me.'

He turned his gaze to her with a flicker of surprise. It seemed to her that he had only just registered her presence. 'Not a word,' he said. 'Not a word, to any fucker. Not to your ma, not to Joe if he comes calling.'

'He won't, will he?' she says, openly anxious.

'No, he won't. But if he does, be careful. Not a word.'

There was a knock on the door.

'Get it,' said Francis.

It was Anne-Marie. 'How're you doing, Bridget?'

'Fine thanks. And you?' She smiled.

'All right. Me and Stevie were going over to Dundalk for a drink.' She pointed at the car waiting at the end of the path. 'You and Francis fancy coming too?'

'That'd be lovely, Anne-Marie. Only we can't. Not today.'

'That's a shame.'

'Sorry. Francis has got a lot on.'

'You won't come for a couple yourself, Bridget?'

'Don't want to play gooseberry.' She giggled, not too affectedly, she hoped.

'There'll be some of the girls down there. We could have a gossip.'

'No. Better stay with Francis.'

'All right, then. See you.'

'Bye.'

She closed the door and went back into the sitting room. It was as if a switch had been tripped in Francis. He sat upright, composed and angry.

'You stupid cow, why did you say that?'

'What?'

'That I've got a lot on.'

'I had to say something, Francis.'

'What if it gets back to Joe? He knows I'm stood down for the minute. What if that bitch is talking to the peelers, eh? Did you think of that? Or Stevie?'

'They wouldn't, Francis.'

'How would you know?' he said, standing and walking out of the room.

9

'Liam's dead. He was taken.' She could hear the panic in her voice, was not sure whether it was for Liam or for herself, but could not eradicate it.

'What do you mean?'

'I mean Liam's been killed. What else can I mean?'

'Sorry. Who took Liam?'

She was stalling for time. Understandable, Bridget thought, though it didn't make things any easier. 'You know who must have taken him,' she said.

'Let's meet,' said Sarah, and they made their arrangements.

A crash meeting in a cheap hotel. Perhaps the first of many, thought Sarah. Not ideal. If this was to continue they'd have to make some more permanent arrangements. Something safer. Meanwhile she fretted whether Bridget would be all right.

She waited impatiently, observing the cobwebs on the underside of the grimy windowsill from the bed on which she sat, taut, one hand gripping the other in her lap, legs slightly apart and swinging for want of anything better to do. These shoes have seen better days, she thought, but this too was displacement.

Liam O'Neill's death would not feature in the grand scheme of things, unless in some bizarre, unforeseen sequence of events his killers could be brought to justice. Joe Geraghty's men were extraordinarily careful. The fact that it was self-evident that the Security Team had carried out the murder meant nothing: there would be no evidence that would make them amenable to prosecution. Liam O'Neill was a nobody in the history of Northern Ireland, simply one of the many disappeared, not even a footnote in his own right. It was the kind of thinking that edged you closer to inhumanity. But the weight of it all.

The timid knock on the door. That would be her.

'Francis told me. Liam was taken. Francis was all agitated. He'd never have told me otherwise. I know I'm not supposed to phone from the village but –'

'Slow down, Bridget. Steady. Just tell me what's happened.'

'Francis has been away.'

'Where?'

'I don't know. Anyway, that's not the point. Then yesterday Joe Geraghty comes round. Afterwards he was upset. He doesn't ever talk about *them*. But he said they took Liam.'

'Did Joe Geraghty tell him?'

'Yes. He said Joe told him to agree to meet Liam and not to turn up . . .'

'Then what?'

'Then Joe Geraghty comes down to ours and tells Francis it's over. Liam's been taken and has confessed. Then been killed.'

'Confessed to what?'

'To being a tout for the Brits.' She looked up at Sarah. 'Was he?'

'I don't know. Anything else?'

'Joe said he killed him. Said it was a matter of honour that he should do it. Said he thought it would give Francis some comfort to know. Was Liam a tout for you people?'

'I don't know. I wouldn't know. I wouldn't be told.'

'And is this what I can look forward to? Is this what's going to happen to me? One day I'll be grabbed and that's the end of me? And you close the file?'

'No, Bridget. Of course not.'

'Why of course not? Why should I believe you?'

'I'll do everything I can to protect you. We need to be so careful.'

'You're telling me.'

'I can't give you any guarantees, but we need to keep to what we've agreed.'

'Because I'm already up to me neck in it. That what you mean?'

'No. If you decide you've had enough we simply say goodbye.'

'What if I decide I want out? If I just leave? Will you help me then?'

'Yes. But it'd be far better if you stayed around for the time being. Far safer.'

'Why's that?'

'Once you've provided some information of real value we'll be in a far better position to help you.'

'And this doesn't count?'

'It counts, but it doesn't help us stop something happening. We need more. You have to see it from our end.'

'I have to see it from your end. Why? Because it's a deal when it comes down to it?'

'It's more than a transaction. But yes, there has to be some value . . .'

'Value?'

'I've no choice.'

'I've got myself caught up with you lot when I didn't need to. That's the blackmail, is it? Give us more or we won't help you get out of this mess.'

'You can stop now if you want and things will go back to exactly how they were before we met. Or if you want to leave now of course we'll help you. If you want to come to England with me this minute I'm there for you.'

'There for me. What does that mean?'

'It'll be better all round if you stay on in there for the moment. We'd be able to help you far more then.'

'You mean you need to see value for money.'

Sarah said nothing.

'I'm here like a sitting duck. That's your deal. Take your chances and you may get some more money. You'll ration out your *help* according to what I tell you. And meanwhile I might end up in a ditch with a bullet through my head.'

'Isn't that why you're talking to me? To stop that sort of thing happening?'

'That's your answer?'

'Bridget, I can't promise you no harm will come to you. How can I? But I will do my best for you. And I would tell you honestly if I thought you were in danger.'

'But you wouldn't know.'

'Not necessarily. But we're not in the habit of losing people.'

'Somebody lost Liam.'

'Neither of us knows what happened. It could be something different. Antisocial behaviour. The Loyalists. They may just have got it wrong. I don't know.'

'And the confession?'

'Everybody confesses when those people get on to you. You know that. Look, I'd be genuinely surprised if Liam had anything to do with us.'

'But you'll find out? And you'll tell me?'

'I'll try to find out. But I can't be certain. What was Liam like?'

'He was a kid. He was selfish. But I liked him. He was a rogue. He wasn't a bad boy. Just impulsive. I can't see how he got caught up with you people.'

'He may not have. It's happened before. The IRA get things wrong.'

'And they get things right sometimes.'

'I know. Which is why we have to be so careful.'

Bridget's head was bowed and she began to sob quietly. 'Francis has lost two brothers now. I just feel sorry for the poor boy. He was just a poor wee boy. What those men'll have done to him. It doesn't bear thinking about.'

The resumption of normality, the application of routine deliberately to numb the senses, to anaesthetize her against what came next. It was an experiment, to quell her heart, which leapt from both fear and tentative, joyous anticipation, to test what a continuation of this life would bring.

In the house damp seeped through the walls. Although he was not there Francis had given strict instructions not to waste peat on the fire after March was out. They had no central heating and she relied upon the immersion and the two-bar radiant fire for hot water and heat.

Outside, it was more like an autumn morning than late spring. The wet cool infused her bones as she walked to the village in her warm coat and the light hung grey and heavy in the sky. It was too settled for rain but there was no sign of the sun.

The walk into Carrickcloghan took just over half an hour. It was a desolate, mean little place now, with everything gone, stripped down, malevolent as it waited to die. Perhaps it had always been like this, but her recollection was different. It had never been a place to come to unless there was a specific reason, but it had been comfortable, to her at least, familiar, quiet and safe, where a body would greet another body and share the time of day. This was how she remembered it. Until the Troubles erupted. Bridget knew her history. What Irish child didn't? The British had been unspeakably unjust and cruel to her people, she knew, and could not be trusted. But all this violence. She had no idea how to compute the politics of it – if politics was something to compute – let alone to explain her continued contact with Sarah. She reduced it to the small picture, knowing all along that that was selfish, an enterprise to see herself out of this place. At other times she thought of it as a small gesture against all this misery and death, an inchoate part of a whole she did not remotely comprehend. Then it came down to a simple choice between two people: did she trust Francis and his way more than Sarah and hers?

Nothing quaint about this place now. The British soldiers no longer patrolled here, not for a long time. Nor did the police. When the security forces came to town it was a heavily armed, green-and-khaki, grim circus. They set up their checkpoints, though, clad in their body armour, pointing their guns at you while you fumbled for your papers. They watched from their outposts, which were sprouting all along the border: heavily defended towers crammed full, it was rumoured, of cameras and telephoto lenses, of infrared sensors and video recorders, of notebooks and computers on which the smallest movements of each inhabitant were recorded and logged. Each man, woman and child had a separate file, whether innocent or guilty or in-between, so the story went, and she could well believe it. A measure of the oppression, so Sinn Féin had it. Yet beneath this scrutiny somehow normal life carried on. Cattle were milked, bread was baked, boys and girls went to school and came home again, machinery failed and was repaired, cars were bought and sold. Still the Provos prospered, as much because of security force attention as in spite of it. Regulation and the rule of law were more the IRA's province here than that of the putative governing authority.

She took the narrow rutted track to her parents' small house, in the middle of a terrace of similar dwellings, built ninety or so years before. She smelt the tobacco, the comforting aroma from her childhood of all those smoked cigarettes, as she walked through the unlocked front door into the sitting room. Her father sat in his armchair, his newspaper open on his lap.

'Hello, da,' she said.

He grunted.

Patrick McNeish had had a grudge against humankind since he had been laid off at the foundry some forty years earlier. Welfare payments, together with the cash earnings of his wife when she cleaned, had seen them through. Bridget had never known a time when her daddy was not in that armchair with a newspaper before him and a grimace on his face.

Her mother was in the kitchen peeling potatoes.

'Your bread's over there,' she said by way of greeting.

'Hello there, Ma,' said Bridget. 'Cup of tea?'

Accustomed over the years to not hearing a reply, Bridget switched on the kettle and fetched the pot from the cupboard above the sink. She warmed the pot with almost-boiling water before setting the kettle on again, swilled out the pot and put the tea in. Two spoons and one for luck. A cup and saucer for her mammy and daddy and a mug for herself. Her mother abhorred mugs. They represented the opposite of refinement, whatever call there was for refinement in Carrickcloghan.

'Your man's not back, then,' said her mother, but it was more a statement than a question. 'Where'll he be now?'

'He's off looking for work, Ma. He's probably down south somewhere.'

They sustained this fiction sufficiently that they could talk to each other, but both knew the truth. Francis O'Neill was a man rarely seen in this house, owing largely to the disapproval of Bridget's parents and partly to his scorn for them. It was not so much the fact that he was a volunteer, her mother had explained, though they were Nationalists, not Republicans. It was that he was an incomer from the big city. She understood what they meant. Cocky to the point of boorish, direct and unsubtle: the qualities in Francis that had repelled her parents and attracted her.

'Hmph,' her mother said, and that was an end to it.

They drank their tea at the kitchen table in virtual silence and Bridget picked up her bread and left. On her way home she stopped by the small house next to the garage where Stevie and Anne-Marie Shaw lived.

'Will you be having a cup of tea now, Bridget?' asked Anne-Marie.

'No thanks. Just had one at me mam's.'

'Your man back?'

'No. Not yet.'

Unlike Cathy Murphy, with her airs and graces and make-up and hair-dos and black leather boots, Anne-Marie was a large, matronly woman. Her four children were at school and she worked in her steamy kitchen. She kneaded the bread dough muscularly before wiping her hands on her apron.

'How's Stevie?' said Bridget.

'He's all right. Busy.'

Bridget did not ask. Stevie's work would be to acquire and conceal vehicles, preparing them for the boys. The mere fact that he was busy would be of interest to Sarah, but Bridget did not dare probe further.

Guilt percolated inside her, along with the fear. Anne-Marie was a good-hearted woman, guileless and devoted to her family. Her hostility to the Brits was unquestioning. And here was Bridget, collecting scraps of information and already calculating their value to Sarah.

'Well, I can see you're busy,' she said.

'No, stay awhile. The pot's still warm. Grab yourself a chair.'

'No thanks. Better get going.'

On her way back she felt tired beyond her years as she walked up the small hill to the cottage. Francis was home, unannounced. The Ford stood in the courtyard.

She fried some eggs for his lunch.

'Where you been, Francis?' she asked, feeling bolder than she once had.

He stopped eating and held his hunk of bread in his hand, looking at her. 'Here and there,' he said, and mopped up the yolk.

When he had finished she took the teapot through and they sat in the front room.

'Listen, Bridget. It's been a tough time. And I'm going to have to go away again soon.'

'When?'

'I don't know. Soon.'

'You won't be . . . It'll not be dangerous, will it, Francis?'

'No. Do I ever get in trouble?' he said with a smile.

'That's good. About before . . .'

'Before?'

'Liam and all that . . .'

'Yeah, well, I was tired. Should have kept me mouth shut. I've had time to have a bit of a rest.'

She said absently, 'Will you have another drop of tea, Francis? I think we can squeeze a little bit out.'

'Not for me. Anyways, I feel better now.'

'That's good. Were you down south on your travels, then?' He looked at her again and she said, 'What? I'm sorry for asking. I know I shouldn't. It's just that I want to know you're safe. Dublin can be a terrible violent place. When you're off out of the city and down country I feel much happier.'

He thought before speaking. 'Aye, well, we were only in Dublin for a day or so. Nothing doing there. Then we went down to Wexford.'

'And did you find work there?'

'Sure, I wasn't looking for work there. Just had a few meetings. Political stuff. You'd not be interested.'

'No, I suppose not. I'm sorry for asking.'

He grunted.

'I'm sorry, Francis. I do understand. It won't happen again. I worry about you, though.'

He did not answer, saying instead, 'Shall we go upstairs, then?'

'No,' she replied slowly.

Somewhere in this conversation they had reached a point and gone beyond it, irrevocably.

'Please yourself.'

She saw him clench and unclench his fist. But he did not move from his seat. Eventually he went to the kitchen to get a beer and she hoped she had remembered to get sufficient cans in. Sarah came to her mind. Should she contact her? Did she dare?

Richard found Chief Superintendent George Donnelly a frightening man. Broad-shouldered but beanpole-tall, he had an incongruous crop of black hair that, depending on how much of the gossip among his junior colleagues you believed, spoke of either an iron will and a clear conscience or the liberal use of hair dye. He walked with a pronounced limp owing to his false leg and also had a prosthetic left arm. He tended to glare, fixing you with what you'd thought previously were rather spaniel-like brown eyes, and speak loudly. From his post in the Special Branch, with a grim resolve and a highly attuned cunning, he ruled over the RUC in the border counties like an imperious king, bending his knee to headquarters only when it suited. His superiors were just slightly less scared of him than the suspects who came under his gaze. Richard counted Donnelly as a kind of friend, and thought his feelings were reciprocated with the same equivocation.

The IRA had tried to kill George on more than one occasion, hence the artificial limbs, the result of the closest call – if you can describe it that way – when his car was booby-trapped. He'd chosen to drive that Saturday rather than sitting in the passenger seat and his wife was killed instead. He'd mellowed over the years but this was a relative thing.

Francis O'Neill, back then relatively new to the area, was

Donnelly's number one suspect for his wife's murder. If his loathing of the IRA was personal, his hatred of Francis was intimate. Richard had never established whether Donnelly's suspicion of O'Neill was founded on evidence or even spurious reporting, or whether Francis, the cocksure terrorist, was simply the closest available target for Donnelly's rage. Whichever was true, Donnelly's desire to crush the IRA was surpassed only by his zeal to see harm come to Francis O'Neill.

Now Donnelly sat in Richard's office.

'What swanky restaurant will you be taking me to for lunch now, Richard?' he said.

'I'm sure you'll tell me all in good time. Been swotting up in the guides on the way over? How long are you in London?'

Donnelly laughed. 'Until tomorrow, at least. If I can string it out to two nights, so much the better. Charles was always good for that. But you'll come over all efficient and business-like on me. I know you. You don't know how to charm us simple Irish folk like your man Charles.'

It was Richard's turn to laugh. 'Why don't we just grab a sandwich from the canteen for lunch? Have a chat, then you can be off to whatever meetings you have and do your shopping. I'll pick you up from your hotel at, say, seven and we can go for a bite after that. Paying our own way.'

'Oh, the Met boys will claim me this evening, Richard. Unless you want to join us?'

'I can't think of anything nicer,' said Richard. 'Sadly, I have an appointment with a ready-meal and the television that I can only shift if it's for a one-on-one with you.'

'Can't stand the pace now, Richard?'

'Never could. If I ever had any drinking boots I lost them long ago.'

They bought sandwiches and coffee in the canteen, brought them back to the office and sat at the table.

'Now then, Richard,' said Donnelly, 'Liam O'Neill.'

'What of him? A bit off your patch, isn't it? Aren't Belfast running with that one?'

Donnelly feigned a splutter. 'Aye. So they say. But I fancy his brother for it. I like his brother very much for it.'

'Sounds unlikely to me. His own brother? Where was he found?'

'Under the bridge on the A5 just south of Bready. He'd been there a couple of days maybe before the call came in. Terrible state. Poor bastard.'

'The family?'

'Refuse to have anything to do with the business. Burial and all that. We could expect as much from Francis. But his mother and father? What goes through these people's minds?'

'They're probably ashamed. Scared of reprisals.'

'I know. But your own son . . . So Her Majesty's Government is in charge of the burial.'

'Could be some criminal thing. He was mixed up in all sorts, so I've heard.'

'You have taken an interest, then. Criminal thing, as if. Look at the timing. Just after he's taken on by your army pals –'

'They're not my pals, George.'

'Of course not. No one's your pal.'

'Except you, George. Naturally.'

'Ha. What did you think of him anyway?'

'Who?'

'Liam. Or are we going to play twenty questions all day?'

'Depends whether this is an interview under caution, George.'

'You know as well as I do that PACE doesn't apply in the same way on my side of the Irish Sea.'

'So you're the investigating officer for Liam's disappearance?'

'No. Let's just say that I decide what the investigating officer investigates. So what was Liam like?'

'That would be saying.'

'It would, wouldn't it? Word is, you didn't think much of him. Told the army to drop him before they got their fingers burned. Of course they ignored you.'

'Why bother asking if you know it all?'

'Because it'd be nice to hear your version. Let's just say I like the sound of your Oxbridge voice.'

'Never went to Oxford or Cambridge. Strictly a red-brick student, me.'

'What do you make of the rumours that it was Joe Geraghty who had Liam seen to?'

'I don't deal in rumours, George.'

'Sure you don't. What if I told you that I'd seen a top-secret report suggesting that Gentleman Joe Geraghty and his boys took Liam?'

'It wouldn't exactly be headline news, would it now? The Security Team does fall to Geraghty, doesn't it? It's their job.'

'See, I don't buy it,' said Donnelly. 'Sure, Gentleman Joe would know about it, I grant you. But he'd manage it differently. Besides, from what I hear Joe is looking to step back from the front-line stuff. Has other fish to fry.'

'Interesting.'

'More involved on the political side, so they say.'

'*They* being?'

'People. Thought you'd know. You're pretty plugged in.'

'I refer my honourable friend to my previous comments about rumours,' said Richard.

Donnelly sighed and said, 'Anyways. Francis was Joe's protégé. He'd say to Francis: you sort out this mess in your back yard. And Francis would have done.'

'You may be right.'

'I notice you don't say that I may *well* be right. You think you know better. So what are your people saying?'

'My people?'

'Your touts. Agents, whatever you call them. All those that you don't tell us about.'

Richard looked hurt. 'George,' he said. 'I've nothing remotely useful to you. All the available reporting has reached you through the correct channels.' All literally true and not unduly, he thought, economical with the *actualité*.

'That sounds a bit legalistic,' said Donnelly.

'Does it really? I'd have thought by now you'd have got used to how we constipated pen-pushers speak. Why do you reckon Francis O'Neill abducted his brother anyway? It hardly seems probable. PIRA would be unlikely to entrust that kind of thing to the man's brother.'

'All the available reporting has reached you through the correct channels,' Donnelly said. 'And this is Ireland.'

'Ah,' said Richard. 'OK.'

'And what's young Francis been up to recently?'

'How should I know?'

'You seem to be pretty well plugged in on him.'

'Do I? And why are you so interested?'

'We wouldn't want an unfortunate accident to befall the sainted Francis O'Neill, would we? Three brothers, now that would be negligent. Just a friendly interest is all. And do you know you have this habit of answering a question with a question?'

'Do I?'

'Ha.'

Donnelly seemed as bored with this as Richard and the pubs would by now be in full swing. The games they were sometimes compelled to play, thought Richard, he hated them.

Just before he left, Donnelly said, 'A little bird told me that friend Francis went off for a holiday a few years back.'

'Oh yes?' Richard said.

'Somewhere in the Far East, I heard.'

'Really? We missed a trick there, then.'

'I also heard that you were seen at Heathrow around then, waiting for a flight off to one of those places. Hong Kong or Bangkok or somewhere similar.'

'Oh, did you? Really?'

'Advice, Richard. Never shit a shitter. Now, is Francis O'Neill one of yours?'

'Wish I could say he was, George. Strictly between us, of course. But I can't.'

'So he's fair game?'

'Depends what you mean. But as far as I'm concerned, fill your boots, George. Within the parameters of the law, of course.'

Donnelly looked at him with grinning distaste.

'Of course.'

The thought crossed Richard's mind once more that George Donnelly was a frightening man. He had no idea whether Donnelly's investigation of the death of Liam O'Neill, or rather the latest chapter in his pursuit of Francis O'Neill, was officially sanctioned by his bosses. No doubt it was a case of force majeure and in the RUC at the time there was no force more majeure than Donnelly.

By now Liam O'Neill's disappearance had become a *case*. It was little different from others.

This person, this once warm breathing being, Liam: what was he really like? He'd found him quite endearing actually. Dealt a pretty shitty hand, he had at least tried to do something with it, however doomed and misguided his efforts. Richard had liked him because in life Liam was so . . . unregarded.

Now he would continue to be. Liam had been hopelessly ill-equipped to survive in the world. And survive he did not.

1993

10

Bridget walked with head down, closing the gate as she left the garden. Clutching her shopping bag to her, she turned off the road and on to the path by the woods. This was the shortest route into the village, though the path was not gravelled but muddy and overgrown. Few people passed this way and Bridget had to swish through the encroaching undergrowth, ducking beneath overhanging branches, laddering her tights where brambles caught her legs. She looked down; she was bleeding. She must look a mess.

She'd left as soon as the two telephone calls had come. One wrong number and a second call six minutes later from a pushy Scottish woman trying to sell her insurance. The signal. She'd learned the drills by heart, never imagining that they would be enacted in real life.

'Whatever you do,' Sarah had said, 'don't try to hide it at home. Do you have somewhere safe?'

'Yes,' she'd said immediately, and they'd agreed on it. It wasn't ideal, but Francis had stopped using the place so far as she knew. She'd given Sarah the spare key. Somehow Sarah or her people had fixed up a hiding place inside it. Now the unreal secret existence she shared with Sarah was about to collide with her reality in Carrickcloghan.

She came to the track that led to her parents' home and looked up it, pausing as she did so, before walking on down the main street, glancing around her as she went. She saw no one. Was she being watched? One of Francis's comrades-in-arms? Or a malevolent RUC officer? Anne-Marie? Or Cathy or

Patricia? Or was it the raw fear that was becoming familiar? Sarah had told her to trust her instincts but to temper them with logic. But her instincts had bled into heart-thumping anxiety and her rationality had been supplanted by a pounding headache that shot pain through the backs of her eyeballs. Eventually she stepped briskly into the snicket that divided the old post office from the next-door house and was momentarily cast back to a happier time. She could almost imagine herself entering through the back door of the shop to find Mr Kennedy standing there in his baggy mustard-coloured cardigan, teapot in hand, waiting for the kettle to boil. But fond imaginings were difficult to sustain.

She turned back and saw only light at the mouth of the alleyway. The point of no return had been passed. She was already dead or safe. The door gave immediately she pushed it. The lock, which had been broken years back, had not been repaired. Inside it was familiar, but unfamiliar. Dust covered the surfaces of the Formica worktops and the stainless-steel sink. All the furniture had been removed, though the outline of the refrigerator could still be seen on the filthy carpet tiles. Mr Kennedy had always kept it spick and span, a proud widower. His easy chair was no longer in front of the hearth, where he used to sit of a wintry afternoon while she cashed up and put the takings in the safe. The small table and chairs had gone too. This, the back room as they had called it, the only downstairs room other than the little shop itself, had always seemed overfull: the furniture, the fridge, the cooker that once filled the gap between the units, the units themselves, old-fashioned even in the early 1980s. But mainly the safe, the incongruous intruder here, sitting like a glowering gorilla in the corner. Mr Kennedy, with gentle wistfulness, used to describe it as a monument to his father's folly.

Here it was, still. This had been the only place it could be. It was too heavy to transport upstairs and neither of the Kennedys would have countenanced its presence in the shop itself. She walked up to it and touched it as if she doubted its existence. Solid and secure it stood, giving no hints of the intervening years. There was nothing outside this room. No soldiers or policemen. No Francis. No Gentleman Joe. She took out her key. With the small clank, the outside world intruded briefly once more. She looked around but it seemed nothing had been disturbed, nothing alerted. She pulled open the door and heard the familiar slight creak.

In the bottom corner of the safe, secreted on the purpose-built shelf concealed from casual observation, where Sarah had told her to look, was the little box. She reached forward awkwardly, careful not to disturb the dusty surface, and retrieved it. Opening the box, she took out the little mobile phone and one of the three batteries wrapped in cloth.

'Don't connect the batteries until we need to talk,' Sarah had said. 'And disconnect as soon as we've terminated the call. It'll save the battery. Each time we meet we'll swap the old batteries for new.'

She slotted the battery in with a click and pressed the 'on' button. She'd practised this with Sarah so many times it had seemed ridiculous. The steps that back then had become automatic and simple now seemed immensely complex. And every moment spent here was a moment in extreme danger, she knew. As she fumbled with the telephone she willed herself to be calm.

The little screen lit green and the device vibrated in her hand. Another stage, however small, successfully negotiated. Another step on the way back to safety. But safety was a relative concept.

There were few preliminaries.

'Where is he?'

Bridget could hear the anxiety in her voice. 'I don't know,' she said dully.

'Do you really not know? Or won't you tell me?'

'I don't know.'

'Sorry. It's just I'm worried that something may be about to happen.'

'I think . . . uh, I think he may be your side of the water.'

'OK. How long?'

'He went away this morning.'

'Were you planning on contacting me?'

Bridget paused. 'I was . . . I was going to.'

'All right. Good.' Bridget could sense in Sarah's voice a forced patience. 'It's just so important that I know. Anything at all.'

'I know.'

'We should meet. Soon. Meanwhile anything else I need to know right now?'

'No.'

'OK. Great. That's all I need. I'll take it from there. Shall we meet the day after tomorrow? Usual arrangements?'

'All right.'

The day after tomorrow meant, in fact, tomorrow. She would rise the next morning and go through a series of routines when she left the house whose purpose was obscure yet on which Sarah insisted. Eventually she would take her seat in what Sarah prosaically called 'our office'. Nothing as melo-dramatic as a safe house. They would talk and then, while Sarah flew back to London, Bridget would take her laborious route back home. Tedious, Sarah admitted, but safer.

She disconnected the battery, wrapped the little thing in its cloth and packed it carefully in its nook, checking again that it would not be found other than in a targeted search, shut the door of the safe with minimum noise, withdrew the key and crept out into the passageway again. She walked slowly up the street to Anne-Marie's just as she had rehearsed, suppressing the desire to scurry home.

She sat, disguising her restlessness with a forced, almost dainty composure, drinking tea as they went through the ritualized mantras and conforming tropes of life in Carrickcloghan. How's the kids? Oh, the weather. Did you hear Barry Flynn's been arrested?

She alluded briefly to undisclosed medical issues – they were not yet confidantes, so would not naturally share the full gynaecological detail. This was how you built a *legend*, as they called it in the spy novels. This way, if she was later quizzed over her absences she would hang her explanation on this hook. She supposed that this was what she now was: a spy. It sounded marginally better than a tout.

It always comes to this, thought Francis. The waiting.

They sat in the car in leafy Leicestershire, this place they had visited several times. They knew it intimately: they had approached the house from every street, walked past, taken photographs discreetly. With characteristic bravado, Jonjo had knocked on the door the previous day with some cock-and-bull story about resurfacing the front drive. The front drive, that is, that sloped down helpfully to the garage. There'd been no answer, though. They hadn't anticipated one. They'd watched the occupant leave earlier that morning. She'd reversed out of the garage carefully in her small hatchback and driven off at eight thirty. Presumably to her place of work, wherever that was. Not their concern. She wasn't their concern. Hunched down in the passenger seat of the van parked in the cul-de-sac, Francis had watched her and then called Jonjo in using his mobile phone.

Some elements of these jobs here were easier. Try parking a van in a cul-de-sac in Portadown where some RUC officer lived and the peelers would be all over you in minutes. Try knocking on a door on the Rheindahlen base and you'd get the third degree. But this was England.

On the other hand, and on balance this was overriding, it was much harder. Getting yourself into this country without being spotted. Getting the stuff in. Getting hold of vehicles. Finding your way round, conscious that as soon as you opened your mouth you were opening yourself up to suspicion. You just bought a sandwich or filled with petrol and you thought the tosser who served you would be on the phone the moment you left.

Staying places. They had what had been called a safe house courtesy of some 'sympathizers', whoever the hell they were. Jesus knew whether they were reliable. So much easier in Europe. No one gave a toss about the English and everyone knew the Irish were cheeky leprechauns who drank a load of Guinness and were benign when drunk. Better still back home: you could do a job and be tucked up in your own bed within an hour or two.

Christ, the English hated the Irish. But not as much as we hate them, he thought.

Yesterday had been the opportunity for Jonjo to look at the topography, close up. He couldn't exactly measure the angles but with his expert eye he could make a swift judgement whether it was a goer.

And it was. Old technology but reliable. Mercury tilt. It had done for Thatcher's old mucker back in '79 – even though that had been the other crowd – and the old go-to would see to this bastard now. Good enough for your RUC sergeant in County Antrim, good enough for some slimeball Tory MP who was cheating on his wife. After the recce walk-through Jonjo had spent the afternoon assembling the device and now all that was left was the waiting. And, of course, Jonjo not blowing himself to smithereens when he put the fucker on. But he was sound as a pound, Jonjo. He could be relied on.

Thursday nights, regular as clockwork, they'd been told. God knows where the intelligence had come from. Francis preferred not to wonder, just so long as it was accurate. Last week it had been. They'd sat in the car round the corner and sure enough right on time at eight your man had zoomed in in his flash BMW. Mikey had walked round the corner just to check it was parked where it should be, then they'd gone off to have their tea. At three they'd returned. The light had been perfect, meaning virtually non-existent. There were street lamps, but the leaves of the sycamore on the corner kept the property's drive neatly in darkness. Francis had driven the van down the close and John Boy had driven up in the car. Jonjo had got out, sauntered up to the vehicle and placed a gloved hand on it before returning to their car with a grin.

Same routine this evening. Except Mikey was in the van. And your man was back for more. Just another Tory fat cat having an affair. The man had done a stint in the Northern Ireland Office as security minister with little distinction between two reshuffles. It had only been eighteen months and he hadn't left a trace before he returned, a pleasant, posh-talking nonentity, to the backbenches. He wasn't even a personal friend of the PM. It was curious why he had been picked as a target. Presumably it was mainly because the opportunity had arisen. The Brits had tightened up on personal security and the number of available targets was smaller. No doubt the recent lull in attacks had precipitated the need to do something, anything. Francis O'Neill's was not to reason why.

He was still fair game, your man. No doubt he was entitled to protection but he wouldn't want the Special Branch boys around when he played away, would he? Or the tabloids, come to that. So he'd be discreet even if the peacock-blue Beemer was a bit conspicuous.

Now it was about waiting.

They didn't speak, John Boy, Jonjo and Francis in the Escort. They were parked in this clearing, listening in to the police frequencies, waiting, waiting.

The anxiety grew in Francis's heart. It was always like this. As you homed in on the moment, as the focus became intense, all else disappeared from view. Joe inhabited a different universe. Liam was forgotten. Bridget might as well not exist. It was all about bringing this home and the trick was to be tensed to the fingertips, alive to everything, without becoming panicky. No distractions, no thinking of the historical significance of what they were about to do, no speculation whether this would be a turning point in the struggle or just another minor politician whose death would feature in the movement's proud record. It was simply a job, like all the rest. Control was what it was about, and Francis was in command, of his team and of himself.

He did not let himself breathe faster. He did not fidget in his seat. He did not glance anxiously or indulge in feigned, unbefitting joshing with the boys. He sat, quiet like them, as the minutes passed and accumulated into an hour and more. Shortly it would arrive: the inescapable moment.

Waiting.

Mikey, sitting in the van ahead, called them in.

A pause, and Francis said, 'Right then, John Boy. Shall we go?'

As they pulled away quietly, with minimum throttle, Francis turned to Jonjo and said, 'All right there, Jonjo?'

'For sure,' said Jonjo, and Francis turned to face the front again. Jonjo was always positive.

They eased on to the main road and John Boy switched on the headlights.

It was the simplest thing in the world. Drive half a mile, turn right, then right again into the street. Stop the car in the darkness. Jonjo gets out quietly. You and John Boy keep an eye out. Jonjo does his thing and then gets back in. You drive off. Simple as.

Of course it wasn't quite that simple. Perhaps they were waiting for you. Maybe without knowing it you were living your last few minutes. Without moving his head, Francis looked left and right as they drove forward at a stately pace. No cop cars, nothing. Francis turned the scanner down to zero volume. Nothing audible now other than the sound of the engine: low revs, John Boy never overdid it. Then the plink-tick of the indicator. John Boy held the car momentarily in the right-turn lane and pulled away smoothly and quietly. Must have barely anything on the accelerator.

Francis continued to peer. Nearing the point of no return. Until they reached the next junction they could, in theory at least, accelerate away.

John Boy indicated again and slowed to a halt as if to check for traffic. Francis noticed his glance but gave no sign of recognition in return. Francis felt the gentle nudge in his back as the car moved forward again. This was it. The engine was no more than ticking over now and John Boy allowed the car to coast past Mikey's parked van down the slight incline of the cul-de-sac, switching the headlights off. There were twelve houses here and at the end was a large turning circle. John Boy turned in one sweep without applying any throttle and the car came to rest exactly under the branches of the towering sycamore. Neatly judged. John Boy killed the engine. He pulled up the handbrake silently. Francis saw Mikey drive off quietly in the van.

They waited a breath but there was no need for further instructions or questions. Jonjo opened the door quietly and slid rather than climbed out of his seat. He did not turn back to close the door. Francis looked about the street. The five houses at the end, arrayed round the turning circle, now looked to him like spectators surrounding the stage of an amphitheatre. How exposed they were, even under cloud with a thin crescent moon. But no lights were burning in the houses and no noise was to be heard through the open window.

They waited again, and Francis continued to watch, his eyes scanning the upper storeys of the houses. He knew John Boy would be doing the same in his seat. Neither spoke; Francis could not even hear John Boy breathing, such was his own concentration.

Minutes. Francis counted off the seconds. He was still peering and was not sure whether he should be reassured or worried by the fact that there was nothing, nothing to disturb this night. Not even a cat strolling past to conduct its nocturnal business, not even a breeze rustling the leaves above them. He had to fight to keep his mind tethered.

Finally a sound. Jonjo climbed back into the car. Francis looked in his mirror and saw Jonjo, shaven head and grim expression, give the thumbs up. Francis touched John Boy's arm. John Boy turned the ignition key and the engine murmured. He let out the clutch slowly and the car coasted forward. He did not switch on the lights until they emerged on to the main road again. He accelerated gradually.

They were away.

1994

II

He remembered that job as he knelt with Mikey on the sitting-room floor, the maps and photographs laid out in front of them. It had been slick. They'd been in the car from Dublin airport when it came on the news. Your man must have got up late, as it was gone nine thirty when the thing blew. Naturally, they hadn't been at the party. Not there to witness the explosion, the sudden flash, the bang you scarcely believed was possible, the momentary dislocation of time, the gnarled metal, the catapulting of torn limbs and organs, the spatter of gore and body parts, the smell of fire and death. It'd been easy for Francis, John Boy and Jonjo. They'd simply gone to Luton airport, parked the car and left the keys in the exhaust pipe. Someone – no idea who – would collect it and take it to the crushers. Mikey, though, had to dump the van and take the long route: a train to Dover, a boat to France, a trek to Brittany and the ferry back to Rosslare. All to avoid having to go through an English airport. His face was too well known to risk the direct route.

Francis was unaccustomed to anxiety, which implied a certain loss of reason, as opposed to a controlled sense of danger and a continuous assessment of risk. But he had long begun to feel twitchy. Mikey had been with them two nights now. He was OTR in both parts of Ireland and a known associate of Francis's. Joe had said this was the only way. In the South the Guards were harassing all Mikey's contacts and he was moving from house to house anyway. Mikey had the planning documents from the previous time he and Francis had visited

England, well before the killing of the backbench MP, and the two of them needed to get this thing in some kind of shape. You'll be as safe at your place as anywhere, Joe had said with his normal grin; but in his tone and expression ran a perplexity at Francis's hesitancy, which in time could curdle to suspicion. Still, thought Francis, this is complete madness.

It was confusing. Joe was cautious. Several times over the years he'd acted as a brake on some of the more headstrong operatives and their hare-brained schemes. But these were difficult times. They were under real pressure. Volunteers were being detained on a regular basis, especially over there. Resources and money were stretched, which was one reason why Francis had been called in, so said Joe. Maybe the Brits were getting their act together. The RA needed men they could trust, in more ways than one. And there was no longer the luxury to secure secluded farms in the South at their leisure. Even the Guards were on their backs when previously the local old boy would have been biddable. In this sense, Francis guessed, the border counties must be the obvious place to retrench. Now, Mikey had been smuggled in, without the knowledge of the local lads, not even Aidan, his notional OC.

'We have to get this fucking nailed down, Francis,' Mikey was saying.

'You don't need to tell me,' he replied.

So many complications with England. So many moving parts. So many things to cover. So dependent on other people you didn't know, especially if you were doing a big one.

There was a rapid knock on the door. Bridget answered it and came quickly into the small sitting room.

'It's Thomas from down the village,' she said. 'He needs to speak to you, he says. He won't say anything to me. Says it's urgent.'

Francis exchanged glances with Mikey, who began gathering the papers. Once Bridget had been sent back into the kitchen both men took the safety catches off their revolvers.

Francis opened the front door and scanned the yard before looking at Thomas Smythe, the teenage son of one of the local helpers. Thomas was agitated.

'Now then, Thomas,' said Francis, 'what brings you out here on such a windy morning?'

'Sorry, Francis. Me da sent me on up. He says to tell you the peelers are on their way.'

'Oh, did he now? And how might he know that?'

'He says to tell you that Bernie called.'

'Bernie?'

'Yes, Bernie. He said for me to take yer man back to ours.'

'Yer man?'

'Yes. I don't know who he was talking about. But he said to tell you not to forget his ma's birthday.'

'To what?'

'Not to forget his ma's birthday.'

'I see. And did he say this was a pressing matter?'

'I don't know. But he said I should take yer man back to ours and he'd call again.'

'All right. Now would you mind just waiting a moment or two here on the doorstep, Thomas, while I work out what you're on about?'

He did not wait for a reply but closed the door. In the sitting room he said, 'Hear that?'

'Aye,' said Mikey. 'Ma's birthday. Bernie. That Joe's code?'

'Yes. It'll be you they're looking for. Local boys'll know you're here now.'

'Aye.'

'Can't be helped, I suppose. Better go with the boy.'

'I'll get the papers, then.'

'Leave the papers here. I'll find somewhere to keep them.'

'Fuck, Francis. You're taking a big risk there. If they find them –'

'I know, I know. Leave me to worry about that. It'd be a bigger risk for you to take them. I'll burn them maybe. You'd better be on your way.'

Mikey pulled on his coat. Francis went to the door and, 'Well, Thomas, it does seem after all that I have a guest who'd like to go with you. You'll take good care of him, won't you?'

'Yes, Francis.'

'Because if you didn't I wouldn't be too pleased now, would I?'

'No, Francis.'

'Well, then. Cheer up, Thomas. It may never happen. Here's the man himself.'

Mikey walked wordlessly out of the house carrying his small bag and sat in the passenger seat of the mud-covered old car. Thomas blinked.

'Mind how you go, Thomas,' said Francis, and closed the door.

'Bridget,' he called into the kitchen.

'Yes, Francis?'

'I'm on me way out for a bit.'

'All right, Francis.'

'There may be visitors. Not a word.'

'No, Francis.'

He went upstairs to the bedroom, quietly opening Bridget's bedside drawer. The large, ornate key that he'd always mocked was there. He'd not seen it in years, he couldn't remember the last time he'd needed the safe. Why had she even kept the damn thing? For old times' sake, she'd said. He'd laughed at her. Her idea of excitement had been doling out stamps and pensions and postal orders to the old biddies in the village.

Though he had to admit, it'd been useful for a while. And now. He'd used the safe a few times, the last time a few years back, for handguns and radios. He didn't deal with minor stuff like that any more. The bloody thing would still be there hulking in the corner, its broody presence evoking old man Kennedy's part-suspicious, part-fearful glare each time he had gone down the alleyway and knocked for Bridget. No one would have shifted that bleeder after all this time.

Best be on his way. They'd be crashing through the door any minute. She'd have to deal with that.

Francis rushed out with a carrier bag under his arm. Bridget sat and waited. She knew what to expect. It was a good twenty minutes before she heard the helicopters. The cars and the vans would be here in a minute or two. The troops would circle the house. She shuddered. These people. These men.

She noticed Francis's coat hanging on the door. He'd gone out without one and would get cold. She delved in the pockets, she was not sure why, perhaps some instinct. She felt the small smooth pebble-like shape and took out his mobile phone. She put it in the pocket of her apron.

The knock on the door came soon enough. She wiped her hands on her apron and walked slowly to the front door. There was a second, harder rap and she opened the door.

'Good morning, Mrs O'Neill. Would your husband be around?'

'And who wants to know?'

'My name's George Donnelly. Chief Superintendent George Donnelly. Mr Donnelly to you. You'll not know me, Bridget.'

Everyone around these parts had heard of Chief Superintendent George Donnelly. And everyone who had heard of him feared him, so it was said, perhaps especially those who had not yet met him. He looked at her with gleeful, almost fanatical large brown eyes, framed by long girlish lashes. He continued to grin, a man in control.

'That'll be Mrs O'Neill to you,' she said.

'Oh, pardon me,' he said. 'Mrs O'Neill it is, then. Well now, *Mrs* O'Neill. Your man about, is he?'

'Social call, is it?'

'Not exactly. I was in the area and thought I'd drop by.'

'With your friends.'

'That's about the measure of it. Not exactly discreet, I know. Still, you and your husband will be used to that, won't you?'

'Well, he isn't.'

'Isn't?'

'He isn't here. So if that's all . . .'

'Not exactly, Mrs O'Neill. We wouldn't mind having a look round. Would we, boys?'

Three soldiers armed with SA80s accompanied Donnelly, along with his scowling bagman. Two scanned the area while one stared straight at Bridget, his weapon crooked in his elbow facing at an angle to the ground and his finger covering the trigger. In readiness. In the muddy yard three further police officers were taking items out of a Ford Transit. Bridget could make out further troops at the edges of the property.

'It's a bit inconvenient, I'm afraid, Mr Donnelly. You see I've just begun me cleaning and it's a right mess inside.'

'We don't mind things a bit untidy, do we, boys?'

'No, I couldn't. And do you happen to have your search warrant on you?'

'As it happens I do, missus. We both know that by the powers vested in me under the Prevention of Terrorism Act blah-blah-blah I don't need one anyway. Now shall we get on with our business?'

Donnelly brushed past her and went swiftly into the house.

His sergeant was less gentle, grabbing her by the shoulders and pushing her inside. He pinned her against the wall and said, 'Bitch.' She smelt his sweat and tea on his breath and could feel the heat of his body. The fear that she had so far managed to sublimate in truculence almost surfaced in panic. She knew he could see it in her eyes. He smiled and said to one of the troopers, 'Keep an eye on her. A very close eye.'

Donnelly spoke over his shoulder. 'Sergeant Peters is a cruder man than I am, you see, Mrs O'Neill. Billy, we're going to have to get you house-trained. I'd keep very still if I were you, Mrs O'Neill, because that young man with the big gun is trained to be awful twitchy with Fenian slatterns. You so much as move out of turn and he's liable to get trigger-happy. Now come on, boys. We've not got all day.'

Bridget stood as the other policemen and soldiers filed past her. The young soldier assigned to guarding her held his gun pointing at her and stared intently into her eyes, as if searching for meaning. He looked so young and so aggressive yet at the same time so frightened. His helmet seemed altogether too large for him, as if he was a child playing at soldiers. How terrible it must be, standing here in the middle of the enemy's territory, afraid that at any moment a wall of fire could end his life. She could well believe he was jumpy. The two of them stood there looking into each other's eyes, locked in their embrace of fear.

The clattering and the shouting went on around them for more minutes than Bridget could count. Finally the search was complete and the party filed out one by one.

'Body search, boss?' asked Peters.

Donnelly gave it due consideration. 'Nah, we'll not bother. We'll leave that pleasure until next time,' he said at length. 'Afraid you really will have to do that cleaning now, missus. Now get on your way, laddie.' He shooed the young soldier out.

Bridget stood by Donnelly at the door. 'Now then, missus. Where would we be finding your husband?'

'No idea. I'm not his keeper.'

'Well, then. So you say. But I'm sure you could tell us a fair few tales about young Francis.'

'And why would I be doing that, Mr Donnelly?'

'So's you don't end up being pulled in for questioning some dark night. So's some overzealous officer doesn't hurt you in his eagerness. So's you don't have to spend a couple of nights in a stinking cell of the kind we can provide up at Castlereagh. I can protect you from all that. I can keep you safe. And you can earn a few quid into the bargain and have a life beyond that stinking pile of shite that is your husband.'

'You make it sound so attractive, Mr Donnelly. But the answer's no.'

'Sergeant Peters was right. You are a Taig bitch. But if you change your mind, here are my details.' He flicked a card on to the pile of papers scattered in the hallway. 'And you can tell your husband I fancy him for that MP over there. I fancy him very much indeed. And I will have him. Tell him that. Or maybe I'll just whisper in an ear or two. I'd tell your husband to watch his back if I were you, Mrs O'Neill. And you too.'

Bridget pushed the door to and slid to her knees. It was a moment or two before they came, the sobs, and she allowed herself only a few. She stood and straightened her apron before walking through the wreckage of the RUC search, the invasion. In the kitchen the cutlery had been taken from the drawers and flung carelessly on the floor. In the sitting room the sofa cushions had been taken out and tossed casually. The television had been upended. On the stairs the carpet had been pulled back and not replaced. A floorboard had been prised up. In their bedroom all their clothes had been emptied on to the floor, along with the bedding. In the open drawer of her bedside table she could see that her key was missing. But it would not be the RUC who'd taken that.

All the while she'd been thinking, wondering what she'd say if they found the mobile phone. Now she took it from her apron pocket and looked at it. She understood it was dangerous even to hold this thing in her hand, let alone switch it on. She realized that the implications were perilous for her, whatever she did or did not do next. Doing nothing was the safer option, for sure. But she pressed the button and the little screen illuminated. She'd had time to consider her decision, even as Donnelly and his thugs were ransacking her house and she stared into the frightened boy's eyes. Now she dialled the number she knew by heart. Sarah answered almost immediately. When she'd terminated the call she rang Anne-Marie from the landline to ask her to come round. She had to reinforce her legend.

Francis ran from the house, all pretence at composure vanished once he turned the corner on to the path through the woods. He clutched the carrier bag to his chest, thinking: what a fecking mess. These papers would be burned but only once the salient details had been committed to memory, and those which couldn't be remembered transcribed in tiny scrawls on cigarette papers that could be secreted beyond discovery by the police. For now he needed the maps and the lists and the addresses and the phone numbers and the photographs. There would be no time to recce again and reconstitute all this if the documents were destroyed. Still worse, though, if they were discovered. He'd be a goner. So hand-to-mouth, against Francis's instincts and everything that Joe Geraghty had taught him about the tools of the trade.

He could hear the rotors of helicopters in the distance, like distant machine-gun fire happening somewhere else. As he ran the sound became louder, then suddenly imminent. He carried on towards the village.

The noise was now deafening and he could see the dark silhouettes of their underbellies in the air, coming lower. He could make out the shapes of camouflaged legs dangling and black boots swinging with the motion of the beasts. There were three of them, evidently aiming to land close to where he was. He hoped that under the cover of the trees he remained invisible to them. He had no time to hide.

The helicopters had landed now, though the rotors still turned and the motors continued to run. They were in the field just the other side of the hedge. He heard shouting, English accents, and smelt kerosene. He slipped his revolver out of his coat.

Slowly the voices became quieter. It was clear now. They had come for him but he would not be there. They might look for him, so he must go on. He was almost there now and could see the road into the village ahead. He set his jaw and fixed his expression, attempting to shrink his world to just this, just the normality of it. Just the walk into the village and back.

There was no one to be seen on the two streets. People hereabouts knew better than to show their faces when the Brits and their helpmates the RUC came calling. Make yourself scarce, that was the drill.

Rash now beyond panic, he did not look round as he slid into the alleyway. He marched to the door through the moss and barged his way in, closing the door behind him as it scraped across the floor.

He drew breath and looked around him in the dim light. He should have brought a torch. Would she notice the key missing? Not a chance. She was in her own world most of the time. So long as he slipped it back once he got home she'd be none the wiser, as he had done the previous few times he'd used the safe to cache things.

He slotted the key into the lock. It would not turn. He removed it and looked at it curiously, noting for the first time in the dim light that its intricate striations and markings were not symmetrical. Inserting the key the other way round, he slowed his heart and concentrated fully. With greater gentleness, he turned it slowly and this time heard the reassuring soft clank. He pulled open the door and reached into the darkness, placing the carrier bag on the shelf. He closed the door and locked it again. He would give it a day or so before retrieving the bag, for safety's sake.

It was now time to put some distance between himself and the documents. He walked out of the village on the opposite side and down the track until he came to a barn, where he waited until he heard the helicopters taking off again.

12

Before one of his regular visits to his old stomping ground, Richard Mercer was summoned to a meeting at the Northern Ireland Office. 'It would be lovely if you could just pop in on your way to the airport,' was how the chirpy voice at the other end of the line put it.

He was shown into the Permanent Under-Secretary's office. Sir John Treanor had not been long in post and, so rumour had it, saw the Northern Ireland Office as a stepping stone to the Cabinet Office, and a pretty precarious one at that. This meeting was clearly well above Richard's pay grade. Sitting on the opposite side of a wide mahogany conference table from Sir John was a man in his early thirties wearing an open-necked shirt and jeans.

'I don't think we've met,' said Richard pleasantly, though he knew full well who the man was.

'Simon Dewey,' he said with a brief handshake but a longer look. Dewey, one of the PM's special advisers, had been parachuted into the Northern Ireland Office to protect his master's interests, or so it seemed to Richard.

Dewey pointedly put down the pen he had been holding and closed his notepad. 'We thought it might be opportune,' he said, 'to share notes. Sound out your views.'

'Fine. About what?'

'The process. The modalities,' said Dewey. 'The thing is, we need to know where we're heading. We need to know whether your interlocutors are actually going to serve anything up.'

'I can't exactly ask them what their bottom line is. I've been specifically instructed not to negotiate.'

'No. Quite,' said Dewey. 'But we need to sort out our positioning, and handling. What's your informed view? With your talking truth unto power bollocks? You must know more than we mere mortals. As you know, we're taking major risks here.'

'Well,' said Richard, 'they're serious. But jittery. They could pull out at any time. At this stage they'll want to know we're serious too.' He paused. 'If they're not convinced we are, and that all we're doing is stalling while the hawks prepare for battle, they may go public. It'd cause them problems internally, but they could judge it'd be more difficult for us.'

'How so?'

'With all the statements about not talking to terrorists.'

'Well,' said Sir John, 'we're not talking to terrorists. You are.'

'Right,' said Richard.

This, more or less, was it, apart from Sir John's dark mutterings that Richard and his like had spent so much time with these Fenian bastards that they'd practically joined the cause.

Richard made his excuses and said he needed to be on his way if he was to catch his flight. A flunkey was summoned from the anteroom of the cavernous office to escort him off the premises.

Richard missed the shuttle he'd intended to take so was playing catch-up as soon as he arrived in Belfast. He was met at the airport by Mick, the detail commander, and taken quickly to the car. None of their colleagues knew they were in the province, so this was a further layer of risk, to be added to the steaming pile that had already accumulated. If George Donnelly or one of his similarly volatile fellow officers were to find out what was going on, the consequences would be unpredictable. But he surely suspected something along these lines, if not Richard's personal involvement. Perhaps it might only be their friendship – if that's how you could describe their strange, tense relationship – that went down the pisser.

While he drove, Mick ran through the arrangements for the meeting. Normally they would have gone to Mick's hotel and his team would have taken Richard through the drills, the route in, the opt-outs and duress signals and finally the exit options, planned and emergency. These were all pretty standard, primarily consisting of Richard curling up and making himself as invisible as possible while Mick and team created a firestorm to enable them to usher him to safety. That at least was the theory. Neither Mick nor Richard wanted to see it tested.

The venue was in County Tyrone and its safety was vouchsafed by Dermot Quinn, the diminutive Dublin professor and middleman in this transaction. He preferred to think of himself as the facilitator of the Channel. It was the home, so Richard had learned, of a successful Catholic businessman with substantial interests in the South but with a reputation to protect in the North. And the logic went that the other side was as keen on confidentiality as Richard's, so would themselves bend over backwards on security.

The door of what was a quite beautifully maintained Georgian house opened and Dermot Quinn smiled, as if Richard were a dinner guest. But nervously. They stepped inside. The hallway's proportions were grand and an impressive curved staircase with polished mahogany finials swept away to the first floor.

'Will you be coming on through then, Richard?' said Quinn as he opened the door to the room where the meeting would take place.

A tall, slight figure rose from the seat where he had been drinking a cup of tea.

'Mr Richard. How the devil are you?'

'I'm fine, thank you, Mr Geraghty. And you?'

'Never better. And remember, it's Joe. How goes it in the world of the securocrats?'

'Fair to middling. And on your side?'

'Well. You know. It's a struggle to make progress. Especially with the headwinds your people are putting up. But I suppose we both have our crosses to bear.'

Richard did not respond.

'Shall we talk turkey, then?' Joe Geraghty gestured towards the table.

'I wish we could,' murmured Richard.

'Tea?' said Dermot Quinn.

'Yes please,' said Richard.

They took out their papers and sat on opposite sides of the table, Dermot Quinn at the end like an umpire.

'We need to be getting all this crap away,' said Geraghty.

'Couldn't agree more,' said Richard. 'But this seems to be where we are.'

'What I need to know, Mr Richard –'

'Richard'll do fine.'

'What I need to know, Richard, is whether your people mean business.'

'They very much seem to, but you'd have to ask them.'

'I'd like to. But I can't, given that we're tangled up in the pre-liminaries. I'm asking myself whether this is worth the candle. Whether it's not some kind of delaying tactic on your side.'

'Delaying what exactly? Your campaign seems to be running at full pelt.'

He ignored Richard. 'Listen. What I really need to know is what your side is prepared to offer.'

'In return for what?'

'Ha. Good question. But I think the first move has to come from you.'

'Perhaps the best way to find out is to state some kind of position. Make a proposition. Then perhaps we can cut some of these "preliminaries", you can start talking to the people who matter, and I can get back to my day job.'

'And I can get back to mine,' Geraghty said with a glint in his eye.

Richard remained expressionless.

'You must know what your government wants out of this. And what they're prepared to offer. Just help us over the starting line here.'

'No.'

'No? And why the devil not? Is this whole thing going to turn to shit just because one petty spook is standing on ceremony?'

'I share your frustration. There are more important things at stake than deciding whether the pencils on the desk should be HB or 2B. But I'm the wrong person to be taking this forward. I am the pencil man. I'm the monkey, not the organ grinder.'

He shook his head. 'I wonder what was going through their heads when they picked you, Mr Richard.'

'I'll take back your dissatisfaction to them. It may be time for someone else to step in. But . . .'

'Yes?'

'Whoever it is, you'll have to prove to them that you want to talk, not just posture.'

'Thank you for that.'

'You're welcome. Just a piece of friendly advice.'

'Friendly.' He laughed.

'Exactly.'

'You don't need to be offering me the benefit of your friendly advice, Mr Richard. You want to be watching your step.' He paused. 'In terms of your career I mean, of course. Just a piece of friendly advice.'

'Of course.'

'Are we done?'

'I'd say so,' said Richard.

Par for the course, thought Richard as he climbed into the car. Had they advanced two steps? Or taken a pace back? He knew for certain that within a couple of weeks or so he would be sitting opposite Joe Geraghty in if not the same house, then a very similar one, having an almost identical conversation, with all its rehearsed fractiousness. This was the way of it, but maybe progress was being made after all.

'I quite like the man, Kenny,' said Joe Geraghty when he was back in the car. 'Better than that milksop we had to deal with before. Aye, I quite like him.'

'Sounds like there's a big "but" there,' said Kenny.

Joe sighed and said, 'That there is. He'll not be the type we can cut the deal with. He has no authority. And not crafty enough. Not mean enough. Not like the other bastard, jumped-up prick though he was. Probably not the appetite either. We'll need to be dealing with his shyster bosses.'

They drove into the city.

'Will you get in touch with Francis for me, Kenny? We need an hour or two sometime soon.'

'Of course.'

'We need to keep the heat up on these bastards. Keep the pot boiling. Francis needs to get a move on.'

'His big job.'

'Aye. This political stuff. It's all very well. But when you get down to it all the Brits understand is force. They need to see the realities. Timing is everything.'

13

He'd dictate the terms. Immunity from prosecution was the start, but just the start. Your man'd moan, for sure. But eventually he'd have to give in. Francis O'Neill was a big fish. Your man couldn't not say yes, whatever sour expression he put on.

Then he'd build on it. New identity, new location. English-speaking of course. Florida maybe, always fancied Australia. Fancy house, flash car, big salary. Would he take Bridget? Not even a question. She could claim ignorance when Joe came calling. With conviction. He never told her anything. So why would he share plans to jump ship? And if he did, why would she still be there? She'd cope. Eventually.

It was all in his head, what he would tell him, and how. First off, this job. Then, gobbet by gobbet, in exchange for further concessions and rewards, he would unveil his whole life for them. A kind of striptease. There he would be eventually, spatchcocked under the floodlights. Friends and comrades sold, the struggle betrayed, the hierarchy shattered. Last of all he'd give up Joe, who would be destroyed, and the fear Francis felt in his presence would dissolve into nothingness.

He'd find some way of sneaking out of the no doubt squalid flat and making the call. The rule was that once formed the unit stayed together the whole time, 24/7. You went out in twos, preferably threes, but never alone. He himself had always reinforced it as ASU commander and this time round would be no different. It made sense. The team was at its most vulnerable to a single leak as it neared the attack and its members were most emotionally fragile. He'd have to pull rank somehow, claiming the need for an emergency call back home, possibly citing twitchiness that they might be being followed. He'd find some opportunity or pretext: this bunch of wasters were beyond the pale and awestruck in his presence in a way that in other circumstances would be gratifying.

That bastard he'd met out there. That's who it'd have to be. He still had his phone number in his head. Remembered it from that room at the police station. Mercer, or whatever his name really was. He was all right. He could deal with him. Not exactly the gullible type, but he seemed principled. Rigid. And that was helpful. He'd stick to his side of the bargain even if Francis didn't. Just needed to watch the small print of what this Richard said.

It was all very well to daydream about these things while waiting in the car, young Antony sitting next to him in the passenger seat. Fine to imagine a parallel life where shortly he might find himself in the land of milk and honey. The price of becoming a Judas for an hour was that he would then be one for the rest of his life, his soul mortgaged to the English crown in a Faustian pact. To make this reverie become real was a quite different thing from indulging it while they sat there. It was not remotely possible. The envisioning of it made him shudder. And besides, as everything else crumbled around him, he still believed. The cause gave him meaning and despite what others did, what Liam, his own brother, had done, he would not betray it. He would not betray his people. It would go against the grain of his whole life, the instinct of every sinew.

Peter and Karl were taking too long. Karl had been sent because of his English accent; Peter told to stay dumb but to nudge Karl should he stray off message. Francis was not anxious yet. But.

He turned to his left and Antony sat comfortable and complacent in his own world, dull eyes looking through the windscreen and a faint, idiotic smile on his lips. He lacked awareness altogether, the ability Francis possessed to hover and scan even when doing something else. That kind of subliminal alertness was mainly instinctual but could be learned through experience. Antony was a child and it was only to be expected. That was half the problem. This lot. Christ, Francis would be glad when Jonjo was with them.

He nudged Antony.

'What?' he said.

'Been a long time,' said Francis.

Antony's head began to swivel, his eyes darting.

'Easy,' said Francis. 'Nice and easy. Stay in control.'

'What do you think it is? Should we be away?'

'Sure we'll give them another couple of minutes. Then we'll start worrying. Just be alive. And don't be turning your head all the time. What do you think all these mirrors are for?'

Francis wound down the window and adjusted the driver's mirror so that it offered a better view of the junction behind them. Not that it would be of much use if it came to it. The Brits knew how to do these things. You had to give that to them. He and Antony wouldn't see them; they'd be bleeding into the gutter before they had time to react. But young Antony wasn't to know and it was good that he should be on his toes.

They continued to wait. Francis turned up the police scanner. Nothing. He switched his mind to what would be necessary if he and Antony had to drive off. Nowhere to stay, no assurance about Peter and Karl's resistance to interrogation. No assurance about anything at all. It would be abort and wet-nurse a panicking Antony back to Ireland.

The shop door opened and Peter and Karl strode out. Karl was smiling; Peter was not. Karl opened the rear door on the passenger side while Peter walked around the front of the vehicle.

'Fecking eejit,' he muttered through Francis's window as he flung his door open and climbed in.

Francis started the engine and, thinking how John Boy would have done it, eased the car out into the traffic.

'Well, gents, we have somewhere to live,' said Karl with a smile.

Peter looked studiously out of the side window.

'What took you so long?' asked Francis quietly.

'Eh?'

'I said, what took you so long?'

'Wasn't that long, was it? Geezer was talking about living in Calcutta. I went there a few years back, when I dropped out. Quite a character, he was.'

'I thought we said in and out as quick as possible.'

'Just making conversation. So's he wouldn't suspect anything.'

'He's letting out this flat, cash in hand. It's suspicious full stop. All you've done is give him a face and a story to remember.'

'And fucking mine too,' said Peter.

'You worry too much, mate,' said Karl. 'Stay cool. Anyway, here she is.' He waved the key in front of him.

'Where is it?'

'Dooley Street. Just turn left at the next traffic lights, right at the mini-roundabout and left at the next junction.'

'Left at the roundabout and right at the junction,' corrected Peter.

'Right. Same difference,' said Karl.

They drove the mile or so to the flat in silence and when they emerged from the car Francis put out his hand for the key, which Karl handed him with a smile.

'Youse two out here,' said Francis to Karl and Antony. 'And act casual.'

He looked at Peter and together they walked to the back of the building, a run-down row of shops. Three of the five were closed and barricaded with metal shutters. The alleyway behind the row of shops was litter-strewn. Tall weeds grew in the gaps in its cracked concrete surface. A large metal bin stank of decaying flesh. It must belong to the fried chicken shop below the flat they had rented.

Francis looked again at Peter, who nodded. They walked back to the front of the building and approached the battered door of the flat, next to the chicken shop's toughened glass door. Francis knocked while Peter looked round casually, scanning. They expected no answer. Francis looked through the letter box, then inserted the thin, worn key into the lock and unlocked the door slowly with a click. He pushed and met resistance. A pile of junk mail had accumulated advertising pizzas, sofa super-stores and DIY mega-outlets. He kicked it aside and stood at the foot of the stairs considering the shit-brown patterned carpet and breathing in the faint fatty stench of long-forgotten fast-food meals and the stale must of uninhabited neglect.

He beckoned Peter, who went past him quickly up the stairs. Francis followed. They checked each room in turn, opening cupboards and looking under furniture. It was stand-ard drill, though verging on the ridiculous. If they were gone, they were gone already. They moved swiftly and were out on the street again within five minutes, gesturing to the other two to get moving. Peter, Karl and Antony took the bags from the car boot and Francis parked the car near the mouth of the alleyway, away from the main street and the front door.

When he returned to the door he found Karl outside.

'What you doing?' he said.

'Calm down,' replied Karl. 'Just having a look. So this is Bir-mingham. Same shithole as everywhere else.'

'Inside,' said Francis, and something in his tone shifted Karl. They gathered in the kitchen.

'Put the kettle on, Antony,' said Francis.

Peter glared at Karl across the room. Finally he could not hold back. 'You arsehole,' he said.

'Hold up,' said Karl. 'Keep your hair on. I know what I'm doing. I was in the army, remember. I've done all the training.'

Peter strode across the room and seized Karl by the front of his shirt. Antony and Francis separated the two men.

'Back off, Peter,' said Francis. 'It's difficult, I know, all these changes. But back off.'

'But this –'

'Peter. Quiet. You're not helping.'

'Yeah. Back off, man,' said Karl.

Francis sighed slowly, then in one movement turned and pinned Karl to the wall, his right hand cupping his chin and gripping his jaw brutally. He squeezed, hard.

'You do what I say. Precisely that, nothing more or less. You'll know from training that your ASU leader is your commander. You do everything he says, without question, without hesitation, without deviation. Is that right?'

'Yes, Francis.'

Francis could see the terror in his eyes. 'I know because I wrote the book. Now, stop treating this like some weekend adventure holiday. That way you get yourself killed, for real, and possibly us too. Understand?'

'Yes.'

'I'm going to be clear with you. You carry on fucking us around and I will take you into the bathroom, tie you up in the bath, cut your wrists and watch your blood drain down the plughole. Then I'll carve you up and fillet you and take out your giblets and put the whole bloody lot in that bin out the back.'

He looked enquiringly.

'OK,' said Karl. 'I get the message.'

Francis pressed harder into his face, fingernails digging into the flesh. 'Get the message? Get the message? What do you mean: get the fucking message? I'm not sending out messages. Just do what I say.'

'All right.'

'Now where's that tea, Antony?' said Francis.

She knew that she had been told to phone only in an emergency. To her, this counted.

'Where is he?' she asked.

'Why?' asked Sarah. 'Do you know something?'

'No. He must be doing something. Is he all right?'

'We talked about this. Your not knowing certain things protects you. Your mind's not full of detail you have to forget . . .'

'I know, I know. But is he . . . ?'

'I'll tell you as soon as I can if anything important happens. I will do what's best for you. I will look after you. I know it must be difficult, all on your own, but the less we're in contact at the moment the better.'

'Did you get them to come to the house? Did you set us up?'

'No.'

'Those men, those vile men. Do they know?'

'Not at all.'

'Are these the people you deal with, though?'

'Normally not directly. There's no chance they could find out anything about you from me.'

'I'm worried about him.'

'I know. Try not to be.'

'Can you guarantee no harm will come to him?'

'It all depends on him. We're both trying to make sure of that.'

'What's going to happen?'

'I don't know. I know it's difficult. You have to accept everything on trust. There's nothing I can say to comfort you. I'm doing my best to achieve what we both agreed and I'm good at my job. But there are so many variables. We talked about this. Public safety has to come first. You just have to hang on in there. Neither of us has any option. This is the most difficult time, the waiting. Just stick with it.'

'I need to meet.'

'All right. Thursday?'

Variables. What variables? She believed what Sarah was saying. But so much of this was beyond Sarah's control. Way beyond. She'd been clear that Francis would be in danger, but much less danger than when he was going about his business without them being aware of it. That part was unconvincing now. Francis was a clever man, he didn't take risks unnecessarily. He'd done it for years without getting caught.

But then. Those people, when he did what he did. Is that really what you want? Sarah had said. Of course it wasn't.

Poor Francis, she thought. Holed up somewhere. Unaware of any of this, unaware anything was wrong, of what would happen to him. She could no longer find any liking in herself for him, but that was not the point. Not the point at all. Poor Francis. She would tell Sarah. No more. Too late. But no more.

Antony drove. Jonjo sat in the front passenger seat. From the back Francis kept a watchful eye on the road, perilous at the best of times with its three lanes and lumbering trucks inducing dangerous overtaking manoeuvres, and on Antony's driving. Foot passengers had disembarked first so they'd avoided being caught up in the slow convoy of lorries spewing out of the ferry on to the roads. It was moderately quiet, even for an out-of-season Tuesday.

'Run me through it,' he said to Jonjo.

'No issues. Straightforward as you could want. Got meself a bacon buttie at Larne and sat and read the paper.'

'Security this end?'

'Nothing. Wasn't stopped.'

'How about landside?'

'Didn't seem to be much. Sleepy old Cairnryan. How's it all looking?'

'It's all right,' said Francis in a tone that he hoped would convey something different to Jonjo. They would need to speak, but not in front of Antony. 'What about the other side?'

'No problems. They're just putting the thing together.'

'Got it all mixed, then?'

'Yeah. And I've got some good boys on it over there. All I'll need to do is connect up the wires and set the fucker.'

'Still on for Thursday?'

'As planned. Same truck. Same reg. Same mobile phone. And we pick them up at Charnock Richard?'

'Right. They've got their instructions?'

'Aye. They wait in the cafeteria until they see me. No contact. Then they go. We watch them down the M6 and then we meet up at Frankley. You tell them where they're to park up. Is it secure?'

'It'll do. How long do you need?'

'Hour or two should do it.'

'All right. Then you and Antony make your way back.'

Francis could see Antony's face in the driver's mirror. He looked hurt. 'No worries, Antony,' he said. 'You're a good lad. You'll get plenty of chances. We'll be five up anyway without youse two. Too many cooks and so on.'

'Right, Francis.'

'Well, then. Time for a bit of dinner.'

They pulled in at the next service station and found a table. Francis said, 'Listen, Antony, why don't you go and get us our dinner now? We could do without them hearing too many Irish voices. Just the one's enough. I'll be having the all-day breakfast . . .' He looked at Jonjo.

'The same. And tea. Cheers, Antony.'

'Aye, yes, tea.' He handed Antony two ten-pound notes and watched him as he walked off meekly to join the long queue.

'He's a good enough lad,' said Francis.

'How's it going?'

'Crock o'shite. God knows if it was up to me I wouldn't choose these bastards. I don't know what Joe and them are up to. Boys and amateurs. And you and me and Peter stuck in the middle. What are the truck crew like?'

'Fecking mad. The driver's sound enough but the other eejit's a mad bastard. Gerry McCluskey. You know the boy?'

'Know of him. Lives down Silverbridge way?'

'That's the one.'

'Thieving heavy plant, that's what he does, isn't it?'

'Aye. What we're doing cuddling up to the likes of him I don't know.'

'Needs must, Jonjo, I suppose. He knows England. He's got contacts. We've so many boys inside just now.'

'Well, he's cracked. His cousin it is, driving the truck. Quiet lad. But Gerry. Real gobshite.'

'We've a fucking Englishman down in Birmingham.'

'Englishman? Jesus.'

'Aye. He's waiting there with Peter. If Peter doesn't do him in before we get there, that is. Member of some ultra-left-wing group. Ex-soldier from the British Army who saw the light. He's vouched for back home. Done some training with the boys, so they say. Karl, he calls himself. Found out the other day his real name's Derek. But that doesn't sound right for a revolutionary, so he calls himself Karl, after Karl Marx.'

'Jeez.'

'Heard anything about Mikey?'

'They're still holding him in Castlereagh, I was told.'

'We could have done with him here. Antony's an all-right kid but . . .'

'Yeah.'

'. . . and Peter's just a fucking hothead. With your two clowns coming over tomorrow, looks like we're going to have a full house. You and me are going to have to hold this together.'

'Aye.'

They looked at Antony, who was nearing the cash register eventually. He smiled back nervously and waved.

'Fuck me,' said Jonjo.

'Yeah,' said Francis.

Bridget and Sarah sat in the two low leather chairs set by the wide picture window for the purpose of looking out on to the Irish Sea, blue and inviting on a day like this under a wide sky. Sarah had acquired this comfortable bungalow on the coast near Downpatrick. Riffing extensively on her Irish heritage, she'd told the neighbours she was a businesswoman looking for a place with seclusion and privacy as a refuge from her manic professional life. The elderly man next door had looked at her enquiringly and she'd said that, no, she'd not been put off by the Troubles. Friends had told her it was all exaggerated, that aside from the flashpoints Northern Ireland was one of the safest and most restful places within easy distance of London. That was how she'd found it, bought this place for a song and now viewed it as home, coming here as often as possible. She was Irish at heart after all, if not by accent.

The reasoning was thin, to say the least. Sarah and Bridget had been using this place for their meetings for some months now.

Before this new arrangement, Bridget had gone to each meeting with Sarah with a mixture of anticipation of the contact and dread of the arrival and departure. She knew a chance meeting on the way there or back could result in her death; still worse was the gnawing thought that she might have been recognized without her knowledge by someone connected with Francis or the Provos. The feeling of peril had accumulated. It was getting easier because of this place and because she now had a cover story, the fictional but unspecified medical condition that she had placed in the other wives' minds.

'Are you all right?' asked Sarah.

'What do you think?'

'It's to be expected. It's tough, especially now.'

'I just want to undo all of this.'

'What?'

'Everything. You and me. Me doing this. All those wrongs Francis did me. Marrying him. Ever meeting him. That's the problem. I just want everything not to have happened.'

Sarah did not reply.

'I mean, I know I can't. But, you know . . .'

'We have to deal with life as it is.'

'That's what I can't do.'

'You're wrong. You're such a level-headed person. You've coped with so much over the years.'

'When I was a small girl in infants school, I was shy. I was in class one morning and wanted to go to the toilet but couldn't say. I sat there and sat there and wet my pants in the end. The teacher told me what a stupid little girl I was, in front of the class. She was right, and there was nothing I could do. Everybody knew, and there was nothing I could do. I feel like that now, just like that. And soon everyone will know.'

'It's not like that. You're doing what's right. However wrong it may feel. Whatever happens from now on. And yes, I would say that, wouldn't I? It's what I'm trained to say. But it's true.'

'Right for whom?'

'Right for everybody. You. Those whose suffering you help prevent. Even for Francis.'

'How do you know Francis is going to kill anyone?'

'You know what he does.'

'They only kill enemy combatants. In self-defence.'

'A policeman, an MP, a ten-year-old boy who happens to be standing next to a rubbish bin?'

'All right. Of course not. But who's to blame for that? Are you saying Francis is? He's only fighting back.'

'I know the history. I know the slogans. I know the charge sheet off by heart, like all good Irish children. I have my own views. But I look at this and think: my opinions are irrelevant. I have to do what I can to stop it. I can't decide the big picture, I'm not powerful enough or clever enough to do that. So I'll do whatever I can.'

'That's just a speech you've learned off by heart. I can't square this.'

'You don't have to. Not at the moment. It's in motion. There's nothing you or I can do to stop it.'

'I could go to them. I could tell them what's happened. Get them to get him back.'

'I doubt they could. But you wouldn't do that anyway. Think of the consequences for yourself.'

'Perhaps I deserve it. Perhaps it's what I want. Perhaps I need to stop thinking about the consequences for me.'

Even as she spoke the words she knew she was lying. Sarah must know too. She looked at the sea, down there, so far away, silent through the double glazing.

As she walked from the bus stop out of the village, Bridget thought she now understood her folly. It had begun in her teens, when she'd allowed herself to be charmed by Francis O'Neill. Perhaps that had been the point at which all of this had been set in motion, with an ineluctable unravelling that would destroy her and Francis too. She was a stupid woman, feckless and impulsive. Sarah, whom she'd regarded almost as a saviour, was in the end just someone to talk to. And not really that when it came down to it. After all, she was a Brit.

Bridget deserved this; but then again it was too late to be thinking any of this. She was beyond, Francis was beyond.

She approached the cottage and became aware of a figure standing outside, smoking a cigarette behind his crooked, shielding hand. Her first instinct was to turn and scuttle back the way she had come, but it would be futile; he had seen her and there would be others lying in wait.

It was Stevie from the garage. He waved, and it seemed an age before she reached him.

'Hello, Bridget,' he said.

'Hello, Stevie,' she replied.

'You was out.'

'Yes. I had to go the shops, see.'

He looked at her. She carried only her handbag. 'Had to get a new battery for me watch. It stopped yesterday . . .' Don't explain too much, she told herself. Don't get drawn in.

'And is it all right now?'

'Yes.'

He nodded. 'Anne-Marie was looking for you earlier on. She dropped by.'

'I'd probably already gone out.'

'It was this morning.'

'And?'

'Anyways, I was looking for Francis. Got a car in he might be interested in.'

'Francis isn't here.'

'Away, is he?'

She looked at him and he looked down, acknowledging, it seemed to her, that this was not an appropriate question. Or had it been a test?

'Well, I'll tell him,' she said tersely. 'Thanks for coming by.'

'Aye, I'll see him when I see him, then,' he said, and went to his car.

As she unlocked the front door she stopped herself from looking round to see if he was watching her.

The night before, everything became calm. Life was simplified, distilled. The talking was done, the planning: all that was left was execution. It was familiar. It was happening to him again. The struggle had become secondary, then somehow irrelevant; what was important was the call to action. Others had disappeared from view, apart from the small assembled crew.

He felt tired, beyond exhaustion. Nervousness was no longer a factor, though he knew that, in the febrile oscillation between doing and waiting the next morning, sweat and anxiety would rise again. And then thirty minutes or so before the final act and flight, inevitably that equally familiar but different wave of fatigue would envelop him before rather than after the last exertion and fruition, which would evaporate suddenly in the clarity of the moment.

Everything was in place. The lorry was parked in the overnight truck stop, Jonjo in the sleeping section of the cab guarding it. Francis had half considered leaving the vehicle on its own. If the security forces were to detect it there was little Jonjo would be able to do on his own to prevent the inevitable. The risks of this operation were not negligible, and Francis did not want to lose Jonjo, of all his people. But if the truck was stolen by common criminals, all hell would be let loose. As it was, Jonjo would be on hand to do his stuff at the crack of dawn.

Antony slept in the other bed in this room. Peter and Karl, a tentative truce holding, were in the other bedroom and the two jokers who had brought the truck over had their sleeping bags in the lounge, which reeked of beer and takeaways. It was quiet, apart from the rumble of traffic along the A41 and the steady rhythm of Antony's snoring. The innocence and ignorance of the young, to be able to sleep on command on a night such as this. Francis would find his own thin sleep, but it would take its time to arrive.

At three twenty-two in the morning he was instantly alert. He was not even aware of waking, so sudden was the transition between the states of sleep and consciousness. He looked at the digital clock and felt under the bed for the revolver he carried with him. Antony snored on.

Francis slid quickly out of the bed, crept across the room and stood behind the door. He wondered whether the others too had heard the sound of voices, or indeed if he had imagined it. As he orientated himself in full wakefulness, he tried to compute what he had heard. The click of a door. Voices, not urgent, insistent or for that matter making any apparent effort to remain unheard. Cheerful if anything. Carefully, he turned the door handle which had a propensity to click. He twisted it until he could inch the door open on to the dark narrow corridor from which all the doors of the flat opened. There was a figure standing in the darkness already. Peter. Karl peered around the edge of the door. Francis gestured him impatiently to go back into the bedroom.

Francis and Peter could hear giggling from the living room. They edged towards the door under which light shone and waited there a moment.

Gerry and Kevin, the truck driver, were sprawled across the armchairs while another figure lay asleep on the sofa.

'What's going on here, boys?' said Francis.

'Got caught in a lock-in,' answered Gerry.

'Oh yes?'

'Yeah. Irish pub. So no worries.'

'And who's this one?'

'That's Pat.'

'Pat?'

'Yeah. He does the ferry run too. He's a good old boy. From Kerry. Known him years. Sound as a pound.'

'And what's Pat doing here?'

'He was going to sleep in his rig. But we thought . . .'

'You thought. Had a few yourselves, lads?'

'One or two. Not much nightlife in Silverbridge,' said Gerry.

'Or Dundalk,' added Kevin, with a laugh. He swigged from a bottle.

'Grand time of it, though,' said Gerry. 'Singing the auld rebel songs and all.'

Peter spoke for the first time. 'Is this some kind of fucking cabaret?'

'Cabaret, right,' said Gerry.

'Cabaret,' repeated Kevin, raising his bottle in a toast.

Francis turned to Peter. 'We'll deal with this quietly, shall we, Peter? Big day tomorrow.'

'Today, you mean,' said Gerry.

'We have to abort now, surely?' asked Peter.

'Abort, abort, abort!' said Kevin, laughing.

'We'll talk about that in a while. We'll clear this up first.'

Kevin vomited profusely on the arm of the sofa.

'And that,' said Francis. 'Get the others up, will you?'

Peter opened his mouth but said nothing.

By the time the others had gathered in the living room Gerry had stood up and Kevin had scraped the sick off the sofa arm into a plastic carrier bag using the lid from one of the takeaway cartons. Both looked chastened, but not abashed. The old man remained comatose in the middle of the room.

For a moment no one said anything.

Karl spoke first. 'I thought you lot were supposed to be highly disciplined. Fucking amateur hour, this is.'

Francis gave him what he hoped was a suitably withering look. He had a point, though. 'We'll sort that later,' he said softly. 'Meanwhile we need to sort this.' He pointed at the man, who had begun to moan. Peter nudged him and gestured to the corridor. When they were there he closed the door and whispered, 'The old boy.'

'Yes?' said Francis.

'We can't just let him go.'

'So what do you suggest?'

'We either abort or . . .'

'Or bump off some old Irish boy? For being in the wrong place at the wrong time? No. Let the poor old bastard piss off and sleep it off. He'll never remember anything.'

'But –'

'This whole thing's been a fucking abortion, Peter. We're too far in. We can't cry off now, we'd get it in the neck back home.'

They returned to the living room. 'You three, get rid of him somewhere,' said Francis. 'I'll look after Tweedledum and Tweedledee here.'

'Where, Francis?' asked Antony.

'I don't know. Somewhere.'

'Just throw him out the front door,' said Gerry. 'Fecking old eejit.'

'I don't think so,' said Francis. 'Few miles away. Other side of town. Anywhere. Do it.'

Peter and Karl lifted him to his feet. 'Come on, pal,' said Karl. Antony opened the doors for them.

When they were gone, Francis said, 'Well, then, boys. Do youse feel up for it today?'

'Up for anything,' said Gerry.

'Good,' said Francis slowly, and slapped him across the face, hard. His hand stung and left a red mark on Gerry's face. 'Now then,' he continued, 'let's not make a big thing of this. Just need to be clear on a couple of things. We'll sort all this out once this is over and we're back home. And don't even think of pulling out now. Youse boys are too deep into it. You fuck off anywhere, you put one step out of line, you're dead. Literally. The boys will come for you wherever you might be. Clear?'

'Yes, Francis,' they said in unison.

'You're not stealing diggers any more. You're with the big boys. You be all right to drive?' He looked at Kevin.

'For sure. Just need a kip and some breakfast. Line me stomach.'

'Well, get off and use my bed, then. I'll wake you when it's time.'

Once Kevin had gone Francis stood in the middle of the room not, for the moment, knowing what to do. He shook his head as if to empty it of all the fog and scratched near the bald patch that had begun to form. Gerry watched him.

'Now then, Gerry.'

Gerry flinched. 'Sorry, Francis. We just sneaked out for last orders. Then the lock-in started. Things got a bit out of hand. You won't be telling them back home, will you now, Francis?'

'I won't be telling no one nothing for the time being,' said Francis. 'It depends on how we go. If it goes to shite there's nothing I can do. Not that I would anyway. So if you don't want anything made of it you make sure this bloody works.'

'Right, Francis.'

'Otherwise I might just tear you limb from fucking limb before you have a chance to get back home. Best behaviour. Right?'

'Right.'

'Get some sleep. You might as well use Antony's bed.'

Francis made himself a cup of tea, switched off the light and looked out on the dawning twilight as he waited for Peter, Karl and Antony to return. Perhaps Peter was right and the whole shooting match should be pulled, regardless of the scorn that would cause back home. The day had already started, before he wanted it to.

14

When Peter, Karl and Antony returned to the flat Francis made another pot of tea. They murmured as they drank it and Francis issued instructions.

'Youse two get a bit of sleep,' he said, indicating Peter and Karl. 'Get those other two up at eight. We need to be moving soon after. Make sure this place is clear and drop off the keys so we don't have to do it later.'

The others listened in silence and shortly he was left in the room with Antony.

'What time is it, Antony?'

'It's a quarter before five, Francis.'

Francis sighed. 'Well, it's a bit early but never mind. There's no point trying to get any sleep or hanging round. We'll wash up and make a move.'

It was five thirty by the time they reached the truck stop. They found a van selling food and bought fried egg and bacon sandwiches and coffee. Weaving between the hulking lorries, they eventually found the red cab with its distinctive yellow logo and the flatbed trailer covered in a black tarpaulin that declared nothing of its freight.

Francis took out his mobile phone. They could hear it ringing inside the cab and it was some seconds before Francis heard Jonjo's sleepy voice. 'Yeah?'

'All good with you?'

'Yeah.'

'We're outside.'

Francis terminated the call. The curtain of the cab was

tugged aside and he could see Jonjo in his vest, frowning with sleepiness, peering out. The locks clicked and Francis and Antony climbed up into the driver's and passenger's seats.

'Sleep?' asked Francis.

'A bit. Not too bad.'

'More than we did, then.'

'Why? What happened?'

'You don't want to know. Long story. It's all right now, though.'

'You sure?'

'Well, it's got to be, hasn't it?'

Jonjo looked questioningly from the rear of the cab.

'Anyway,' said Francis, 'we'd better get a move on.' He held up the bags containing the sandwiches. 'Brown sauce or ketchup?'

When they had finished and Jonjo had washed and shaved inside the toilet block, Francis instructed Antony to patrol outside the truck. 'Don't look obvious,' he said.

'Where could we dump this lot if we decided to abort?' he asked Jonjo.

'You serious?'

'Kind of. Not really. Hypothetical. But with Fred Karno's Army here who knows what might go wrong?'

'In theory, anywhere, so long as you haven't set the bastard. Some service station, I suppose. It'd not be noticed for a few hours with a bit of luck. But you'd have to call it in. Can't risk some civilian setting it off. Be a mess, though, whatever. You'd have to be well clear if you didn't want to be picked up. Never been involved in a job that was called off this late.'

'Me neither. Like I said, it was hypothetical. I hope. We'll all be safe and sound at home by tonight, watching it on TV.'

Jonjo flung his sleeping bag and rucksack into the front of the cab and shifted the mattress so that he could gain access to the panel below. He unscrewed the fixings and pulled the panel off. Francis twisted his body in the front seat to get a better view.

Jonjo attached a clip-on torch to the headlining and knelt in the confined space, his knees spread wide so that he could reach down into the space below. Francis could see a nest of wires, wildly deranged it seemed to him. Jonjo knew what he was doing.

'It's a normal fit-up,' said Jonjo. 'The boys have wired her all up through the chassis of the flatbed. Did a load of welding. Should be undetectable. She's all wired through to here. All I have to do is connect it up. We tested the circuits the day before yesterday. She's sound as a pound. Now the next bit is mine. Best if I concentrate on me own. You just sit there and listen to the radio or something. I'll give you a shout when I'm ready.'

He stripped down to his vest again and pulled the curtain shut. Francis could hear the click of the torch behind him. He switched on the radio and tuned in to Radio 4 as the *Today* programme began.

It was seven thirty when Jonjo put his head round the curtain again.

'Right. I'm done.'

Antony, dozing in the passenger seat, jolted awake.

Francis looked at his watch. 'You made good time. Right then, Antony, do you want to get rid of all this crap while Jonjo shows me the necessary? Then we'll be making a move.' He handed Antony the empty Styrofoam beakers and the greasy paper bags. 'On you go,' he said.

'Now then, Jonjo.'

'I'd rather stay the distance, Francis, if it's all right with you.'

'No need, Jonjo. Like I said, too many cooks. We can't go three up in this rig.'

'Let me do it, then.'

'No. I have to be on board as we deliver this. That's my job. Anyways, you said it. It's a standard fit-out. Just remind me of what to do and it'll all come flooding back to me.'

'But . . .'

'I won't fuck it up, Jonjo. I don't fuck things up. If I thought I might, you'd be there. Now, what is there to do?'

Jonjo shone the torch into the compartment where he had been working. 'It's simple enough. You've practised it. You see this switch I've screwed into the bodywork here?'

He shone the torch into the hole and Francis knelt on the driver's seat to look back in.

'Yeah.'

'That's it. That's the final connection. Flick it and she's live. She'll detonate at whatever time the timer's set for.'

'Right. And the timer?'

'Already done. Set for twelve thirty, like you said.'

'If I need to change it, where is she?'

'Under here.' Jonjo reached below the rim of the compartment and gently withdrew a digital timer, connected to the innards of the vehicle by two wires. 'Now, you'll have to be careful here so's you don't break the connection. And you know how to set it?'

'I should hope so.'

'If you need to change the time you have to do it before making the connection.'

'Yes, yes, I know right enough. I won't need to. But just so's I know.'

'Right. It's a new battery on the timer so you won't need to check whether it's going.'

'And then?'

'Once you've set her you need to screw the plate back on top of the compartment. You see these contacts here?' He pointed to some soldering on the cover of the compartment.

'Yeah.'

'When you screw the plate down tight that makes contact with these little buggers here . . .' He pointed at two small soldered points in the frame of the compartment on top of which the plate would fit, from which wires led down into the dark.

'And once that's done she's well and truly trapped. Almost impossible to defuse. But for Christ's sake don't screw the plate down before you press the switch. Because you're fucked then. You can't open her up to have another try. You do that and the whole fucker goes sky high.'

'Got it.'

'You all right with this, Francis? I'd much rather do it meself.'

'Course I am,' said Francis, though he felt sweat trickle at the back of his neck.

After Jonjo had changed clothes in the toilets at the truck stop, Francis drove them in the car to the nearby railway station.

'You boys need to be on the next flight back to Dublin,' he said. 'I want you gone before she goes up. You've enough cash?'

'Sure,' said Jonjo.

'Francis,' said Antony, 'can I stay? I want to be in on this.'

'No. There's too many of us as it is.'

'You could send Peter back. Or one of the others.'

'No, Antony. You'll get your chance sure enough. Now just be on your way. I'm on a double yellow here.'

He watched them into the station and got back into the car.

Before he turned the ignition key, he paused. This was his moment, if he was to have one. Shortly he would be back with the shambolic cabal that was his team and there would not be another chance before he set foot in Ireland again. If he set foot there again. So it had to be now.

He'd made preparations, collected the pile of one-pound coins that he was fingering in his jacket pocket. He'd rehearsed what he'd say. If he truly felt it was all shot he could go to a public telephone and call that Mercer boy. The number he had remembered since Singapore.

The RA was his family. A bloodline that reached through the centuries to him, an inheritance of passion for freedom and loathing for the English yoke. He'd been nurtured in the cause, educated in the ways and necessities of the fight by his cruel begetter, Joe Geraghty.

Families feuded. Brothers betrayed you. Your kin could be cruel to you, to the point where you doubted. You doubted their desire to look after you, you doubted your sanity.

But no, he was not about to become a traitor to this family. Unlike Liam, he was not a tout. He did not have that in him. He was straight and true. He would follow this through, those were his orders, whatever the consequences for him.

He drove to the flat and announced to the others, 'Let's get this fucking thing done.'

They made good time to the M1. Francis sat next to Kevin in the cab of the Scania truck. The others were in the car, periodically speeding ahead to scout the route before dropping back behind the truck to scan for the police.

Kevin's bravado had worn off. His hands gripped the wheel and his eyes were fixed in a stare on the motorway in front of him.

'You all right, son?' said Francis.

'Yeah. Sound. Just want to make sure this goes right.'

'You're doing fine. Not too fast, not too slow. Drive neat so's you don't attract attention.'

'This fucker's not going to go up with us in it, is it?'

'You think I'd be sitting here if I thought so? Jonjo knows what he's doing. She's good as gold.'

'If you say so.'

'I do. Now where have the others got to?'

'I can see them in the mirror. Here they come.'

The Vauxhall overtook them at a steady pace. Francis watched intently. There was no sign of the signal they had agreed on in the event of problems: a quick flash of the hazard lights. The car accelerated away as it began to rain.

'Shame, that,' said Francis. 'Such a lovely day.'

They left the M1 at the junction with the M25, travelling east.

'This is nonsense, man,' said Kevin. 'It's quicker straight down the MI, then on the North Circular.'

'This is our route,' said Francis. 'We stop at the services and wait.'

At South Mimms they parked as far away from the other vehicles as they could. There were no trucks here, only coaches. It was just after eleven. Kevin was muttering, nervously looking all around. 'Soon be over,' said Francis gently. The car with the others in would be somewhere ahead, conducting a final sweep of the target in preparation for Francis and Kevin's arrival there in about twenty minutes' time. Before that, they would make a mobile telephone call to confirm all was clear and that the traffic en route was reasonable. Not until they arrived at the electricity substation in Wembley would Francis prime the device. When they had finished and by the time they were well on their way back to Ireland millions of Londoners would be without power. Rail services in much of the capital, as well as large tranches of the Underground network, would be closed down. There might be some dead at the substation but that was just unavoidable. Collateral damage. Omelettes and eggs. Francis's bosses had calculated that London could be crippled for weeks. That was the theory.

'You need the toilet?' said Francis.

'No. I'm all right,' replied Kevin.

'Well, I do. I'm fecking bursting. Be back in a moment.'

He could see the look of dismay on Kevin's face as he left the cab.

Standing at the urinal, he still had that feeling there was something wrong. Most obviously with this operation, but with the whole thing too, with Joe and the RA altogether. Something was unsettling everything. A frisson of fear spread a juddering frost down his spine. His sweat turned cold on his back as panic took hold of him. He had been thinking so hard

that he had become oblivious to everything around him. Run!
The word echoed in his head.

It lasted only a split second. As he turned everything was
normal. Just blokes having a piss and queuing at the wash-
basins. He went to wash his hands.

''Scuse me,' a voice behind him said in one of those whining
English accents.

'Yes?'

'You using that, or what?'

An elderly man wearing a flat cap looked at him impatiently,
staring him down.

'Ah, yeah,' said Francis. 'No. Sorry.' He took his hands from
the dryer, which had already stopped, he now realized, and
walked out to join the mass of bodies shifting one way and the
other between the food outlets and the shops. The usual service station commotion of ignorant people exclusively intent
on getting wherever they needed to go.

Another fucking wobble. Get a grip, man. It's all right. It's
all right. He was mouthing the words. Fuck you all, you bastards, he thought as he gathered speed. We're going to do this
and it'll be on you all.

He was running by the time he reached the truck, which was
still standing on its own at the edge of the parking area. He'd
found purpose again, the clouds had lifted. He climbed on to
the running board, but to his surprise the door was locked. He
was about to shout to Kevin when he was gripped firmly from
behind and forced to the ground, his arms pinned painfully
behind his back and his face ground into the asphalt.

A voice shouted, 'Armed police. Do not move. Do not struggle.'

Francis sat in the rear of the police car as it sped through Kil-
burn. Paddington Green was the inevitable destination for
dangerous people like him. He wore a white coverall made of

resilient paper, and blue plastic bootees, and was handcuffed to a similarly clad detective. Swabs and fingerprints had been taken from him at the scene. In the front of the car, next to the uniformed driver, sat another detective, senior to the silent, burly young man beside Francis. The radio chattered with life and the two men in the front murmured to each other about the route they were taking. Several other police vehicles were ahead and behind in the blurred cavalcade of blue lights and sirens. He felt surprisingly calm. It's almost over, he thought.

The older detective turned in his seat and said, 'We're taking you to Paddington Green, sir.'

Sir? Had he actually said 'sir'? Or was it 'son'? No, definitely 'sir'.

Francis neither replied nor met the eye of the policeman. He stared resolutely at the back of the seat in front of him.

'You'll have a chance to speak to your lawyer there. I understand someone is on their way. Meanwhile I'm unable to question you under caution. However, I am permitted to ask you in the interest of public safety whether there's anything we need to know to prevent injury, loss of life or damage. Do you have anything to say?'

'No comment,' said Francis in a monotone.

'The device in the cab. Our people on the scene believe it has not been primed and poses no present risk. Is that correct?'

'No comment.'

'Is the device booby-trapped in any way?'

'No comment.'

'Is there anything else you'd like to say at this point? It may not be admissible as evidence but I will make a record of it anyway.'

Francis considered for a moment.

'Yes?' said the policeman.

He thought further.

'No comment.'

15

Bridget learned about it first from the late news. Five Irishmen arrested by the Anti-Terrorist Squad. Reports of a huge bomb made safe. Shaky images of a fleet of cars driving at speed into Paddington Green police station, sirens blaring, blue lights flashing. It was not so difficult to work out. It had happened at last and he was safe. At least she assumed so: the reports indicated that the arrests had taken place peacefully, with neither resistance nor injury.

He was safe, she kept repeating in her head. What had she done? He was safe: that was the important thing. He would be years in prison, he would emerge a broken old man. What had she done? And where did it leave her? Her hands shook.

Soon she would be far away. She had done it, betrayed him, and now she must leave. She'd made her choice. Sarah had told her to sit tight in those first few days. To try not to contact her unless it was an absolute emergency. No one would do anything in the immediate aftermath and it would be more dangerous for her to behave abnormally. But what, she'd asked, would count as normal? Sarah could not answer the question. If she perceived herself to be in clear danger she should go to the nearest RUC station and Sarah would sort it out from there. She wasn't about to do that.

It would all run like clockwork, Sarah had said. Then it would be over.

She would walk out of this house. She would not look back and it would be all she could do not to break into a run. She had no idea what would come next. A darkened car, a private plane, a house in the country, a different country altogether? Until then she would not sleep. She would leap from her bed several times each night, expecting Joe and Kenny and the local boys to be waiting for her downstairs, silently bearing the news of her fate with bared teeth.

She put a tea bag in a cup and, waiting for the kettle to boil, went upstairs to fetch a cardigan. She felt so cold. When she returned to the kitchen she noticed she had not switched on the kettle. She now did so. She'd left the cardigan somewhere. Having climbed the stairs again, she realized she was wearing it. As she walked back down she heard a click and stopped still on the stairs. Had they detected her betrayal so soon?

There was no further noise. She edged downstairs and then it dawned on her. The familiar sound of the kettle clicking off. She went into the kitchen and made her tea, giggling irrationally and suddenly finding that the giggle had turned into an uncontrollable shiver. She went into the sitting room and switched on the television, hoping for more news.

About half an hour later she heard footsteps on the front footpath. A knock on the door. She stood quickly, then thought: be natural, whoever it is, whatever it is that happens next. They would take her like they took Liam. Sweet young Liam. If it's to be, it's to be, she told herself.

She took her untouched cup of tea into the kitchen and poured it down the sink, before opening the front door. There were Stevie and Anne-Marie. They looked serious.

'I can see you've heard the news,' said Stevie.

'Yes.'

'Well.'

'Was he . . . ? I mean, is he . . . ?'

'So I'm told.'

'Is he safe?'

'No one knows exactly what happened. But they don't think he's hurt.'

She did not say anything.

'They said not to worry.'

She smiled thinly.

'They said to stay calm. I'm to make sure you've everything you need. They'll be in touch soon. Meanwhile you'll be safe. If the peelers come, say you want a lawyer present. They'll want to search the place no doubt. Say nothing.'

'All right.'

'Bridget,' said Anne-Marie.

'I know,' she replied.

'What can I say? We'll look after you. You never know. He might . . .'

'Yeah.'

'The police'll be here sometime,' said Stevie.

'I know.'

'Come with us,' said Anne-Marie. 'Stay with us tonight. I'll get the boys to double up and you can have Ryan's room.'

'No. I don't want to drag you into this.'

'We're in this together. Shoulder to shoulder. Come with us.'

'I won't, thanks, Anne-Marie. I need to be here, where we live. To wait for him to come home.'

'But . . .'

'No. I don't mean it like that. I just need to be here.'

'I can stay with you.'

'No. You've your kids to think of. It's all right.'

'Maybe you could come to ours in a couple of days. When it's all sunk in.'

'Maybe. Thanks a million. It's not that I'm not grateful. I know you'll look after me and the boys will.'

'We understand, don't we, Stevie? I'll come around again tomorrow.'

'Thanks. That'll be grand. And give my love to Cathy and the others.'

'I'm real sorry, Bridget,' said Stevie. 'If there's anything we can do . . .'

And then they were gone. She went to the sitting room and watched their figures in the dark as they walked down the front path, heard the clank of the gate closing and the car doors opening and shutting. Stuck to the spot, blankness forced into her facial expression, she stood and watched as the car lights came on and they pulled away. Then the shuddering began again, in waves.

Harriet King was jollier than he had expected. He'd been schooled to talk to no one until Harriet arrived. Not afterwards either. He was to speak to his barrister only in the company of Harriet, and even then she would lead proceedings carefully. It was, so he'd been told, something the barristers resented but something they had to suffer if they wanted the high-profile cases. Harriet was the only one of those people who was trusted and if the golden-tongued egos were offended at having to defer to a mere solicitor, so be it.

Harriet King eschewed the trappings of celebrity, or notoriety, dressing in plain pleated skirts and sensible blouses, with flat shoes. Unfashionable steel-rimmed spectacles. No make-up. Her thin straight brown hair was cut short. Would he have judged a male counterpart as readily by his appearance? For certain: he'd met his share of foppish, flamboyant little popinjays with their highlighted mullets, shoe lifts and double cuffs, paid a fortune to represent your interests, or that's what they claimed to be doing. Even on the other side of the Irish Sea they were to be found in abundance in both the Six Counties and the Twenty-Six.

Severity did not seem to feature in Harriet's repertoire. She was beamingly courteous with the custody officer and in the opening interview that she permitted before being able to consult privately with her client she joked pleasantly with the senior investigating officer, DCI Spence. Her amiability was not reciprocated. The interview lasted less than fifteen minutes. The cops, it seemed, were going through the motions, trying to confirm Francis's identity, which resulted in a predictable no-comment interview. This, Francis presumed, was to be the pattern of the next few days. Finally Spence had said, 'Cup of tea? And presumably you'd like the chance to confer with your client, Ms King.'

'Thank you, Alan,' she said. 'Can you make mine Earl Grey, please? Lemon, no milk.'

Now they sat in a room on their own. Harriet sipped at her tea while Francis swigged from a can of Coke. Even his choice of drinks had been transmitted through the medium of his counsel.

'You've said nothing to them so far?'

'No,' said Francis. 'Apart from "no comment".'

'Let's keep it that way. Inside the interview room, that is. Outside, restrict it to just practical stuff. Food, showers and so on.'

'I know the drill.'

'Good. Now you can – and must – discuss anything and everything with me. Anything that might be remotely relevant. And only me.'

'Yeah, I know. When will they charge me?'

'I'm hoping they won't. Realistically, I think they'll give it the full forty-eight hours, so they have maximum time to collect evidence with minimum constraints. My team and I will be going over the fine detail of everything they do. If there are any procedural irregularities we'll jump on them.'

'There won't be, though.'

'You never know.'

'Are you representing all of us?'

'My firm is. But I personally am representing you alone. That gives the two of us a higher level of assurance. And it may provide some wriggle room later on.'

'What do you mean by wriggle room?'

'Put it like this. I don't want there to be any conflicts of interest as we move forward. Assuming they do charge you. I don't want to have to exclude myself from defending you.'

'Why would you do that?'

'If we found later on that one of the other defendants wasn't entirely singing from the same song sheet as you.'

'If there's a tout, you mean?'

'Your choice of words. We're just keen to avoid any potential conflict of interest.'

'We? Who's this "we"?'

'Formally, I've been instructed by you. But don't imagine I'm here entirely by chance.'

Francis chuckled sourly. 'There's not much happens entirely by chance.'

'Quite. We'll be concentrating on the disclosure exercise.'

'To find procedural mistakes?'

'Yes, that. And what lies at the bottom of this.'

'Who, you mean?'

'Exactly. One of the first things I want you to do is to think hard about the events leading up to today. Was there anyone on the team who struck you as flaky?'

'All of them.'

'All right, but was there anything that happened that makes you think now: ah, that was why? I'll be attacking on all fronts on disclosure but I need to know from you anything that you think particularly worth pursuing. If there is someone at the bottom of this –'

'It's possible there may not be?'

She considered for a moment.

'Unlikely. It's usually boringly predictable. The aim of the exercise from our point of view is to try to flush out the truth, to find out what is undisclosed to us.'

'And that'll get me off?'

'It may do. Sometimes they drop cases if the pressure's too great. But even if not . . .'

'They'll want to know back home.'

'Yes. I'm sure you'd want to know too.'

'Too right,' said Francis with emphasis. 'Do my family know I've been arrested?'

'I'm reliably informed it's all been sorted out. Your wife is being looked after. They'll take care of her. Meanwhile think about how things panned out. Anything out of the ordinary. I need to know where to probe.'

She cleaned the house from top to bottom. Anything to stop thinking about it. Anything to forget the fear just for a moment. She emptied the wardrobes with a furious energy she hadn't known she possessed, before taking a cloth into their darkest corners and climbing on the stepladder to reach the tops and wipe off all that accumulated dust. She dragged down the net curtains that hadn't been washed in years. She exhausted herself by day, subsiding into a slump on the settee in the evenings. She ate little or nothing and still could not sleep.

People came to call, with sympathetic murmurings and casseroles. She ate none of the food and the strain of their presence and the effort required to play the bereft volunteer's wife, still loyal to the Provos, stretched her even more taut. The dissembling threatened to break her altogether and to scatter her to the winds. And the fear. Was the priest come to soften her up for the boys waiting down the road? What did that glance of Cathy Murphy's mean? Did her mother suspect the truth, and could she be relied upon if the RA came calling?

Kenny came down from Belfast.

'Joe wanted me to make sure we're looking after you all right, Mrs O'Neill. He sent me personal, like. You remember me?'

'Thank you. Of course I remember you. You took me to the shops. How're you keeping?'

'I'm doing fine, Mrs O'Neill. Joe was awful sorry. He'd have come himself. He's just so busy.'

'I understand.'

'He'd have written you a wee note. But . . .'

'It doesn't matter. I can see that he couldn't.'

'You'll be getting your money weekly now, Mrs O'Neill. Stevie down the garage'll bring it. And if there's any problems, you'll be getting in touch.'

'Thank you, Kenny. And how should I be contacting you if I need to? Not that I think I will.'

'Talk to Stevie. He'll call me. Don't phone him. I'd be wary about using your home phone.'

'Aye, I will.'

'The boys are doing their best to get Francis out. There's a long haul ahead, though.'

'Am I to visit him, then?'

'You just tell Stevie when you're ready and we'll sort it all out for you. Tickets and all. Someone will go over with you to make sure you're all right.'

'And will that be you, Kenny?'

'No, it won't. It'll be someone else probably. More, y'know . . .'

'Yes.'

'I hear you've decided not to go and stay with Stevie and Anne-Marie, or for her to stay with you.'

'That's right. I don't want to put them to any trouble.'

'It wouldn't be any trouble, I'm sure. It's up to you. But we're always here to help. You need to give it some serious thought.'

'Thanks. I will.'

'We will find out how this happened, you know.'

'Yes,' she said.

'And if someone's been talking out of turn –' he engaged her with an earnest look – 'we will find them and they'll wish they'd never lived.'

She said nothing.

'But that's not your concern, Mrs O'Neill. Don't you worry about it.'

'Thank you.'

'Joe asked me to give you this.' He handed her a thick envelope. 'Joe said to tell you it's in recognition of Francis's . . .'

'Thank you,' she said. 'I appreciate it. Please thank Mr Geraghty for me. Now will you have a cup of tea before you set off back?'

They met in the Downpatrick bungalow as usual. Sarah was more brisk; for Bridget's own good, she said.

'We have to get you back as soon as we can. No long unexplained absences. Not now. Now's the time to make quick decisions.'

Bridget felt incapable of decisions, quick or slow.

'You say they visited you.'

'Kenny dropped by. Said Joe sent his regards. They'll get me organized to go and see Francis.'

'No questions?'

'No. There will be, though, won't there?'

'If you stay there will. You could decide not to go back home at all. Leave from here, now.'

'Was it just Francis you were after? Was that what it was all about? He's not the big man. There are bigger fish than him.'

Her eyes were red from the crying, she had neglected herself and was a mess, and she had trouble holding the mug of tea without spilling it. She was a sight, Sarah's concerned eyes told her that, but she knew it anyway. She'd not eaten for days and had taken to muttering to herself. She felt angry with them all, Francis, Joe Geraghty, Sarah, Kenny, Anne-Marie and the girls. They'd put her here. She didn't know who she was most scared of: the RA, George Donnelly or Sarah's people. She turned away towards the window.

'They'll want to talk to you again, you know,' Sarah was saying. 'Possibly Joe Geraghty himself. You need to be ready for that. Or you can come with me now. I've made preparations, if that's what you want.'

Bridget continued to look out of the window, kneading her fingers.

'There'll be others too. The police will want to speak to you.'

'What about?'

'Francis's whereabouts. What he was up to.'

'What'll I say?'

'Don't worry. They won't expect you to say anything. It's for completeness' sake as much as anything. Just tell them exactly what you'd say if you and I weren't in contact.'

'I wouldn't say anything.'

'Well, then. These people won't know anything about you and me. I've no idea who they'll be. Except in all likelihood they'll be from the Met, not the RUC.'

'Will I have to give evidence?'

'No. If the judge says we have to reveal your identity, we'll drop the case.'

'And Francis will be released?'

'Yes.'

'Won't they know there's a tout?'

'Cases can get dropped for all kinds of reasons. But it won't come to that. Anyway, you'll be away from there by the time the case comes up in court.'

'When can I leave?'

'Now, if you want.'

'No, not yet. But when? Where will I go? What will I do? Who will I be?' She saw the uncertainty of it all. Suddenly that new, enticing life away from this seemed even more terrifying than just staying put. 'I need more time.'

She had no idea what she would do with more time. Probably drive herself completely insane. She would be no clearer in her head in ten minutes or ten days or ten months from now. But she could not bear the decision, not yet.

'All right. But there's not much of it. Don't close me out. Let me help you through this. Don't go flaky on me, Bridget. You need to make a move very soon. It's a big decision to stay.'

'It's a big decision to go.'

Sarah would return to her little flat and fret about Bridget. She would not sleep. Should she have been more forceful, dragged her out of the house and into the back of a van, taken her to a place of greater safety? Bridget clearly did not know her own mind, but nor for that matter did Sarah.

Maybe Charles had been right back then in that case conference when he was handing management of the section over to Richard. He'd spoken as if she wasn't in the room. 'Need to get this one handed over pronto to someone else. Can't see much potential, but the woman won't know she's on the books until she's been handed on. And it'll be easier for a man to exert the necessary discipline.'

He'd looked at Sarah as if challenging her, and she'd looked away. Strange how she could be assertive in the field but found it impossible in the office. Its frames of reference, its set-up, its language were all masculine.

'Don't worry,' Richard had said when they'd left the room. 'Before too long we'll be able to ignore him. Not worth wasting our breath. You and I know how good you are. Charles wouldn't know a good source if it sat in his lap. There's no point arguing with him. It's your judgement that's important.'

'Water off a duck's back,' she'd said, and not meant it.

Maybe Richard had been right. Maybe Charles had been.

Things had changed at work when she and her husband divorced. Before, the job had been just that: a job with a difference, requiring a heightened commitment, but a job. Increasingly, though, it was as if she had taken a lover, those furtive telephone calls with colleagues, those sneaked weekend assignations with her workstation while she pretended she was meeting a girlfriend for lunch and shopping, those feigned transport delays while she perfected a submission.

After her divorce it turned into an obsessive marriage. She worked late each evening, despite her casual banter in the office she felt each setback and challenge deeply, she dreamt of her agents – her people, as she insisted on calling them in her head. When she met colleagues for a drink she had to be careful not to talk about the office the whole time, yet conversations seemed invariably to circle back there.

Tonight she would return home late and make a quick bowl of pasta, taking her meal, with a glass of white wine, into the living room. She would sit unlistening and unseeing in front of the television. In her mind she would run through the frames of the slow-motion train crash she had set in motion. Then she would go to bed and watch the ceiling.

Which one of them had it been? His money was on the Englishman Karl. He'd discounted Jonjo and Antony for the moment. It could well be one of the two clowns, Gerry and Kevin. Peter? Probably not but you couldn't reject the notion completely. He'd been even more like a cat on hot bricks than normal, from the very off.

Steady on. Hadn't something simply happened along the way to compromise them? Some stupid mistake or some random occurrence?

He turned in his bed. It was these thoughts, not the noise and light that an institution generates even into the middle of the night, that kept him awake. Not the echoes of distant doors slamming, the coughs of patrolling screws in the corridors, the shadows moving under the doors. Not the smell, of male sweat and shit and piss, intermingled with boiled vegetables and fried food. They were nothing. He had it easy here. This was not hard yacker. It wasn't like the H-Blocks. He was segregated from other prisoners and his high-security status afforded him other comforts too, including a palatial remand cell. His guards were scrupulously polite and correct. Instructions from on high, no doubt; Harriet King would leap on any possible evidence of maltreatment. His meals were hot, edible and regular. Back in the Maze you had the literal fear of death. Here Ms King was your guardian angel. Almost.

No. It had all been too neat. There had been no chance involved. One of those fuckers was a tout.

Another day, another series of interviews. No comment no comment no comment. Grin. No comment. Cup of tea, Ms King? Mr O'Neill? No comment. They were allowing the forty-eight hours to tick away. Did you . . . ? No comment. Were you or were you not . . . ? No comment. What did you . . . ? No comment. Where were you . . . ? No comment.

Finally, then. The time of arrest had been given as eleven fifty-two a.m. DCI Spence came into the room, took off his blue pinstriped jacket and placed it carefully on the back of the spare chair on the other side of the table, then sat down. He rolled up his sleeves as his sergeant, who had been conducting the interviews in his absence, recorded his entrance for the benefit of the tape.

'The time is now,' he said, looking at the clock on the wall, 'eleven forty-four. I hereby charge you under the Explosive Substances Act 1883 with conspiring to cause an explosion of a nature likely to endanger life or cause serious injury to property, or making or having under your control an explosive substance with intent to endanger life or cause serious injury to property. You are under no obligation to say anything but anything you do say will be written down and may be used in evidence. Do you have anything to say?'

Bridget was taken to see Francis by a junior member of his defence team. She was silent and obedient as Jonty navigated her solicitously through the procedures at Belmarsh. She was barely aware of what was going on and suddenly there she was in a large, gloomy strip-lit room that seemed somehow like a cafeteria. It was modern – the prison had only recently been built. The walls were brilliant white and it was carpeted. The tables and chairs were bolted to the floor. A window the length of the far wall looked out on to the London hinterlands and there was a smell of boiled cabbage. The tables, except for one, were unoccupied and apart from Bridget and three guards there was only one person there: Francis.

His jaw was set and he looked grim. He looked up at her and she felt tears forming. She coughed and resisted the urge to rush to him. He sat before a table beneath which he continuously wrung his hands.

'All right?' he said.

'All right,' she replied.

'Will you not sit down, then?' he said, and she obeyed him.

She looked at him. He had maybe two or three days' stubble

and now he was doing his best to look cheerful, of all things. Would he know it had been her? Would he be able to see through it all? Would she betray herself somehow? The fear daggered through her again. He levelled his eyes at her and instead of suspicion she saw the fearful boy within. His eyes seemed to beg.

They had little to exchange but platitudes. So they exchanged platitudes. Perhaps buried deep beneath the clichés, even beneath the intent, invisible to both of them, lay meaning. It could be here that she found trace memories of the young brash boy she'd known, that one she'd fallen for.

It was as they were nearing the end of visiting time that she said it, carelessly. 'I'll stand by you. However long it takes. You know that.'

He looked at her.

'I will,' she insisted. The peculiar thing was that as she said it she believed it.

The weather in Downpatrick was miserable today. Sheeting rain hammered against the large picture window. Not that they were looking at the view as they sipped their tea, hands cupped around their mugs. The radiators ticked quietly as they warmed.

'The police interview,' said Sarah, 'was it terrible?'

'No. They were on their best behaviour. An Englishwoman and a man. They phoned me the evening before and told me what they planned to do. I turned up at the station with the lawyer and they just sat me down. They were only going through the motions. They didn't expect me to say anything. The lawyer told me to say "no comment" to everything anyway. They were polite enough. They gave me a lift home afterwards and the search had been done while I was being interviewed. They left everything neat and tidy.'

'And you've seen him?'

'Yes. Went over to London and all that.'

'And how was that?'

'It was . . . all right.'

'So –'

'Excuse me, Sarah,' said Bridget quietly. 'That's not what I need to talk about. It was all right. That's all. Nothing came out of it. Nothing to spoil what we've been doing. Satisfied?'

Sarah looked at her.

'But – I've made my decision. This is over. I'll be staying. I can't do this. I can't come away to wherever and whatever, knowing no one, leaving everything behind. I'm just too scared. I know you think it's the wrong decision but I've made it.'

'Go on,' said Sarah.

'It isn't like I love Francis. I did once. Oh, we loved each other. But love doesn't come into it. We're husband and wife and that's how you lead your life round here. You make your bed and you lie in it. For better or for worse. Anything else is just fantasy. So this has to stop.'

'But what's just happened –'

'What's just happened just proves it. Everything's changed. He needs me now.'

'But –'

'I know. What they say he did makes me sick. What he is makes me sick. When he puts his hands on me I feel sick. But I have to be loyal. Make up for . . . Though I never can.'

'You've done nothing wrong, Bridget. He's the guilty one. You weren't planning to set off a bomb. You owe him nothing. You don't have to wait. You've every right to make a new life.'

'But I haven't. I can't escape. This is where I grew up. This is me. I'm not going anywhere. I'm not whatever you're inventing for me.'

'I'm not inventing anything. You need to think of your safety.'

'You said it would probably be all right. It'd blow over in all likelihood.'

'I said the chances were it'd be all right. But they're unpredictable. You have to be aware of the risks.'

'I'll take my chances. Perhaps I deserve to be found out. Perhaps I need to be punished.'

'Of course you don't. You've done a good thing. You know that.'

'It doesn't feel good. And I've done it, good or bad, and now I'm to pay the price.'

'You're not going to tell him, are you? Or them?'

'Maybe I should. But I don't think I'm that brave. No, my price will be paid in the years and days and hours I'm waiting. Waiting for him to come out and them to find out.'

'Punishing yourself, you mean?'

'If you like.'

'For doing the right thing?'

'It's not that simple, though, is it?'

'It is from where I'm standing,' said Sarah.

'I saw him there, in the prison. He was that young boy again, proud and brash but behind it all just a wee kid, needing me to protect him.'

'He doesn't require protection. It's just the little-boy-lost thing. All men pull it at some point. He doesn't deserve you. You've got to think of yourself, Bridget.'

'No. We've finished. You've got what you wanted and you can forget about me now.'

'I won't forget about you. You've got to realize how ridiculous you're being.'

'Ridiculous, am I?'

'Well, yes. I've always been honest with you. So yes, ridiculous is the right word. Understandably so, I'll admit. It's tough.

But look at it rationally. If you were doing the wrong thing in talking to me – which I don't accept for a second – you've done it now. Francis has been caught and there's nothing you can do about that. You do him no good at all by staying and you do yourself no good either. You want to leave and by staying you put yourself in a dangerous place. Very dangerous: you could be committing suicide.'

'Maybe that's what I want to do.'

'I don't believe that either. You think we were so wrong?'

'No, not wrong,' said Bridget. 'It wasn't wrong. It was . . . wrong for me. It's my fault. I have only myself to blame.'

'And staying will put it right?'

'I don't know. But it feels like the only way.'

In unison, they took another sip of tea.

'I shudder to think of it,' said Bridget. 'The risks I've been taking.'

'I've looked after you with as much care as I could.'

'I know.'

Sarah paused. 'This is where I'm supposed to say: OK, Bridget, it's fine. Your choice, you're a grown woman. No hard feelings. No one's fault. You've been incredible.'

She looked at Bridget until her gaze was returned, before continuing. 'But no. You stupid bitch. You stupid bloody bitch. Don't be so perverse. So selfish. What is this crap: I've got to be there for him? This is my penance? I've got to play the little woman, more like. I've got to melt because Francis O' bloody Neill flutters his eyelashes and puts on a pained expression. I ignore everything he's done to me in the blink of an eye. I've got to play the classic downtrodden beaten wife because, actually, that's what I am. It doesn't wash.'

'You're upset.'

'Upset? I'm fucking furious. And terrified. About what may happen to you.'

'You said –'

'I know what I said. And it's all very true. In my business we look at risk. We manage risks down to acceptable levels. And the risks of them detecting you are, what, very low? Negligible? Perhaps not that low. But the level of acceptable risk in some situations is zero. I've half a mind to slap you, Bridget O'Neill.'

'I'm sorry I've let you down.'

'It's not about me, I keep telling you. It's not about Francis. It's about you. I'm serious when I say I've a mind to slap you. To overpower you and take you back to London.'

'You can't.'

'No. I can't. I'm held hostage by someone who'd started taking possession of her life but then thought better of it. It's too difficult after all.'

'Staying's difficult.'

'You said it. That's why it's so absurd. You're actively deciding to do not only the wrong thing but the thing that's most difficult and dangerous too.'

'That's your view of it.'

'Contradict me, then. Tell me I've got it all so fucking wrong.'

'You're not wrong, as such . . .'

'As such. I know you're under stress. I know you're confused. I know I should be apologizing for my unprofessional behaviour and take you through the rational arguments for and against. But bloody hell, Bridget. Just ignore that fog in your head and do what I say.'

'No,' said Bridget. 'I've made my mind up. I'm going now.'

The thought shot through him like a bolt, like a dose of the shits, making him feel weak. His knees bent involuntarily and he wanted to throw up. He knew.

Joe. It had to be Joe. The boys back home were always

talking about Joe's manoeuvring and politics. All rumours, Francis had thought, all talk. Until now. In spite of his gentility, Joe was a warrior. Cold in that way. The touch of his slender fingers belied his special brutality. Francis had felt that ferocity as a boy, alternating with gentleness. With Liam, no doubt the pulling of the trigger had been preceded by a soft caress.

That cold-blooded ruthlessness would have been useful in negotiation. The sacrifice of a few for the greater good. The bigger picture. It had been that man Mercer who'd said that one day Francis would be expendable. Perhaps he'd been right. Perhaps, after Liam, Francis had outlived his usefulness. Perhaps Joe thought he'd lost his nerve, become brittle and biddable. Reached the end of the road. So he'd given him up as part of some crazy trade that somehow he could rationalize. Joe's mind was like that. Byzantine. Dark and full of hidden places. It was all too possible. Would that be flushed out in Harriet King's little disclosure exercise?

Francis sat in the little room with her as she burrowed in her pile of papers, the condensed summary of the many cartons of documents, tapes and videos that had been delivered to her office by the CPS.

'Help me, Francis. Help me,' she murmured as she looked. 'Somewhere in here . . . Somewhere. They've done a good job. But somewhere. There has to be something.'

'Don't they have to give you all the evidence they collected?'

'Up to a point. You know all about public interest immunity and ex parte hearings, though, I imagine. The English courts are as much a minefield for us as the Northern Ireland ones.'

'So we're buggered.'

'Not necessarily. Sometimes they're sloppy. It just takes one small mistake and their whole case can unravel. But not here, it would seem. Not yet, at least. Help me, Francis.'

'They reckon they've got plenty of evidence without bringing their tout to the witness box.'

'Yes, apparently. We'll attack it, though. Examine how they acquired each piece of information, look for procedural errors. But all these recordings and the video footage . . .'

Francis knew he could not afford to assist Harriet King too assiduously. He could not risk his dealings with Richard Mercer in Singapore coming to light. He did not at all want the job of explaining that away.

He would find out on his own. Whatever it took. He would conduct his own tout hunt, from within prison. Eventually he would find out and have his vengeance. At the moment vengeance sounded a very satisfactory word for it. Biblical. Righteous. Violent.

'What's clear,' said Harriet without raising her head, 'is that they've known about this from the get-go. In a lot of detail. The resources they were able to put in. The recording devices and cameras at the flat in Birmingham. The fact they tracked the truck from Ireland. The armed police teams already in place at the service station. They were well prepared. Any ideas?'

1995

16

'Well, then,' said Kenny, and sat back and smiled. 'You understand we have to do a very thorough investigation.'

'Yes,' she said. 'Can I top up your tea for you?'

'No thank you. Hardly touched this one. No, we have to
find out what went wrong. So we have to speak to a lot of people. Put together a sequence of events.'

'I see.'

'Including you, Bridget.'

'Oh.'

'Nothing to be concerned about. Just a few simple questions. That's all.'

'All right.'

'It's for the sake of completeness. I'm sure you want this cleared
up as much as we do. Find out what put Francis behind bars.'

'Of course. But you see, I don't know anything. Francis
never talked to me . . .'

'No, he wouldn't have done. It'll have been his way of protecting you.'

'Yes.'

'All I'm doing is building up a picture of what happened
before and after he went over. A lot'll be irrelevant, trivial. But
it may just fit in with the bigger picture and tell us something
new. That all right by you, Bridget?'

'I suppose so.' Then, more boldly: 'Yes, of course it is, Kenny.'

'Now, Bridget, Mikey came to stay for a couple of nights.'

'It was strange. No one's ever come and stayed before.'

'What did they talk about?'

'I don't know. I mean, I knew it must be to do with . . .'

'Business?'

'Yes. But I didn't hear a word. Francis told me to stay in the kitchen and I did.'

'For two days?'

'Yes.'

'You didn't pick up anything by chance?'

'No.'

'Weren't curious? Weren't tempted to listen at the door?'

'Certainly not. Francis is always very clear with me about . . . business.'

'Did you go the shops or anything?'

'No. Francis told me not to leave the house and I didn't. I had me radio. And me book.'

'What did you eat?'

'Eat?'

'Yes. If Mikey landed without you knowing he'd be there you might not have had enough food in the house.'

'Francis come home the night before with a couple of bags of frozen stuff. Told me I wasn't to go anywhere. We did run out of milk. Had to have black tea.'

'Did you use the phone at all?'

'No.'

'So no contact with anyone? No visitors?'

'Not until Thomas from the village –'

'We'll get to that in a minute. Did you speak to Mikey at all?'

'Just to say hello in the morning. And maybe a couple of words when I brought tea or food in.'

'Where did he sleep?'

'In the spare room. We have only the two bedrooms.'

'Did you go in there at all?'

'No. Not until he left.'

'Did he leave anything in there?'

'No. Not a thing.'

'Did the boys have the odd drink, now, Bridget? I know Francis likes the odd drop. Maybe a beer at the end of the day?'

'No. There was none in the house. Francis didn't get none.'

'What did Francis tell you about what he and Mikey were up to?'

'Nothing. He never does.'

'You must have been curious.'

'No. And if I had been there'd be no point. I couldn't ask him.'

'Nothing about something big?'

'No.'

'About going over to the other side?'

'Nothing.'

'All right. What did you make of all this, Bridget?'

'Make of it?'

'What did you think they were doing, Francis and Mikey?'

'Nothing. I had no idea.'

'You must have wondered.'

'I already said. I've been with Francis all these years. I've learned not to wonder . . .'

'Aye. Well. Tell me what happened later.'

'When the police come?'

'That's right.'

'Thomas come up from the village and knocked the door. I answered and Francis spoke to him. There was a bit of a commotion.'

'A commotion?'

'Yes. Thomas stayed outside and Francis was thinking about what to do. He went in the sitting room and I heard voices.'

'Francis and Mikey? Could you hear what was said?'

'No.'

'Were they arguing?'

'I don't think so. But they were anxious.'

'Could Thomas hear any of this going on?'

'I doubt it. He was outside the front door.'

'Go on.'

'In the end Francis come out with Mikey. Mikey got his bag and went off with Thomas. Francis told me to go back in the kitchen. A few minutes later he said he was going out and I was to expect visitors.'

'You knew what that meant?'

'Yes. The police.'

'What happened then?'

'Francis went.'

'Did he take anything?'

'I don't know. It all happened so fast.'

'And when did he come back?'

'About four hours later.'

'Did he say where he'd been?'

'No.'

'What happened while he was away?'

'Well, you know . . .'

'I don't. Tell me.'

'They came. This Mr Donnelly. They were asking after Francis. I told them I didn't know where he was.'

'Did they ask any other questions?'

'Where had he been recently? Who had he seen? What was he doing? I said I didn't know to everything and they stopped asking questions.'

'What did you make of this Donnelly?'

'I didn't like him at all.'

'Did he ask you anything else?'

'Like what?'

'Like asking you to meet him again, or giving you any phone numbers?'

'No.'

'All right. And that was it?'

'Apart from the search. There was a whole bunch of them, police, soldiers. They made a terrible mess.'

'And did they find anything?'

'I don't think so. But they kept me in the hall.'

'And have they been in touch with you since?'

'No.'

'No one else either?'

'No.'

'And you haven't contacted them?'

'No. Why would I do that? The London police interviewed me the other day.'

'We know about that. You had your lawyer there?'

'Yes.'

'And since then?'

'What do you mean?'

'Anne-Marie Shaw's been round to the house several times.'

'I know. I just locked the door and hid away upstairs. I couldn't bear to see no one.'

'When did she come?'

'No idea. I just lay on me bed and come down for me meals. I lost track of time.'

'Someone saw you at the bus stop.'

'I had to go the supermarket.'

'Don't close us out, Bridget. We want to help.'

'I know.'

'Now is there anything else you can think of, Bridget? Anything else that may be of relevance?'

'I don't think so, no.'

'All right, then. I'm sorry to ask you all these questions. You must think, what's the point?'

'No. You have to do what's necessary.'

'We need to be thorough. Listen, what we need to do now

is to go through everything bit by bit and then I may have to recheck a few details with you. Would that be all right?'

'Of course.'

Guilty. It was predictable. An English court, with all its prejudices. Then again, he was guilty in their terms; with all that amassed evidence, he'd have found it difficult to contest the fact. All those taped conversations in the flat. The video of them meeting Jonjo at Cairnryan. The recordings from the car. Even Jonjo instructing him in the cab of the lorry on setting the device. Kevin and him bickering over the route to the target. They'd been made to look like fools each day in court. Karl preening himself outside the flat. The Asian shopkeeper's testimony of his bizarre behaviour as he picked up the key. Antony's head swivelling in the car, on film, as they waited outside. The episode with the old drunk. It was a soap opera for the tabloids and he'd been the hapless leader of this bunch of wasters. They were clowns. But guilty clowns.

Forty-one years, though. The verdict had been returned within twenty minutes. Indecent haste, his barrister had said outside court as he mooted an appeal. Why bother sending the jury out if it was such a foregone conclusion?

Just words. But forty-one years. He'd expected it, known it to be the going rate, but when the judge said it: Christ. He couldn't quite believe it. He'd be well into his seventies when he came out. There'd be plenty of time to ruminate on who was responsible. He'd find out, even from here, and he'd let them know back home.

Harriet King had met him the day after the court case ended.

'I'm sorry, Francis,' she'd said, her jolly-hockey-sticks smile absent.

'It's all right,' he replied.

'Joe Geraghty sent you this note,' she said, and passed him a piece of paper.

It contained the usual platitudes. Noble sacrifice blah-di-blah, look after your wife blah-di-blah, doing our best for you blah-di-blah, your family are proud of you blah-di-blah. Joe wasn't the one facing a forty-one-year stretch.

'I can't let you keep it,' she said when he'd had time to read it.

He handed it back. 'I understand,' he said, and he did.

Now he was in his cell in Whitemoor, settled into a routine that, with the odd minor alteration over time, would see him through the next four decades. It was comfortable, though, it had that going for it, but he looked to the future with dulled eyes.

He couldn't stop thinking. Mikey had been conveniently pulled by the RUC two weeks before the job but at his first hearing had been released on a technicality. From a Belfast court. They said he'd high-tailed it to the Free State that very day. That's who it was. Mikey had been talking to the Brits.

She visited him once in that prison in Cambridgeshire. She was becoming used to being on her own. Without him, without Sarah. She booked a budget flight to Stansted airport and took a bus to Dublin airport, after someone from the village gave her a lift to Dundalk. In England she caught a train from the airport to March. There she took a taxi to the prison. The taxi driver, as she climbed in, was cheery and joked with her. Once he heard her Irish accent he said nothing more and glared at her when she paid her fare.

She was processed, in a way that suggested to her that the sins of the prisoner would certainly be visited on all his acquaintances, especially those with the temerity to visit him. She joined a group of other visitors in the holding area, none of whom she recognized, none of whom talked to the others. It was a bleak room with hard seats. Young women with long, stringy hair bowed their heads and picked at their loose ends. Elderly men sat upright and stiff, twiddling their tweed caps in their hands. Children looked bored.

After forty minutes a severe-looking guard came in with a clipboard, making ticks on a list as people shuffled through morosely, muttering their names. Bridget was examined. Her handbag and pockets were emptied of anything that could be construed as either dangerous or contraband and she was given a list of instructions to which she would need to adhere. The guard promptly read the list out loud to her as if she did not credit her with the intelligence to read.

Francis was a prisoner under special conditions, which meant that Bridget had to submit herself to an intimate search. This was conducted by the female guard in a cubicle, not exactly violently but with a peremptory brusqueness that made Bridget blush full-red with embarrassment and shame. And then into the room itself.

Francis sat at a table, his left foot stamping rhythmically. He was staring at the floor. She approached and sat down, and smiled. He looked up at her but did not return her warmth.

'Got here all right, then, did you?' he asked.

'I did, yes,' she said quietly. 'And how are you, Francis?'

He looked at her with bewilderment and she thought as usual he was about to start. But he lowered his eyes and said, 'I'm all right, I suppose. Considering.'

'I brought you some things. But they took them off me. They have to check them. They said you'd get them sometime.'

'Aye,' he said.

'Me ma and da send their regards.'

He stifled a laugh. 'Sure.'

'Joe sent his boy down to see me –'

'Don't you be talking about Joe here,' he hissed. 'They're listening to every word we say.'

'Sorry, Francis.'

'OK. No need to get het up.'

'I'm doing all right. It's strange being on me own. Francis?'

'Aye?'

'I'll try to come and visit you as much as I can. Why won't they send you back to Ireland? There's Maghaberry.'

'To make it as difficult as possible for us. To make me suffer. They're vindictive, the English.'

'Yes. I suppose they must be.'

'Anyways, I don't want you visiting. I don't want you coming here. I don't want you seeing me.'

'But –'

'No.'

'Then I'll only come a few times a year. Once or twice. For your birthday and before Christmas.'

'No. I need to do this on my own.'

'But Francis. It's –'

'Don't you think I know how long it is? I don't want you coming here. You should do something with your life. Find someone. Go live somewhere else.'

'And why would I want to do that? I'll write you and in a couple of months you'll feel different. I can start coming then. I'll put some money by.'

'No.'

'But Francis, if you won't have me visiting, I'll wait for you. I don't want anything else.'

He shook his head.

It was only a few days after she had returned to Ireland that Kenny visited again.

'Joe would have dearly liked to come and visit,' he said.

'That's very kind. But I know how busy a man he must be.'

'That's true enough. But he would like to see you neverthe-less. In fact . . .'

'Yes, Kenny?'

'He's down south today. Caught up in a meeting. Not so far away.'

'How far?'

'About an hour's drive. If you'd care to do him the service of coming over with me, he'd love to see you. That is, if you have the time.'

'Well . . .'

'Of course if you've something on Joe'll understand. It was just on the off chance. I can drive you over now and we'll be back in no time at all.'

'No, Kenny. Of course. It'd be nice to see Joe.'

'Let's be going, then, eh?'

So this was how it happened. A few pleasantries, a lie told softly, pull the front door to with a click and that would be it. No good-byes, no calls to Sarah, no histrionics, no struggles as you're forced into a van. This was it, that click of the front door you'd heard a thousand times before, and into Kenny's nice car. Disappeared.

'So you've been across to see Francis,' he said by way of con-versation on the drive over.

'I have, yes.'

'And how's he doing?'

'Oh, you know.'

'It must be hard.'

'It is. Not as hard for me as it is for him. You cope. You have to.'

'Still. Can't be easy.'

'It's not. But there's no choice. I have to do the right thing.'

'Aye. That you do.'

The place was beyond Monaghan somewhere. Bridget had no real idea where they were, what with all the turns and the narrow roads with their tall, dark shadowing hedges. It felt as if her imprisonment had already begun.

It did not surprise her that there were no houses nearby. There were numerous anonymous outbuildings but nothing

250

that indicated this was still a working farm. The house itself was large and built of red brick. There were no cars on the drive.

'Well, then,' said Kenny.

The front door was not locked.

'Hello,' he shouted jauntily as he walked through the large, parquet-floored hall.

'In here,' came Joe Geraghty's voice.

They walked into a large dining room, with dark, old furniture, lightened by beams of sun filtered by net curtains.

'Well now, Bridget,' said Joe Geraghty, 'how're you doing now? How are you bearing up? I was so sorry to hear about Francis. He's like a younger brother to me, sure he is.'

'I know, Mr Geraghty. I'm all right.'

'Now, now, Bridget. It's Joe, you know that. So, before we have a chat, can I fetch you anything? Cup of tea? Coffee?'

'No thanks, Joe.'

'Right, then. Kenny?'

'Yes, Joe?'

'You'll give us a few minutes? Make sure we're not disturbed? And we could do with a couple of glasses of water.'

'Right you are.'

Joe Geraghty invited Bridget to sit at the table. He sat on the other side.

'I hope you don't mind me taking notes now, Bridget,' he said, opening an A4 pad. 'Only, my memory . . .'

'Of course not.'

'I'm sorry to have to. It takes away from the spontaneity. I'd have preferred for the two of us just to have a little chat now. But I need to be precise, you'll understand.'

'It's all right.'

He smiled. 'You'll know how seriously we all take what happened to Francis?'

'Yes.'

'We're determined to get to the bottom of it. I don't normally involve myself personally in this sort of thing any more, but I'm making an exception here.' He consulted his notes. 'Well, then. It may be something and nothing when it comes down to it. It's obviously not something and nothing for poor Francis, locked away over there, but what I mean is that it might all be bad luck. An innocent mistake somewhere along the line. A slip of the tongue. A momentary lapse. Something like that.'

He paused. He had been looking at her steadily the whole time.

'These things happen. But on the other hand, if there's something more sinister at the heart of this, we have to deal with it. I'm sure you agree.'

'I'm sure I do, Joe.'

'So, shall we get down to it?' he said.

There was a moment of silence as he took two further sheets from his leather folio and examined them. He looked up at her.

'These here are Kenny's notes. We have to be quite meticulous. We want no miscarriages of justice here. We'll leave that to the Brits.' He smiled grimly. 'Now then,' he went on, and began the process of running through each sentence of Kenny's report, looking quizzically before asking her to confirm, refute or elaborate. She could almost believe him to be a kindly old judge, with his grey hair and watery eyes.

For the first time she noticed a fine grandfather clock in the corner of the room. The afternoon and her life were ticking away quietly in this unseen, comfortable corner of the world.

The old truisms are true, Sarah had said. We humans are quite simple when it comes down to it. We lie through our mouths and betray ourselves elsewhere. Generally we can control the facial muscles and expression to support the deception. The further away from the head, the more difficult it becomes. Watch out for tapping feet. Keep your hands still, preferably in your lap. Don't be afraid of seeming nervous. What else would you be?

Bridget had never thought it would come to this, even though, since Sarah had been in her life, her every waking moment had been suffused with an underlying, suffocating fear.

Joe Geraghty proceeded at his own stately pace, unhurried and determinedly inscrutable apart from the occasional raised eyebrow or intake of breath calculated, Bridget guessed, for effect.

Finally the hour approached six. Geraghty sighed with apparent contentment and smiled. 'Well, Bridget,' he said. 'I think we've covered all the ground. You've been very helpful.'

'Thank you.'

'No, no. It's me who should be thanking you. Very useful. Much food for thought. You've a very good memory. Very comprehensive and detailed. I think I've as much from you as I'm likely to need. Francis is lucky to have you for a wife, Bridget. You've stood by him all these years. It can't have been easy. And now this.'

'It's not been so bad.'

'You're too modest, Bridget. I know what you must have sacrificed. You never had children, you and Francis.'

'No.'

'Any particular reason?'

'I'd rather not say.'

He seemed to think for a moment. 'Aye. Well, what goes on between husband and wife in that regard is private, I suppose. Shall we be getting Kenny to fetch you back home now?'

'Yes please. If you're sure . . .'

'On the other hand, I wouldn't want to have to trouble you another time. Kenny and I are off tonight doing a few more enquiries. If you'd be happy to stay over here we'll be back in the morning. There may just be one or two extra questions. Mrs Lomax keeps house and she'll look after you.'

'I think I'd rather just go home, Joe. You can call me any time for a follow-up.'

'That's very kind of you. Only it'd be easier for me if you'd stay on here. I'm awful busy and I'd like to wrap this up as soon as I can. It shouldn't take long tomorrow. An hour or so maybe. Then you'll be free to go. Free as a bird. You don't mind?'

'Of course not. But I have none of my things with me.'

'I'm sure Mrs Lomax can sort you out with anything you need. She'll cook you a tasty dinner too, I can vouch for that. That's all right, isn't it?'

'Yes, Joe. Of course it is.'

'Good girl. That's wonderful. I must be getting off. See you tomorrow morning.'

They sipped at their Scotch.

'So,' said Kenny, 'do we wheel in the Donegal Polygraph?'

'There's no place for levity here, Kenny. It's a serious business we're about.'

Jimmy Lafferty and his team had been trained assiduously by Joe in the art of extracting confessions from those unwilling to part with them. They had dealt with Liam before Joe had applied the coup de grâce.

'I know, Kenny,' continued Joe. 'Gallows humour. It's been a long day. It's a big step to call Jimmy and his boys in. Are they prepared?'

'Ready and waiting. I just need to drive her over there.'

'Do they know who they're dealing with?'

'No.'

'And they could be stood down?'

'They know the score.'

'All right, then. What do you make of young Bridget?'

'Difficult to call. Nothing she's said jars with anything else we've heard. But you never know.'

'That's true enough. Do you think she knows anything about the phone?'

'I shouldn't think so.'

'Hmm. I may ask her. What do you think that's all about anyway, the phone?'

'No idea. Who could he have been calling?'

'That's the question.'

'The call was made to an Eircell number. Bought from a backstreet shop in Limerick. No idea who bought it.'

'Could it have been Mikey who made the call?'

'No. Francis said he had the phone the whole time.'

'His operational phone, and all. Have we asked him about the call?'

'No. Could he have been calling the Guards?'

'And just how would that work, Kenny? I don't think so. But I may just see what Bridget has to say about it. What about Stevie Shaw's woman going round there?'

'Bridget says she was in the bedroom, upset.'

'Yes?'

'I can't say she wasn't there.'

'Aye. It's plausible enough. Something and nothing, I suppose. Do you have a gut feeling?'

'No. Do you?'

'That's the thing. I usually do and I'm usually right. But not this time. So what should we do?'

'I don't know.'

'If there's a tout somewhere we have to find the bastard. So?'

'Pull her in and see what she says? Otherwise we'll always be wondering.'

'There is that,' said Joe. 'But where would that get us? If Jimmy and the boys are on the case she'll either say what she thinks they want to hear or deny everything. Either way we're no further forward. If she confesses we can't be sure and if she doesn't we'll still suspect her. It's like throwing a witch in the river.'

'She might tell them things we can verify.'

'She might at that. But whatever, it's a death sentence for

her. If we had evidence, even a little, I wouldn't mind. But just at the moment, with these talks and all . . . I'm just not sure. I think I'm just going to have to play it by ear. See how it goes tomorrow. If I get the sense, then we'll call the boys in.'

'Do you think it could be her, Joe?'

'No, not really. But you never know. Those English bastards. The thing is, we have to find someone for this. If we don't it'll be difficult to carry everybody with us. The next few years'll be difficult enough anyway. If we can't make head nor tail of it, then Bridget may have to do. She's not from a Republican family, which says something. She's been married to Francis all those years, but can we trust her loyalties? We may just need to shake the tree. Stir the pot. Probably not Jimmy and the boys just yet. But we'll keep the pressure on her. See what happens. Keep the boys close, on standby.'

'Well, then, Bridget. How did you sleep?'

'Not too bad, Joe.'

'That's good. And what did you do last evening?'

'Mrs Lomax cooked us a nice meal and we watched television.'

'A nice relaxing evening in watching TV. What could be more pleasant? Sadly, Kenny and I were burning the midnight oil.'

'I'm sorry to hear that.'

'No, it's all right. I want to sort this out. It's important to me. Now, where were we? Ah yes. What do you do when Francis is away, Bridget?'

'Do? Nothing.'

'You must do something.'

'Just normal stuff. I do me shopping and cleaning, listen to the radio, watch TV, read me book. Same as when Francis is around.'

'Nothing else? It must be lonely out there.'

'No. I'm used to it now. I like me own company.'

'No friends, then?'

'No. Apart from Anne-Marie, Cathy, Patricia and them.'

'And your parents – they don't exactly approve of Francis, do they?'

'They're all right with him.'

'They don't like us, though, do they? They're not fond of the Provos, are they?'

'They're not that interested in politics, that's all.'

'I'd have thought that where you come from you have to be political. Occupied by the colonial power, not five miles from the so-called Free State. But it's up to them, I suppose. All I'm interested in is whether they'd talk out of turn.'

'They wouldn't. Anyway, they don't know anything about Francis. Less than me. I don't tell them anything.'

'I could always just talk to them.'

'You could at that, Joe. You could at that.'

'You're probably right, Bridget. No point bothering the old folk. And what do you think of what we're about, Bridget?'

'What do you mean?'

'The struggle. What do you make of us?'

'I'm behind you, Joe. Behind you 100 per cent. I've supported Francis all these years.'

'That you have. No doubts?'

'No. I don't know about politics. But I'm with the cause.'

'And didn't you worry about your man? Before all this?'

'I did, Joe. But he was doing the right thing. He was fighting for us. And I wouldn't go talking to no one about him.'

'No one's said anything about talking to anybody, Bridget,' said Joe encouragingly.

She returned his look. 'But that's what you're trying to find out, isn't it? Who talked to who about what?'

'All I'm trying to do, Bridget, is to find out the facts. Does that worry you, Bridget O'Neill? Do you feel threatened?' He smiled.

'No. Or yes. I do. I want to find out the truth as much as you. But I don't understand these questions. I don't know anything.'

'I know, Bridget. Occupational hazard, I suppose, that I should upset some people along the way. Don't think too badly of me. But I do apologize. When we do find out who was responsible I can assure you there'll be no mercy, Bridget. But for now that's not what we're about. Now then, I need to focus in on when Thomas came knocking at the door.'

'I don't remember much of it, Joe. It all happened so fast.'

'I know,' he said soothingly. 'Just tell me what you remember. And be sure now, let's not be imagining extra details just to please, shall we? Now, Thomas comes to the door. Was he anxious? Was he flustered?'

'He was. But I suppose he would be. You don't think he . . .'

Joe Geraghty chuckled. 'I don't think anything, Bridget. I've told you. I'm just getting the facts. Once I have them, that's when I'll begin thinking. So Thomas is outside. You're in the hallway. Francis and Mikey are in the sitting room. You can't hear anything. They both come out and Mikey goes upstairs for his bag and goes off with Thomas. That right?'

'Yes.'

'So it's you and Francis. What happens next?'

'He tells me to expect visitors and I know it's the police. He goes and gets his coat and leaves me there.'

'Does he take anything with him?'

'Like what?'

'I don't know. A bag or something?'

'I can't remember. It's just a blur.'

'I understand. Were you worried?'

'I was, Joe. Out where we live the police don't come by often. When they come with their helicopters and guns and vans . . .'

'I know. You've been through all this with Kenny. I'll not

rake it all up again. Apart from this. What did you make of George Donnelly?'

'Do you know him?'

'We go back a long way. I'm a Belfast man. In theory Donnelly and I shouldn't have anything to do with each other. But George Donnelly meddles.'

'I didn't like him.'

'I didn't expect you to. Not many people do. Not even his own people. He scares the living daylights out of them. You don't want to be messing with him.'

'No. But if you mean, did I –'

'No. I'm sure you didn't. And if you did I'm sure you wouldn't be telling me now, would you?' He smiled at her kindly, as if to indicate that the question required no answer. 'No, of course not. I'm not bothered about Chief Superintendent George Donnelly. Not at all. I'm sure you wouldn't be so stupid as to give that rascal the time of day. All I'm trying to do is to get an exact picture of the sequence of events. Mikey, Thomas, Francis, where was everybody at any given moment? Now, about this phone.'

'What phone?'

'The wee little mobile.'

'I don't know anything about a mobile.'

'Oh, I thought you told Kenny about a mobile. Ah well. You didn't see Mikey use a phone? Or Francis?'

'No. I didn't know they had them.'

'A tiny little thing. Dark grey. You could hide it in the palm of your hand. Even pretty little hands like your own, Bridget. It folds out. You don't remember a phone like that?'

'I think I'd have remembered.'

'So do I. Be very careful now, try to remember. You'd be doing no one any favours leaving out the detail, least of all Francis.'

'No. I saw no phone,' she said decisively.

'Ah well. Fair enough. It was a long shot. Never mind. Let's be getting you back home now, shall we? I'll get Kenny to bring the car round.'

'Thanks, Joe.'

'No, thank *you*, Bridget. You've been very patient with us. And at such a traumatic time.'

Bridget collected her handbag from the bedroom. Kenny sat in the car, the engine running, while she and Joe said their goodbyes.

'If there's anything more I can do, Bridget, you can always contact me through Kenny.'

'Thank you, Joe. And if you're passing the house . . .'

'That's kind. I'd love to drop by for a cup of tea sometime, but I'm rare busy. Don't think me rude.'

'Of course not.'

'A piece of advice, though, Bridget. Don't close us out. We're family. We stick together.'

'Right, Joe.'

'People can get the wrong idea. So don't close us out, now.'

'I wouldn't do that, Joe.'

'Good. And how was Singapore?'

'Pardon?'

'Singapore. Wedding, wasn't it?'

'What do you mean?'

'It's all right. Francis asked permission before you went. Friends, wasn't it?'

'That's right. It was years ago.'

'I told Francis not to say to anyone else. It was strictly between the two of us. The three of us now.'

'I see.'

'Went well, did it?'

'I'd never been outside Ireland before in my life. It was exciting, but it all seems so long ago.'

'Were there a lot of people?'

'It was a big do, yes. But I kept meself to meself. I'm not one for crowds.'

'And Francis?'

'You know Francis. He had to do the normal stag things.'

'Aye. The odd drink was taken, I dare say.' He laughed. 'Was he all right?'

'He was fine.'

'Not behaving strangely?'

'No. He was his normal self.'

'Grand. It'll have been a bit of a rest for him, then.'

'I suppose so.'

'That's what I intended when I said he could go. None of those peelers hounding him. You weren't stopped on the way in or out, were you?'

'No.'

'Did he meet anyone?'

'He met lots of people.'

'Anyone in particular? Did he spend more time with any one person? Talk about anyone in particular?'

'No. He just had a good time.'

'Fine. And you, Bridget?'

'Me?'

'Did you make any friendships? Meet anyone in particular? Anyone who's kept in touch since?'

'No, Joe. I kept meself to meself. I was glad when we got back if I'm honest. I don't like all that fuss.'

'No. Well. I won't keep you any longer, Bridget. Safe journey home.'

Two days later it was the police again.

There were no helicopters this time, just a small group of nervous young English soldiers and George Donnelly and his sergeant.

'How may I help you, Mr Donnelly?'

'An invite inside would be a start. And a nice cup of tea. It's bitter out here.'

'Oh, I don't know. It's better than it's been the last few days.' She looked at him.

Sergeant Peters muttered a sentence under his breath.

'Now, then,' said Donnelly. 'Manners. If Bridget here doesn't want us to come in, then we'll conduct our business here on the doorstep. We're all nicely wrapped up. Apart from you, Bridget.'

'Mrs O'Neill,' she said sharply.

'Mrs O'Neill. I beg your pardon. Will you be fetching a coat or a cardy? You look frozen to the bone.'

'I'll live.'

'All right, then, Mrs O'Neill. How's your man doing?'

'All right. No thanks to you people. He shouldn't be inside in the first place. He's innocent.'

'Well, you're entitled to your own opinion. I hear he won't accept visitors.'

Bridget said nothing.

'That's a real shame, isn't it? He could do you the service of seeing you every so often. Seeing as you're standing by him. Or perhaps you're planning a new life.'

'I'm sticking by Francis.'

'It's a long time. A very long time. A woman such as you would have plenty of chances . . . Still, I didn't come here to chat about you and your husband now, did I?'

'I don't know. Why did you come?'

'We were talking of visitors. Had any other visitors recently?'

'Me ma comes by when she can get a lift out. She's not so good on her legs these days. Couldn't do the walk, especially in this weather. And the priest drops by every so often, to see how I'm going on.'

'And have you had any – special – visitors?'

'Apart from you, no, I don't think so.'

'Are you sure now, Mrs O'Neill? Think hard.'

'No. I don't think so.'

'Word has it that Gentleman Joe was in the area just a couple of days ago.'

'Gentleman Joe? What kind of name would that be?'

'Fella by the name of Joe Geraghty,' said Donnelly pleasantly. 'Tall man. About my age, maybe a little older. Grey hair. Distinguished.'

'And what business would it be of yours, Mr Donnelly?'

'Every breath Joe Geraghty takes is my business, Mrs O'Neill. He's one of the big noises up in Belfast, is Gentleman Joe. And I'm told one of his boys was at your house the other day. When Mr Geraghty's on my patch it's very much my business. When he's here I own him.'

'Told? By who?'

'Ah, now that's for me to know, isn't it? What did you talk about?'

'Well, my private conversations are for me to know about, aren't they? Or are you accusing me of some crime?'

'So Joe Geraghty's boy did come and visit you? Heard you went off in a car with him. Off to see Joe Geraghty?'

'I wouldn't be telling you.'

'I'm just trying to have a civil conversation with you, Mrs O'Neill.'

'It doesn't seem very civil to me, Mr Donnelly. Accusing an innocent person of lying. Or is that part of your job?'

Donnelly shook his head. 'It seems I've outstayed my welcome, Mrs O'Neill.'

'Oh no,' said Bridget. 'It's nice to stand here chatting on the doorstep.'

'Hospitality's changed round these parts since the old days.'

'Is that a fact?'

Donnelly and his team climbed into their vehicles and left.

Bridget drew the curtain behind the front door. She waited another hour or so before pulling on her winter coat, picking up her shopping bag and walking into the village. Before visiting her mother, she dropped in to the garage to see Anne-Marie.

'The police come calling. Can you get Stevie to tell Joe Geraghty?'

Joe sat with Kenny in his office, the upstairs rooms of a well-protected terraced house along the Falls Road.

'Hmm,' he said. 'It might have been Francis himself. Some deal with the Brits that's gone tits up. Doesn't add up, though.'

'I know. It's Francis who's on the wrong end of a forty-one-year stretch.'

'Hmm. Christ, I'm bored with this. Do we have enough to be asking Mikey a few questions?'

'I think so, boss.'

'You think so, Kenny? You think so?'

'No. I'm sure. I mean, the arrest.'

Joe Geraghty sighed. 'I don't like it. I don't like it at all. But all right. Looks like you need to prepare for a little trip down south. Get Jimmy geared up again, will you? And a couple of vans. You'll go down tomorrow. You know where Mikey is?'

'Yes. He's staying –'

'I don't need to know, Kenny. You just make your arrangements ahead of time. I suppose we'll use the normal place in Donegal. You go over there while the others pick up Mikey. And Kenny . . .'

'Yes?'

'No foregone conclusions here. Tell Jimmy to treat him nice. I don't want him harmed. You talk to Mikey yourself. Report back to me. We can take it from there.'

2000

17

It was raining heavily on Francis O'Neill's last night in the Maze. He'd served six years of his forty-one. Driven by a swirling wind, the rain was flung against the window of his cell like gravel. In the office where the final formalities were completed, a Portakabin near the main gates, it pattered on the flat, felted roof as forms were completed and civility was just about maintained on both sides. No warmth, though. No fond farewells, no rueful humour, no sense in the eyes that at last it might be all over.

It pelted on the roof of the car like tin tacks as they drove away, for ever, the windscreen wipers struggling to clear the continuous line of water as it washed across the M1, the tyres sweeping through the surface water with a liquid swish. Through the window that he kept open in defiance of the rain and wind the air smelt dank. It was gloomy overhead and the light from the car's headlamps smudged and spattered whitely.

Now as he lay on his bed the rain came in rhythmic waves across the roof above and water dripped from gutters that could not contain it.

He had chosen to come home rather than to run the gauntlet of a raucous reception at the Felons Club. There would be time enough for celebration. He needed to replicate his prison conditions just for now, to begin to adjust. He lay on the bed, as he used to lie in his crib, the door shut, looking up at the ceiling, though it was a different ceiling. Home.

She was downstairs. He could hear the sound of crockery and her moving about the kitchen. Quite unlike the hard metallic clanks of the prison and the sound of pacing boots at night. Apart from her and the sound of the rain, it was silent here. He was outside life, outside time.

He supposed he must go downstairs. He could not delay it for ever. He stood and ran his fingers through his hair. It was cold in the house and he felt somehow more vulnerable here than in prison. He missed the warmth of his cell and its self-contained security. Everything he needed had been to hand and, over the years, diligently organized in the limited space: his books, his radio, the small laptop computer he had latterly been permitted, his chair.

'Will you have a cup of tea, Francis?' she said as he entered the kitchen. It was warmer here, with the heat of the oven. She wiped her hands on her apron. 'I've been doing some baking. A nice fruitcake. It's still warm. Will I cut you a slice?'

'No thanks,' he said. 'Not hungry.' He looked at her and changed his mind. 'No. I will, Bridget. Cut me a slice.'

They sat at the small table, a fold-out affair that took up most of the space. Francis ignored his tea and his cake and stared out of the window that looked on to the overgrown back garden.

'Still raining,' he said.

'I was wondering what you'd like to have for your tea now. I bought some lamb chops. I know how you used to enjoy them.'

'Aye. That'll do fine.'

'How did they feed you in there?'

'Not too bad.'

'Not like home, eh?'

'No.'

'Are you glad to be out, Francis?'

'What kind of a question is that? Of course I'm glad.'

'I suppose it'll take time.'

He did not reply but sipped his tea.

'That'll be cold now. Will I make you another cup?'

'No. I think I'll get a bit more rest.'

'All right, then, Francis. Will I give you a call when your tea's ready?'

'Aye,' he said.

He'd been transferred from England to the Maze in early 1999. It had been clear then what would happen. At first he'd maintained his insistence that she should not visit, but later he relented. She was not sure why: it was possible that the counsellors they'd dispatched to the prison had persuaded him. His successful rehabilitation would depend partly on his being psychologically correctly set, his mentality appropriately reconfigured for a life beyond captivity, beyond the Troubles. It could even have been a stipulation of his early release, for all she knew.

She visited him monthly. It was invariably a dispiriting experience to sit with her husband and listen to the silence as he, head slightly cocked as if he were curious, looked beyond her to the window and the hills beyond.

His long sentence meant he was one of the last to be released. How had they come up with the dry arithmetic that governed these things? Had Joe Geraghty sat across a table from some faceless British mandarin and traded with these years of prisoners' lives? Probably. She supposed this was the way such things were resolved. Compromises and fudges, all codified with careful language on bits of paper hidden away in government files in London and Dublin, their facsimiles stored faithfully by Joe Geraghty and his colleagues in their archive, all dutifully signed off, all painstakingly observed as the years crept by.

One saving grace of his late release was the lack of publicity. The first few had attracted celebrity and notoriety in equal measure, as Republicans whooped and hollered and the right-wing English press blustered and roared in indignation. Francis, despite his earlier momentary tabloid notoriety, had crept out under the radar.

He'd been home now for nearly five months. There had been the inevitable trip to Belfast and the celebrations there, during which, to her, he'd seemed uncharacteristically subdued. Not that he hadn't accepted the backslaps and the beers, but there seemed a malevolent quietness about him these days.

The quietness came with a sullen glare that often scared her. The fear of this man that she had always felt was now different: less direct, more insidious. For the first three months after his release they had slept in different rooms. He had not asked for it but she'd judged he needed his space to recuperate and to reintegrate.

Then she had tentatively suggested he should move from the bedroom that was spare in furnishing and ornament, as well as being normally unused, to the one they had shared before his arrest.

'Francis, are you all right in that little bedroom?' she asked.

'It's all right,' he grunted.

'There's nothing there but the bed and the chair.'

'What more do I need?'

'Won't you come back in our room? I thought you might prefer to be on your own for a while. But it's been a long time.'

The fact that he'd shrugged and acquiesced caused her more concern than had he baulked or shouted at her. Since that day they had slept in the same bed and she had felt his simmering, wakeful presence beside her. He would lie stiff, breathing softly, turned away. Now she regretted having invited his unsettling silence into her bed. Their bed, she corrected herself.

He remained in the house most of the time. Initially she'd thought it was to do with the winter weather and the fact that he was no longer accustomed to the open air. Before his sentence – even after his spells in the Maze – he'd been full of energy and, when he wasn't away with the boys, enjoyed tinkering with the car or tending the vegetable garden at the back of the house. On his behalf she'd had to turn down all the invitations to go to the pub in Forkhill or Crossmaglen. Anne-Marie invariably suggested that Bridget go on her own, but she always declined.

'It'll pass,' said Anne-Marie.

'Yes,' said Bridget. 'I hope so.'

He stayed inside, reading his science-fiction books with their gaudy covers and watching the television with steady eyes and no emotion on his face. Since the sessions in Belfast he'd not touched alcohol. He rarely spoke. It had done him no good, her staying. She was as irrelevant to him now as she'd been before.

At breakfast Francis spoke for what seemed like the first time in an age. 'I'll be going up to Belfast for a couple of days tomorrow. See me ma and da and a few people.'

'Oh aye,' she said questioningly. 'Will I come with you, Francis?'

'No,' he said, but not sharply. 'It wouldn't interest you.'

He packed his bag that night, ironing a clean white shirt and pressing his old wedding suit as best he could. The trousers were tight in the seams and the jacket could be buttoned only with difficulty, but it would have to do. He cleaned his best shoes and put them in his bag too.

He left at six and was at his parents' house before breakfast time. His mother popped out to the corner shop for the makings and prepared him a large Ulster fry. His father raised his eyebrows in amusement.

'Don't get this treatment meself, now, Francis.'

'Don't be so silly, Sean,' said his mother, sipping her tea. 'It's a special occasion, having our Francis here. Now are you here for anything particular, Francis?'

He smeared a piece of potato and bread with vivid yellow egg and bright red tomato ketchup.

'This is smashing, Ma,' he said. 'Set me up for the day. Do youse two ever think of Liam?'

His father grimaced; his mother put her teacup carefully on its saucer and looked down.

'Now, then, Francis,' said his father. 'We don't want to be bringing all that up. Your mother . . .'

'No, Sean. It's all right. I do think of him. A lot. I wonder how I brought such a boy into the world. I wonder what we did wrong for him. I feel sad. But you can't deny what he did. He knew the punishment.'

Francis looked in her eyes and said, 'And you're sure that's the way you feel, Ma? You're not in front of the neighbours, now.'

There was a gentleness in his tone that made her look at him.

'Of course I'm sure, Francis. I'm not pretending. In a way I don't blame him. It's those British soldiers I blame. They killed Liam as sure as they killed Paddy.'

'It's all over, Ma. The RA is in the past.'

For a few moments the only sound in the room, aside from the ticking of the clock on the mantelpiece, was of cutlery on their plates as Francis and his father completed their breakfasts.

'I'm going to look a few people up,' said Francis eventually. 'See if there's anything I can do. Old pals from the day. There must be something for me.'

'I'm sure there must be, son. What kind of thing?'

'I don't know. I read a lot in prison. I've had a lot of time to think. There must be something I can do. There's plenty of others as have made the switch.'

'Aye, son,' said his mother. 'And we'd be proud of you if you did.'

He made some telephone calls, arranged to meet old comrades over a cup of tea or a pint. Generally, they shook their heads and sucked their teeth.

'Difficult,' they said. 'He's a busy man, so he is.'

'Well, just get word to him. He'll make time for me.'

Eventually, he did. Francis was summoned from his parents' home late one evening. He put on his suit and tie before leaving the house. He was driven to the office on the Falls Road, where the upstairs lights were still lit. In their youth, he'd been in the Belfast Brigade with the boy on the door. Boy: like Francis, he must be pushing forty now. Barry had become stout and his crew cut befitted his sentinel role. They smiled and shared a joke, and Francis submitted to the body search easily.

'Sorry, Francis. No exceptions, the bosses say.'

In the outer office Kenny stood over a young woman in front of a computer screen. She typed while he dictated. Kenny looked up.

'Well, look what the cat's dragged in,' he said with evident pleasure. 'You've been keeping yourself to yourself.'

'Aye,' said Francis.

Kenny embraced him and Francis acquiesced. The human warmth felt pleasant.

'How's the wife? Now, wait. Bridget. Lovely girl. How's she doing?'

'She's all right.'

'Stood by you all these years. She's a cracker, that one.'

'Aye.'

'Press release,' said Kenny, looking over his shoulder at the woman typing. 'That's what we're about these days.' He said it with apparent mild amusement, not rancour. 'The boss is looking forward to seeing you. Just go on in.'

He walked through into Joe Geraghty's office, dark aside from the table lamp that cast a dim light around the room and bright light on the papers scattered over the desk's surface. He did not see Joe at first, but there he was rising from a leather sofa to greet him.

'Well, if it isn't Mr Francis O'Neill himself,' he said. 'It's good to see you, Francis.'

They shook hands.

'You too, Joe. You're looking well.'

'Thank you, Francis. You too. Put on a couple of pounds, but that's understandable. After what you've been through you should allow yourself a few luxuries. And how's the country life treating you?'

'All right, Joe.'

'And that darling wife of yours?'

'She's fine.'

'We did our best to look after her while you were inside. We always do, but I made sure we took very good care of Bridget.'

'Thank you, Joe.'

'Don't mention it. A wee drink, to mark the occasion?' He held up a bottle of Scotch.

'No thanks, Joe. I've given up the sauce.'

'Really? Have you taken the pledge now, Francis?'

'No. Nothing like that. Just lost the taste for it.'

Joe Geraghty shook his head. 'Now there's a thing. Not sure I ever could.'

'How's it going, Joe? The politics and all?'

'You know. Power sharing's back on. The Prods and the Brits are on about decommissioning, but we have a few tricks up our sleeve. It'll be all right. We're not going to sell ourselves down the river. Not after what we've sacrificed.'

'No.'

'It's a different world, Francis. We're doing all right, I suppose. But it's a rare strange old thing. You've to get used to it. These people, with their ways. It's no different, Westminster or Dublin. They're all the same . . .' He paused. 'Then again, you can't afford to become too much like them. You have to continue the struggle, but in a different way.'

'It must take some getting used to.'

'It does that, Francis. It's no hardship, don't get me wrong. But sometimes I think the old days were simpler. We had a mission and we set off together to do it. Chain of command. Action. Nowadays you're swimming in treacle. But we've to look at the bigger picture, where it's getting us.'

'I suppose.'

'And how are you doing, Francis? I've been thinking about you, you know. The boys have been saying they don't see much of you.'

'I'm getting there, Joe.'

'Well, that's good. Is there anything you need of me? Or is this just a social call?'

'I was wondering whether there was any way I could get back into things. Get involved somehow.'

'What were you thinking of, Francis?'

'I'm not sure. I'd like to help. Maybe on your staff, on the security side –'

'Kenny and the boys have more or less got that covered off. But if he decides he needs someone we'll certainly bear you in mind. Of course he's always been a bit less . . . high profile, shall we say . . . than you.'

'What about something more political?'

'What did you have in mind?'

'I'm not looking to run before I can walk. I was thinking of maybe a nomination as a councillor down in Armagh or maybe Monaghan.'

'There's boys down there been working for years as councillors. You can't expect us to shift one of them for you.'

'I've been working for years too, Joe.'

'I know. But it's difficult.'

'I'm an intelligent man, Joe.'

'Never said you weren't.'

'I know the theory. I've read up on the politics. I've had time to. I know I have to start at the bottom.'

'Well, for a start, join your local party. Then see where it takes you.'

'But you can give me a leg-up.'

'Is it a question of the money, Francis? Working as a local councillor doesn't earn you anything other than the expenses. And it's a thankless task.'

'No. It's nothing to do with money.'

'Is your money being paid on time, now? If you want, I can see what I can do about a little increase. And perhaps a bonus payment. In recognition and all that . . .'

'No. I've said. It's not the money. I want to do something useful. There's plenty of others as have made the transition.'

'Me, you mean? You're looking at me like that. Of course you are. Don't blame you. But that was then and this is now. We're in a different era.'

'Are you telling me I couldn't do it?'

'Not at all, Francis. Listen, there'd be issues.'

'What issues?'

'You were a high-profile volunteer. Locked up in England. You're notorious.'

'So? All of youse on the Army Council were military men. Now you're political. Are you telling me the English wouldn't stand for it?'

'And then there's the Mikey thing.'

'The Mikey thing?'

'All your accusing about Mikey.'

'Well, if it wasn't Mikey, who was it, then?'

'I don't know, Francis. But it's in the past now.'

'He was a tout, I tell you.'

'He wasn't, Francis.'

'How come he got released by the Brits, then? Answer me that. They wouldn't let him go unless there was a reason.'

'Mikey wasn't a tout.'

'How can you be so sure? The RUC don't just lose evidence. All those forensics that linked him in. Administrative error. You don't believe that any more than I do.'

'That was us, Francis,' said Joe Geraghty gently.

'What do you mean?'

'It was us. Let's just say we had someone close to Special Branch. They hadn't transferred the forensics to the central store. They were working off duplicate samples that weren't properly logged. The original forensics of several cases were being stored in the Special Branch office. We got in and grabbed everything and in among it was the stuff for Mikey's case. The Brits kept it quiet. So it was "administrative error" in the court case.'

'You really believe that? It must have been a set-up.'

'I do, Francis, I do. I've checked it out meself. And Mikey's not happy. We're just trying to keep him in the tent now.'

'In the tent? Is that some kind of political speak?'

'Well, we don't want him outside pissing in, that's for sure.'

Francis said nothing.

'Listen here, Francis. I'll see what I can do. I'll talk to some people, pull a few strings. Leave it with me. I might pop down and pay you and Bridget a visit sometime and we'll talk about it. Meanwhile, I see that Kenny's hovering. I need to be off. Another bloody meeting.' He smiled wearily.

'Well, then, what are we to make of poor Francis?' said Joe.

'He's in a state, isn't he?'

'Aye, floundering, I'd call it. Wants to go into politics, so he says.'

277

'What did you say?'

'I had to tell him how the land lies. He'd be eaten alive by some of these young whippersnappers. He's not happy, but he knows how things stand. I'm not so worried about that as his thing about Mikey.'

'Shit.'

'Quite. Here I am trying to talk Mikey down from the ledge and Francis is bad-mouthing him. I can do without this. Is there any point dusting off the old security inquiry?'

'What would the point be? We'd simply come up with the same conclusion. Or non-conclusion. And get up Mikey's nose into the bargain.'

'It might satisfy Francis. No. I agree. Silly idea. It couldn't have been Mikey, could it?'

'Of course it could have been. But unless he admits it we get nowhere, do we? I can't see it, though. If he'd been working for the Brits he wouldn't be after Francis's blood. He'd be keeping quiet.'

'Unless it's all empty threats. Theatre.'

'Doesn't sound like that on the street.'

'I don't buy it any more than you, Kenny. I'm just bloody searching for answers. So what do we do about Francis?'

'I really don't know.'

'You're not going to like what I have to say,' said Joe Geraghty, his eyes full of benign intent, three weeks later.

'You've found nothing for me. You don't want me back.'

Joe sighed. They were sitting opposite each other in the small sitting room. Bridget busied herself in the kitchen, while a burly man wearing a dark suit and an earpiece whom Francis did not know stood discreetly in the hallway. The door was closed and Joe spoke quietly.

'What can I say? That's about the measure of it. Though it's

278

not a matter of wanting or not wanting you back. It's just the reality of it.'

'People are moving over all the time. And I'm liked round here.'

'Admired, maybe. Feared a little. Look, everyone respects what you've done. But liked? I'm not so sure, Francis. I have to be honest with you. And as for the transition, it's hard. It's not instant. I did it myself a few years back and I found it difficult. It's no easier nowadays. You have to create this clear dividing line.' He chopped his hand down on to the table as if to demonstrate. 'And now's not the best time.'

'You didn't, though.'

'Right enough. I stayed involved because I had to. Someone had to hold it together. And I took special care of me own boys. Like you. Made sure the best men were put on the best jobs. They couldn't deny me that. That was my price for moving to the political side. They were different times, I keep telling you.'

'You still sent me and others on to the front line.' Francis spoke the words quietly, in resignation rather than anger.

'Had no choice, Francis. Surely you can see that? We had to keep the conflict going, to bring them to the table. And we needed our best men on the task. Which meant you, among others. I was hoping you'd stay clear until we'd negotiated something.'

'But someone turned us in.'

'Let's not get started on that again, shall we?'

'Well, some fucker was touting for them. Fucking hell, Joe.'

'You have to put that in the past, Francis. Let it go.'

'Let it go? Easy for you to say, Joe.'

'Well. You're entitled to your opinion. I've said it, easy or not. Stop being stupid, Francis. We have to keep our good people on the straight and narrow.'

'Meaning?'

'Just that, Francis. I'm not casting about idle threats. Least of all to one of me own boys. But for the sake of Ireland we have to hold this together. We need to be disciplined. Which brings me on to Mikey.'

'Aye?'

'Yes. Mikey's not a happy man. With all the accusations going around.'

'I've not been spreading rumours.'

'No, you haven't. Not recently. But it started with you. You dropped the stone in the pool. We had Mikey in, you see. He had a bit of the treatment. Came through all right. Was angry, but he was all right with it. But it became known that he'd been talked to. And the rumours don't go away. Mud sticks. When you got out, it all flared up again. Plus, he's not happy with the new arrangements. He's not a happy man at all, our Mikey.' He shook his head.

'So?'

'So this, Francis. First off, he's not happy with you. He won't see reason where you're concerned at all. I wouldn't be surprised if he came visiting.'

'That would be all right by me. Bring it on, I say.'

'Well, it wouldn't be good from our point of view. Internecine squabbles. Violence. Not a good look. We want Mikey to stop being a pain in the arse. We want him well and truly back with us.'

'Why don't you just take him out?'

'Ah, Francis. If only you knew. We do less and less of that sort of thing. Normalization, it applies to us as well. We don't want to make Mikey a martyr either. He's plenty of friends, you know.'

'So?'

'So, your visit got me round to thinking. I need to do something to see you right. I'm thinking a fresh start might be in everyone's best interests.'

'Fresh start?'

'Yes. We thought you should perhaps take yourself off out of the heat. We'd help you, of course. Sort you out a nice quiet place. Down south somewhere. Find you a job. We can square it all off. Keep you well out of Mikey's way in case he gets awkward. Discreet. Under the radar. We'd make sure there was no comeback. And every so often you could visit your ma and da back in Belfast. Just give us the word and we'll set it up.'

'What choice do I have?'

'I can see your predicament, Francis. I've asked meself the same question. What choice does Francis have, now?'

18

In the end the move was straightforward enough. Kenny rang to say that they had this place set up down in County Kildare and would he and Bridget like to pack. The boys would see to everything else. They'd turn up one night soon. He couldn't say exactly when. No farewells to Bridget's folks, though. She'd be able to visit them sometime, but only after the move had been done and only under certain conditions. Not a word to anyone. Someone in the city would let Francis's parents know. Someone would sort it with Anne-Marie and Stevie and the rest of the locals.

The place they were allocated was a council house set on a hill in a huge estate of almost identical homes. Someone in the council had fixed it, though Francis was never told who. The boys came late one night and packed all their belongings into a truck. There wasn't much. They'd been told to leave the car; Stevie down the garage would sell it on and they'd be sent the proceeds in due course. Some boys Francis didn't know drove them down in a fancy German car. They travelled through the night by a circuitous route through Kells and Mullingar, avoiding Dublin. They arrived past one in the morning. The driver handed Francis the keys to the house together with a card with a telephone number on it.

'This is your helpline,' the other boy said humourlessly. 'Any trouble, you call that number. Ask for Dessie.'

'Are you Dessie?' asked Bridget.

'Are you being funny, missus?' he said. 'No. Anyways, you just call that number. You want to go back to see your family, you call that number. Anything at all, you call that number.

Got it? The local Gardai may pay you a visit. Don't be worried if they do, they're squared off. Joe says we're to take good care of you. You'll find everything you need in the house. Your things'll get here tomorrow. Goodbye now.'

The black Mercedes sped off.

They carried their overnight bags to the front door. Francis let them in. The electricity was on and the house was warm and carpeted. That was something at least. In the kitchen there was a kettle and two mugs, and milk in the fridge. A small plastic box containing tea bags stood on the worktop. Upstairs someone had set up two folding beds with clean bedlinen. There were threadbare towels and a half-used bar of soap in the bathroom.

In the dining room Francis found another envelope. He had been allocated a social insurance number and the address of the factory where a job had been found for him was also enclosed. He was expected there on the next day but one. There were medical cards, too, for him and Bridget. He picked up the telephone. It was not connected. The boys had taken both their mobile phones, so he'd have to sort something out in the town tomorrow. He was tired and needed to lie down.

This, then, was home.

Bridget didn't miss the cottage or the routine that had become ingrained over all these years. Still less did she miss her parents, though obligation meant that at some point she would have to return to see them. She did not quite understand why they'd had to leave at all, let alone under cover of darkness. She did not ask, and Francis volunteered no details.

She hated this house, numbered 1,700 and something, suitably anonymized and anonymizing, in the big estate on the hill that led from the town. The estate did not have a central road running through it. Rather, it seemed to be designed to confuse, with streets running in all directions, houses clustered around wide green areas on the wind-blown hill where horses were tethered and children of all ages played. No climbing frames, though, no goalposts: simply expanses of raggedy grass in which youngsters ran enthusiastically while teenagers smoked and looked on, bored.

The noise. There were two sorts. The general, the night-time drunken shouting across the green, the starting of cars at all times of the day and night – sometimes a chase over the grass leaving a muddy trail of tyre marks – the banging and clattering of doors and smashing of glass, and the occasional whinnying of the poor horses, which somehow she found soothing. And the more particular, the neighbours on both sides arguing, the shouting at children and the music, the slamming of doors. It was the constancy of it, day in, day out.

It stank too. The old cottage smelt, she had found belatedly when she began to go away. When she returned from some fine hotel or Sarah's centrally heated Downpatrick bungalow, she always inhaled the smoke, the peat of generations. That had been comforting in its way. This place stank of fried and burnt food, urine and excrement and the chemical afterburn of whatever drugs had been prepared in the bathroom or on the kitchen worktop.

It was quite comfortable, she would tell Francis when he asked. He always said they'd move on once they'd found their feet and located something better, but she knew they never would.

His only animation came late at night. He had begun, quite suddenly, to crave intimacy again. And surprisingly to her, it was not the disappointed, half-hearted intimacy of the balding, nondescript middle-aged, formerly energetic man, but the frenzied, desperate lunges once again of a man in full.

'Did you betray me?' he asked in the middle of the darkness one night.

'Francis, what are you talking about?'

'Answer the question. Did you?'

'God, no, Francis. I've stuck with you these years. What do you take me for?'

'I don't take you for anything. You didn't talk to anyone? You sure?'

'No, Francis! No.'

He grunted, and was silent for a while. She thought he might have fallen asleep.

'That day,' he said suddenly.

'Which day?'

'When Mikey was at ours. The police came.'

'Yes.'

'You speak to them?'

'No. We've been through this.'

'My mobile.'

'What mobile?'

'I left it in the house. I know I did.'

'I didn't see any mobile. Joe Geraghty asked me about your mobile too.'

'What did you say to him?'

'Same as I'm saying to you. I didn't know about any mobile. Would the police have found it?'

'When I got back it was in my coat.'

'So?'

'It wasn't there earlier.'

'Are you sure? Could you have missed it?'

'I don't know,' he said plaintively.

'It was all mixed up.'

'I don't get mixed up.'

'Could the police have got it? And put it back in your pocket somehow?'

'I don't fucking know. I just told you.'

285

They faced each other and in the half-light cast by the street lamp she could see his intense gaze. She returned it with an affected tenderness. It was as if he was actively seeking a reason to accuse her, to strike her, to kill her.

Perhaps that was it. Somehow George Donnelly had learned of Mikey being there and they'd somehow managed to get hold of his phone and replace it. The phone was all they'd have needed, after all: his clean phone, specially acquired just for this attack, to be thrown away straight afterwards. But how? He must have had it with him. His memory of events was beginning to fade, or at least the certainty about his recall, which had previously been unshakeable.

No. It hadn't been the phone. It was Mikey. He still had to be the main candidate. Perhaps not. Perhaps the Englishman. But he hadn't known enough.

He couldn't get beyond it. Casting from his mind again the dark inkling that it might not have been Mikey who'd betrayed them, he rang the number and asked for Dessie, giving his cover name, Raymond.

'Yes?' was the terse response. 'How're you doing?'

'All right. I'm doing all right.'

'Well, then?'

'I need to speak to someone.'

'Someone. Anyone? This isn't the fecking Samaritans.'

He did not recognize the voice. 'Not anyone. I need to speak to . . .'

'Well?'

'Not your man. I don't expect to see him. But his mate.'

'His mate?'

'The boy who works with him.'

'You're speaking in fecking riddles, man.'

'It's important.'

'I'm sure it is.'

'Do you want me to give the name here, over the phone?'

'What do you think?'

Francis wished he knew who this boy was, wished he was in the same room as him so he could tear his vocal cords out of his throat.

There was a sigh at the other end of the phone. 'I'll see what I can do. Call back tomorrow.'

He terminated the conversation.

Eventually, he got his meeting. Eventually. After several calls in which intermediaries tried to fob him off, he heard Kenny's weary voice.

In the end Kenny said, 'I'll come down and see youse.'

'It's all right,' Francis replied, 'I'll come to you.'

'No, you won't,' said Kenny. 'No way.'

'Halfway then. We can find somewhere in the big city. Get your boys to set it up and get someone local here to let me know.'

'No,' said Kenny firmly, with a touch of irritation. 'You stay put. I can't say when exactly. I won't call in advance. It'll be some evening.'

'If you don't show up in a week or so should I give you a call?'

'Have a bit of faith in me, Raymond,' said Kenny. 'I will be there. I don't know when. I've a lot on. Don't you be going on phoning again. I've told you, I will be there. There's no fecking emergency, is there? Where's the fecking fire?'

It took ten days or thereabouts. Kenny appeared at the front door while they were eating their evening meal. A large car stood at the pavement and two henchmen grimly guarded it against the attentions of the local children. Kenny wore a suit. Francis sent Bridget off to do the ironing in the kitchen.

'This low-key, Kenny?' said Francis.

'Needs must, Francis. You wanted the meeting. I've things to do in Dublin. Found time for you. If my clothes don't suit I'll get back to my hotel.'

'It just kind of breaks my cover.'

'Your problem, Francis. You wanted the meeting. What's this about?'

Francis explained while Kenny sat with an expression of exaggerated patience. He'd got to thinking. It couldn't have been Jonjo or Antony, could it? Jonjo was sound and Antony didn't know enough about what was going on. He was just along for the ride. And they'd both been pulled at Birmingham airport. Jonjo had been the bomb maker so he'd copped for a big sentence. The Englishman, Karl? Now that was a real possibility. Francis had never liked him, but he had to be careful to keep his personal likes and dislikes out of this. Karl had been flaky from the off. Completely unprofessional. Mind you, so were those two jokers Gerry and Kevin. And they knew more about the whole thing than Karl. Had to. But then again, they didn't know about the Birmingham flat beforehand, did they? Peter. He was the dark horse. Before the trip Francis would have trusted him completely, but he'd been even more jittery and argumentative than normal. No. Couldn't have been him. Then again, they'd all ended up with long sentences. Everything wended its way back to Mikey. Who had been the only one of the original ASU to get away scot-free.

Kenny looked at him. 'I can see where you're coming from, Francis,' he said. 'But you've got to drop this. Stop torturing yourself. It's in the past. Gone. There may never have been a tout in the first place. The Brits may just have got lucky.'

'Lucky? How?'

'I don't know. You tell me.'

'People keep saying that. Why do you want to put me off? You know you don't believe that any more than I do.'

'We did a careful investigation afterwards. Joe was involved personally. He oversaw it. There was nothing there. Nothing at all. We hauled Mikey in. He's clean as a whistle. We've been over this. It's time to let it go.'

Francis paused.

'And Liam?' he said.

'Liam?'

'You've got Liam giving the army little titbits and you lay on the full works to crucify him. Now you've got some fucker who gives all of us up and you sweep it under the carpet.'

Kenny sighed. 'That was then and this is now, Francis. Different time, different place. Liam was caught with his fingers in the till. Joe had no choice.'

'Were you there?'

'No. I stayed in the car. Waited for Joe. He was mighty cut up at having to do it. Took his responsibility. That's the measure of the man. The boys saw Liam meet his handler. Portstewart. They were behind him. Martin Dempsey thought he was suss, so Joe agreed to have him followed.'

'Tell me about it. Were you on the job?'

'No. I was away at the time, looking after Danny. Pat was on the detail. He told me about it after Joe did Liam. It was in the car park by the strand. The wind was blowing off the sea. Liam was standing there at some railings. Then this car pulls in. Ford Granada, and a big Vauxhall after. As soon as the door opened, Pat knew it.'

'How come?'

'According to Pat, the passenger door opens. He's at the back of the car park. Starting to feel uncomfortable. There's two exits and he's close to the second one, but the opposition are probably tooled up. Pat stays because if he moves they'll be on to him and fuck knows what'll happen. The passenger door opens and this leg appears. The fecker doesn't get out straight away. He's talking to the guy in the driver's seat or something. All Pat can see is this trouser leg. Jeans. But ironed, sharp as you like. You can see the edge of the crease from the car, knife blade. Brown brogues. It's enough for Pat already. No Irishman would iron creases in his jeans. But there's more. These two other fellas get out of the other car and start parading round the car park. Macho men, moustaches. Then your man finally gets out of the first car, goes up to Liam and they both go back to the Granada together. Everybody drives off then, Granada in the lead. Couldn't have been clearer.'

Francis stood and walked to the front window, pulling back the curtain so that he could see outside. The black car was still there, with the two guards glaring about them.

'Francis, leave it. There's no way we're going to find out what happened with you in England.'

'Easy for you to say.'

'Aye, I suppose it is. We've to live for the future.'

'And Joe. Is he living for the future?'

'What do you mean?'

'He's done all right out of this. He did his deals.'

'Don't be talking like that. It could be dangerous.'

'Sounds like you're threatening me.'

'Fuck no, Francis. How far back do we go? All I'm saying is, these nasty rumours, once they get going. You were one of Joe's boys. He'd do anything for you.'

'I don't know, Kenny. We both know what it's like to be one of Joe's boys.'

'Don't go there, Francis. I am warning you now. Do not go there. It'll get you nowhere.'

'You just forget it?'

'Of course. Of course I do. What choice have we got? There's maybe too much to forget, but we've no choice.'

2005

19

Richard Mercer had long before been assigned to matters other than Irish terrorism. There were different existential threats now. But in March two telephone calls in quick succession prompted him to take four days' leave, to tidy his affairs at the office and to think hard. He was required, not by official function – certainly not, he'd never have got this sanctioned internally – but by personal obligation, to return briefly to the worlds of Francis and Bridget O'Neill. The second of the calls indicated they were in danger.

He spent several hours poring over maps until he felt he had it all off pat. He went to the storage facility where he kept much of his old gear, and dug out some old jeans and a disgustingly shabby jacket.

He packed the clothes and some scuffed but serviceable shoes into an old suitcase. Always make sure you're wearing good shoes: you never know when you may have to make a run for it.

He went to the foreign exchange desk at the bank and withdrew an inordinate amount of euros, as much as he could afford from his savings account.

'Big holiday?' asked the cashier, he thought innocently, just to make conversation.

'You could say that,' Richard said, and smiled.

The next morning he flew to Dublin.

Terry Cochrane had had a fixed expression of alarm on his face even when Richard first met him in the 1980s. Then he worked for a second-hand-car dealer on the Seven Kings High Road; later he obtained his own pitch further along the same road and this was where they had had most to do with each other. Hookey motors were a regular requirement in Richard's trade.

Terry had never planned to return to Dublin. But he got divorced and his mother fell ill. For her to move to London was out of the question. So he sold up, bought a similar business in Tallaght and found a comparable flat in Howth.

Terry met Richard at the arrivals gate at Dublin airport. They took a cab to a nearby hotel and ordered a coffee in the lobby, the waiter looking askance at Richard.

'Fallen on hard times, have we?' Terry asked.

'What do you mean?'

He raised his eyebrows and grinned. 'The clothes. The stubble.'

'No. Just necessary for what I have to do.'

'I don't want to know.'

'No, you don't. The car?'

'In the car park, out the back. Just as you said. Legal and in good mechanical order. I checked her out again myself last night when I heard from you. Shocking bodywork, though. That's why I can't shift her.'

'Has it got enough heft?'

'Heft, is it now? Sure she'll motor well enough if you need her to – 2.5 litres, straight six and the engine's sweet as a nut. Plenty on the tyres. If you need to do your getaway stuff she should see you all right.' He grinned again.

'I'm hoping not to have to.'

'If there's any trouble I'll deny all knowledge. Say she must have been nicked off the lot. She's been parked out back there for a month or more. No one would notice her gone.'

'Fair enough.'

He handed over the keys and left. Richard finished the rest of his coffee and went to the car park. It was easy to find the old BMW. Its red paint had dulled to a faded matt finish. Once this had been the pride and joy of some affluent Dublin businessman. Now it was almost fit for scrap. He turned the ignition and it started immediately, the engine rumbling and the car settling into a rattling shake. It would do.

He stayed the night in a cheap hotel in Bray. His clothes and demeanour would not stand out. Its long, narrow corridors were ill-lit by bare, low-wattage bulbs and the room had a single bed and a washbasin but no more. The window rattled in the wind coming off the Irish Sea and he slept fully clothed under pink polyester sheets; rather he lay awake, kept alert by the clanking of the pipes that ran the length of the window wall and the street light shining through the gossamer-thin purple curtains. In the morning he paid with cash.

After a greasy breakfast he set off, skirting Dublin and heading west. He was travelling against the flow of traffic and made good time. He drove into the centre of town and then up the hill to the estate, to check whether it matched his study of the place online the day before. It did. It was a monstrous labyrinth of decrepit council housing, once white-faced but now grey and dismal. It rained on and off, and in this dead hour of the morning, between people going to work and lunchtime, the only sign of life was the tethered horses, shaggy and dappled black and muddy white, eating grass contentedly.

He allowed himself two passes by the house itself, a luxury he could probably just afford. Who knew who on the estate was sitting at windows, watching for strangers? Drug dealers on the lookout for the Guards, sharp-eyed old men or bored housewives? He drove back to the centre of town and then, without stopping, further west to wait for his time. He travelled as far as Portlaiose, where in the best gruff Dublin accent he could muster he tersely bought a meat pie and a can of Coke.

Finally it was time to move.

He drove through the town and up the hill. The days were lengthening now, but he still needed the headlights at five thirty. It would be around teatime for them. The rain had gone and a breeze sped long clouds through the grey, darkening sky. As he drove past the houses, into their thousands, he was reminded of the estates he'd lived on in his childhood in the frozen North-East. The horses continued to chomp away unperturbed. Small, dirty children played barefoot on the kerb, studious as they prodded the drain covers with their sticks. Older kids, nervous and aggressive as they watched the car pass, sat on a wall and smoked.

The car coasted to a halt. He looked around briefly but did not allow himself long. Three lanky youths watched him with interest as he got out and locked the door. He knocked hesitantly, in part to play the role of a harmless and unkempt man on a piffling errand, but mainly because he felt hesitant. He could, just about, scarper to the car, clear off and not do this, he calculated. But then the door opened and it had to play out.

Francis O'Neill's eyes widened and Richard thought he took a step backwards into the house.

Richard raised his eyebrows, not wanting to talk within earshot of the boys. Francis nodded dumbly and Richard stepped through the front door into the smell of bacon. His stomach rumbled audibly. Francis led the way down the narrow corridor and barked, 'In the kitchen.' At first Richard imagined he was being addressed, but behind Francis's bulk he saw a slight figure move away quickly.

They were alone in the small main room, which had two armchairs and a television at one end and a table and two chairs at the other. There was an indeterminate smell of cat's piss, or cigarettes, or both. Francis had filled out, to put it in the politest of ways. He could rightly be described as obese. The skinny, hard-edged youngster from the first mugshots had become someone quite different. It seemed he had lost his leanness of mind and spirit in the same process. Richard found himself staring at a middle-aged man who looked down at the floor, not with the haunted zeal of the revolutionary but with the cowed expression of the worn down. Richard thought for a moment that Francis was close to tears but realized that his eyes were just bloodshot and red around the rims. His complexion was sallow and puffy. Drinking too much and no longer fit enough to shrug off the effects of alcohol, that must be it.

Francis cleared the plates on the table to one side in an untidy pile before gesturing to Richard to sit down. He still had not spoken. Looking at each other they sat simultaneously.

'Well, then,' Richard began.

'What's brought you here?' Better, thought Richard. He could hear the challenge in that voice barely softened by his time down south.

Richard gave it a moment or two. 'I know. There's no business to do . . .'

'Too fecking right. Never was. Never will be. I've nothing to offer you. You've nothing to offer me. Unless you're going to give me a million euros out of the goodness of your heart.'

'Not a million euros, no.'

He continued to stare at Richard, somehow emboldened. After a while he said, 'So? What the fuck are you doing here?'

'I needed to see you, Francis, to tell you something.'

'To tell me something?'

'Yes. Something important. To warn you.'

'To warn me? Are you threatening me again?'

'No. Quite the opposite.'

'So why couldn't you just pick up the phone?'

'I could have, I suppose. I didn't think it was right.'

'Didn't think it was right.'

'It might have been dangerous too.'

'Dangerous. Like coming here in full view of the neighbours isn't dangerous?'

'I see your point. But I've taken precautions.'

'You see my fecking point? You're talking in riddles.'

'I'm sorry. There's not much time so I'll come straight to it.'

'Yeah. You do that.'

'Mikey Sullivan.'

'Mikey. What about him?'

'He's after you.'

'He's been after me for years. That's why I moved down here. I could deal with him anyways, but I can do without the aggro. Mikey's not a problem.'

'I think he may be. The reason I've come is because I've been told he knows where you are. Precisely. This address. And he plans to do something about it.'

'Why should I believe you?'

'Why shouldn't you? I don't want anything from you.'

'Who told you, then?'

'I don't think either of us expects me to tell you that.'

'When?'

'I found out a couple of days ago. I'm led to believe that Mikey Sullivan plans to do something in the next couple of weeks or so.'

'My people will look after me.'

'I'm glad you're so sure of that. I'm not quite so confident.'

This was the difficult part. He couldn't tell Francis O'Neill that it had been Joe Geraghty who had authorized the leaking of the information to Mikey Sullivan. A sop; a trade to rein

Mikey in and cease his continuing involvement with the dissident groups. He would have his moment with Francis and retire, that seemed to be the theory. A shaky theory in Richard's view.

Francis was clearly thinking. 'So what am I supposed to do? Up sticks again and move away?'

Richard raised his hands in denial of ownership of the consequences. 'I don't know. That's up to you. But I didn't want it on my conscience. I felt it right to warn you.'

Richard watched Francis calculating what the angle was. He glared like an irate, poor poker player. They were approaching the truly tricky phase of this visit.

'So that's it,' he said with a rising inflection that was not quite a question. 'You've said your piece and now you can go.'

'I thought you might need a bit of help on your way.' Richard put an envelope on the table. 'There's 10,000 euros there. It should get you started.'

He stared.

The door to the kitchen opened. Richard had never met Bridget O'Neill before but there she stood, looking at him. Francis did not turn at first but finally did as Richard gazed at her.

'Christ,' said Francis.

He hadn't suspected, but now he knew.

'You're Richard, then,' she said quietly.

'That's right.' Richard strained to remain outwardly relaxed, though he had become tense and prepared. He was not armed and this could go terribly wrong.

'Christ,' said Francis again.

'You're sure?' Richard said, redundantly, to Bridget.

'Yes,' she said, and continued to look at him.

'You're ready, then?'

'I was told not to pack –'

'That's not what I meant.' He said it as gently as he could in the circumstances. 'We should be going.'

'I'm ready, yes,' she said, and began the short walk between the kitchen and where he now stood at the door to the hall.

Richard watched Francis intently for a sign that he might grab her. But she negotiated the journey without hindrance and passed Richard on her way to the front door, where she waited. No handbag, no belongings. He glanced back at Francis, who seemed to regard him calmly enough. Then he heard the scrape of the chair. Francis was standing. Bridget looked back in horror. His face was red, his fists were clenching and unclenching. This was it.

At Richard's signal Bridget opened the front door. They walked out together, running the gauntlet of the eyes of the young men who had gathered. This was not the kind of place you happened upon and strangers were not common here. They walked down the front path towards the car. Richard let Bridget in the passenger's side and unlocked his own door. They fastened their seat belts and he pulled away slowly. At the next junction he turned the car around carefully and they passed the group of boys again. The boys watched intently as they made their sedate progress down the hill. A minute or so later they were buzzed by a moped ridden by a boy with no helmet who couldn't have been much older than thirteen. He grinned and gesticulated as he weaved across the road in front of them. Richard thought better of putting his foot down hard on the accelerator. They inched their way off the estate and towards town and evidently the moped rider became bored.

Once out of town he accelerated fast. They were pushing 120 kilometres an hour along these single-carriageway roads. He wanted to get away and enjoyed the concentration of it. He and Bridget had not exchanged further words until this moment.

'Glad that's over and done with,' he said.
'Yes,' she said, in some doubt, it seemed.

The only way she'd been able to walk that small but infinite distance across the room was by imagining she was holding her child's hand. He was a sweet wee thing – she'd decided he was a boy, with Francis's cheeky smile but her mild nature. She took him by the hand and led him – or did he lead her? – slowly across that room, that matter of metres as wide as an ocean. As she sensed Francis behind her, she flinched inwardly but took strength from her boy's grasp – his small, soft, trusting hand in hers – and felt a duty to protect. It's all right, she murmured inside her head, to him. Sarah would be waiting somewhere, so she'd said on the phone. But Francis has met Richard, which is why he'll come, and he's got something else to talk to Francis about. Don't worry, I'll be close by, she'd said. It'll be all right.

Epilogue

It is all in the past, a past that seems to Sarah sometimes distant and sometimes as immediate as the last minute. Much of the time it's as if it never happened.

She lives now in the Peak District, not so far from where she grew up. The small inheritance from her parents has enabled her to retire modestly on an actuarially reduced pension. She does not pine for her old work although she misses her colleagues. It is the newspaper that has brought it back so suddenly.

Francis O'Neill vanished shortly after Richard's warning. He left no trace, always had been a canny operator, and she hopes he might have evaded Mikey Sullivan and be leading some sort of life now.

She'd met Richard and Bridget at a roadhouse on the way to Cork, where they'd changed cars. There had been no time for emotional reunions, time was tight for their flight. They'd spent a few days together and then the machine had kicked in with its systems and processes. She'd seen Bridget periodically afterwards but with decreasing frequency.

Now Bridget is somewhere out there in the world, safe, with a new home, a new name and sufficient money to live comfortably. Sarah has never asked for any of the details, but for a time received regular reports that she was well. Now, since Sarah has left, she no longer hears anything. It is right this way. She does her best not to wonder.

She picks up the paper again and looks at the article about the newly appointed minister in the Northern Ireland Assembly,

Joseph Geraghty, MLA. It is a shock after all this time. Joe smiles in the accompanying picture, photogenic and media-friendly as ever, and over his shoulder she can make out his ever-present chief of staff, peering shyly. Seeing Joe Geraghty is not what has shocked her, he is frequently in the public eye after all.

It was 1987 when they first met. She was only twenty-nine herself, among the first women unleashed on to an unsuspecting IRA. 'Those of the fairer sex,' Charles had said, 'should in my view be protected from these people. But my view is by the by.' Thankfully it had been, much like Charles.

She'd set her sights on him early on. Something about him that she gleaned from the early reporting, a flavour of this boy. She knew it was superficial and potentially dangerously misleading, but she'd liked the photo of him on file: a chubby boy with a hesitant smile. Never been arrested, but known to be one of Gentleman Joe's boys.

Their first meeting was the most delicate of pulls. She made sure the RUC team that accompanied her could at least pretend to be gentle souls and he acquiesced well enough. She had little time: the police wanted to wrap up the checkpoint as quickly as they could. She kept it simple and direct but, she hoped, not brusque as they sat together in the rear of the Transit van.

'I'm not police, though you'll have guessed that. And I don't expect you to say anything. Probably better if you don't in fact. You need to keep your head clear. I've not told these guys anything about what I'm going to say. But they're not stupid. The point is that I trust them, with my life. Whatever you may think, these are good people.'

He opened his mouth.

'No, I don't want to debate it because we don't have time. Perhaps some other time. I know you don't like violence. I know you think all of this is getting your people nowhere. And you're right on that score. I know you're desperately unhappy and afraid. I know you can't see a way out.'

He did not refute these unsupported assertions. It was a start.

'This is your way out,' she said.

She deliberately didn't give him a telephone number. She said she would see him again sometime. He hadn't uttered a word.

There were follow-ups, with the same crew, over the next few weeks. He spoke to her. He did not glare at her in silence or trot out the drilled responses. Finally she ventured the idea of meeting somewhere else, somewhere he would have to turn up of his own volition. He agreed. It was that simple. It was that simple when it worked.

She remembers waiting for him in the car park. There was anxiety enough in the period beforehand but none was necessary once the agreed time arrived. He was punctual, always was throughout their relationship, and appeared as if from nowhere. She knew then he was right for this. He valued professionalism; it was part of what underscored the relationship.

His other motivations became clearer later. At first the exchanges were transactional: he passed information, she tested it with questions and then logged it. No money changed hands. It was tacit both that this would have been too dangerous and money was not what had drawn Kenny into this relationship in the first place.

Kenny had elderly parents and a younger brother with cerebral palsy whom he adored. They provided his anchor and a large part of his reason for speaking to Sarah. Soon their sessions together became hours during which he would speak, very possibly for the first time, about young Danny. He would be in tears, enmeshed in the IRA, fearful that one day he would be locked up or dead and unable to care or provide for his brother. He no longer wanted to be part of it, yet was captured in its embrace and Gentleman Joe's particular tyranny. Joe Geraghty paid lip service to Kenny's needs, soothing him gently with promises to keep him out of the firing line, but they were only words, Kenny knew.

So they shaped a future together, Sarah and Kenny. Kenny would insist to Joe that he no longer take a front-line role in operations but would offer other support. He would claim, with justification, that he needed to take time out to look after Danny and could not offer the instant and total commitment that active service required.

According to Kenny, Joe said with a smile, 'Going soft on me, Kenny, are ye? It'll not do, I can tell you. It'll not do. But I'll think on. I could do with some more help myself. I'll think about it, Kenny. But I'm not happy.'

'Stick to what you've said, Kenny,' said Sarah. 'He'll come round.'

'You don't know him. He's an evil bastard.'

'I know that much. But if you give in to him now he'll own you for ever.'

'He does already.'

'No, he doesn't. This is your chance to take your life back. Hold your nerve. If he insists, we'll have to think again. But hold your nerve, Kenny.'

He looked at her and she saw belief in his eyes.

He did. Eventually Joe had given in. The shooting in which Colm Hawley had died and Kenny was injured was a factor. Kenny became Joe's right-hand man, dealing with the practical annoyances of his life. Over time he made himself indispensable as Joe's responsibilities increased. He refused to become directly involved in Joe's security inquiries, ostensibly because of his family commitments but in fact because of the legal complexities in which Sarah had schooled him. By dint of his functionary role he became a key agent. He told her about Joe's view of the future. 'Francis O'Neill's the boy to watch,' he said one night in 1988. 'Joe's told him to stay in South Armagh because he's got big plans for him. And Francis is an animal.'

Later, he described Joe's intent to secure his own future. 'Got to back both horses, Kenny,' he'd said. 'Got to back all the fecking horses in this race. You stick with me, Kenny. One word out of turn, one wrong smile to one of the other Army Council boys, and I'll crucify you. You belong to me, never forget that.'

Kenny and Francis had been inducted into the Belfast Brigade at around the same time. He seemed not to realize that tears were running down his cheeks as he told the story. 'He's a brutal man, Gentleman Joe. It's ironic, that title. Everyone knows Joe. You'll be in your bed and he'll pounce suddenly in the middle of the night. He'll stroke your face or he'll drag you out by your hair. Possibly both. You learn not to sleep, but there's nothing you can do about it. I don't know whether it's to make you his, or whether he's just like that, but the fear just stays with you, always. Francis is just as afraid of him as I am. I hate the bastard.'

Kenny told her of Francis's planned trip to Singapore, which Joe Geraghty had confided to him. He told her too late – he'd been at home with Danny – of the taking of Liam O'Neill. He warned her that Francis O'Neill had been entrusted with a spectacular near London, but he had none of the details. She had to go elsewhere for that: to Bridget O'Neill. He'd been primed to whisk Bridget away if Joe Geraghty decided she should be interrogated by Jimmy Lafferty's boys. He related Joe's perspective on his secret discussions with a spook called Richard Mercer. His last piece of intelligence, long after he'd retired, was to tell Sarah that Joe Geraghty had told Mikey Sullivan the O'Neills' whereabouts.

In 2002 it ended, amicably, when Kenny's father died. Sarah, somewhat equivocally, offered Kenny the chance to leave, together with his mother and Danny. It did not surprise her that he declined. Like her, he knew that they would cut too much of a striking profile in their new lives. Joe and the boys would find them if they wanted to. So he'd stuck with it and was still sticking with it now. Some money – not too much – found its way circuitously into his bank account each year courtesy of an obscure index-linked investment putatively connected to an insurance on his father's life; and that was now the extent of it.

Apart, that is, from the day in 2016, just before she retired herself, when they'd met at his request. It had been strange to see him in London, in the lobby of a five-star hotel over coffee. He was there on some kind of political business.

'Can't you screw the bastard? Get rid of him?'

'What do you mean?' she'd said.

'You've got enough on him. You could ruin him, surely?'

'I've got to consider where it'd leave you, Kenny.'

'I'm past worrying about that. He's still the same bastard, you know. He should be destroyed.'

'Why don't you just move on? Resign and do your own thing. Forget about him. You could do something else. It's not as if you're trapped any more. He can't do anything to you.'

'Can't you see? Of course I am. Regardless of what he can or can't do. I'm stuck, until he's brought down.'

'I can't do that to you, Kenny. You know it'd all come out.'

'I don't care.'

'Besides . . .'

'Yeah. Thought you'd say that. Can't afford to disrupt the process.'

'Well? Are you saying we can?'

It had been amicable enough, considering the circumstances. The old warmth had come flooding back, never expressed in word or action – to do so would have been to destroy it. He'd known before the meeting what she'd say. He'd simply had to try. And there he still was.

On each anniversary of that first stop near Belfast airport she drinks a quiet toast to him, and to Bridget too. Usually it's just a raised mug of tea. Sometimes, though, she is taken back there by a news item, back to that strange world that was once so familiar and normal. Another act of violence, apparently random but in fact in the name of another of those ideologies that see death as a means to an end: a bomb in a marketplace, a man with a machete in a street or a truck zigzagging along a pavement. Different than it was, of course, but it reminds her of those dark, anxious days. She thinks of Bridget and Francis, both of them alone out there somewhere and, she hopes, free of the fight.

Acknowledgements

These acknowledgements include those who, over the past three years or so, have helped bring my novels to publication and make me feel that I'm on the way to earning the title 'writer'.

Many thanks to the whole team at Viking, for whom brilliant is not an overblown term. Poppy North, Annie Hollands, Stephenie Naulls, Lesley Levene, Keith Taylor, Katy Loftus, Patricia McVeigh and Isabel Wall, plus undoubtedly countless others whose names I don't know, have been so good at their individual jobs but also work superbly together. And the huge added bonus is that they're such nice people. A special mention must go to my editor, Mary Mount, who has without doubt made this book a much better one than if I'd been left to my own devices. She's shown patience, unerring judgement and friendship in navigating us to our current position. I'm flattered by her confidence in me.

Likewise for the exceptional Curtis Brown team, and likewise I'll risk naming names. I'm extremely grateful to Catherine Cho, Kirsten Foster, Kate Cooper, Alice Lutyens, Eva Papastratis, Camilla Young, Jess Coleman and Nadia Mokdad for their forbearance and skill. The mastermind of this effort is my friend and agent Jonny Geller, who has shown such faith in me and such enthusiasm, and has kept me going when I have (more than once, more than ten times) doubted myself. I owe a special debt of gratitude to Jonny, who works with such a blend of charm and integrity.

I should, though they may not want me to, mention my former employers. Despite possibly feeling uncomfortable – I simply don't know – about my deciding to write, and about this novel in particular, they have shown real grace in their dealings with me over it and no obstructiveness. We may disagree over some things, but that disagreement is civilized.

Finally, though this is not in the normal manner of book acknowledgements, I must show recognition of the suffering of the people of the islands of Ireland and Great Britain before, during and after the period euphemistically known as the Troubles (and it isn't, as many people seem to believe, over yet): the innocent victims and the guilty; the stupid boneheads and the very clever; the brave and the brutally, unscrupulously devious. I do not write with a 'message' in mind – I'm far more interested in how so-called ordinary individuals somehow become extraordinary – but if there is one thing that we can take from our centuries-old experience in these islands it is the (in all but the smallest number of cases) utter futility of political violence, which seems at times to be calculated to defeat its own ends. It is the (not so) ordinary people who suffer from the perverse, vaunting ambition of their leaders, and it is they who should count.